Black Milk

Black Milk

DAVID HARTNETT

Jonathan Cape
London

First published 1994

1 3 5 7 9 10 8 6 4 2

© David Hartnett 1994

David Hartnett has asserted his right
under the Copyright, Designs and Patents Act, 1988
to be identified as the author of this work

First published in the United Kingdom in 1994 by
Jonathan Cape
Random House, 20 Vauxhall Bridge Road, London SW1V 2SA

Random House Australia (Pty) Limited
20 Alfred Street, Milsons Point, Sydney,
New South Wales 2061, Australia

Random House New Zealand Limited
18 Poland Road, Glenfield,
Auckland 10, New Zealand

Random House South Africa (Pty) Limited
PO Box 337, Bergvlei, South Africa

Random House UK Limited Reg. No. 954009

A CIP catalogue record for this book
is available from the British Library

ISBN 0–224–03972–5

Typeset by Deltatype Ltd, Ellesmere Port, Wirral
Printed in Great Britain by Mackays of Chatham plc, Chatham, Kent

'Too near the ancient troughs of blood . . .'

I

First it is light then it is dark. You go into the dark through a hole in the side. The hole is long and slow. It slides away light and it slides away home. You go into the dark in lines. They watch you go, standing in the light. While their servants run and curse and hit. Then Alicia and Chaim and little mother and me are together in the dark.

Alicia woke to a slight shift, a tremor in things. Swaddled by the darkness and stench of the wagon she could not at first detect its source. The boundaries between her body and the world had become blurred. Then she felt Chaim move, a little jolt that meant his head had lolled briefly away from her shoulder. She knew now that the shift originated somewhere deep inside the black body of the train itself, as it slid and rattled through an unseen, shrouded landscape. She tensed slightly, gliding her right hand across her breast to support her son's head. Again the tremor, like a change of rhythm. It was unmistakeable this time: they were beginning to slow down. Then almost at once she sensed something else: the darkness was dispersing. High up on the wall opposite, the barbed wire ventilation grille glimmered a soiled grey. Morning must be close, the third of their journey. Soon light came seeping into the wagon through countless cracks. Among the forms that stirred or lay prone in its chill wash, Alicia could detect the curled-up bulk of Uncle Henryk, dozing and muttering in the straw by the latrine bucket. To her right, against the wooden bulkhead, Grandma slumped, mouth open, an elastic thread of spittle dangling down from lower lip to shoulder. They would wake soon. Like the strangers with whom they had travelled they would wake and want to know *Are we there?* Chaim would wake. *Where are we mother?* And she would lower her eyes, unable to answer, longing for the darkness to return.

Then the light comes back through the hole. But it is dark light, different. And they are standing in it again, watching. But different. Then you go out in a crowd. Into the dark light. And their servants are here too. Running and cursing and hitting. Afraid of the ones who watch. You can't see your breath but it isn't as warm as it was at home. And you walk in a crowd away from the hole that slides away home.

Josef Rosenfeld rubbed his eyes until the lids swam with shifting mosaics: black on white, white on black. All days were long but today had been longer. First the argument with the Chairman about the provision of medicaments for the orphanage; then the suicide downstairs just as he had begun his official weekly report; and now the new deportees from the West: Hamburg, Cologne, Vienna. Not that he hadn't known about them for days, with precise lists from Amtsleiter Schaefer as to provenance, numbers: one thousand five hundred and forty three of which one thousand and six were from Cologne; three hundred and ten from Hamburg and the rest . . . Vienna was a name he didn't care to rehearse too often. Even after all these years. So he had busied himself with the vexed matter of housing. Strange that Schaefer should be so precise in furnishing statistics, so vague as to how these statistics must turn into people needing shelter, food, warmth. In the early days he had made the mistake of confronting the Amtsleiter with this paradox but fortunately the Chairman had intervened before too much damage had been done. Later he had taken Josef aside and treated him to a favourite phrase: They propose; we dispose. Today the disposing involved a vacated school, a ruinous tenement near the hospital and perhaps fifty rooms or clusters of rooms, scattered over all four sectors. The school could house the Cologne contingent, the Hamburg refugees would have the old hospital outbuilding while the Viennese . . . He glanced up at the clock above the filing cabinet. Tonight, before curfew, he would slide the cabinet gratingly aside and step again into his secret world. Black mosaics, white. A stark geometry of witness and lament. It was his core these days, his centre of gravity. As Mystical Theology had been. Once. In what he had taken to be difficult times, unhappy even. When he would turn to a figure like the Kabbalist Isaac Luria for pure solace. But that was before he lost his faith, before . . . From Solomon's office below there came muffled shouts and curses. His assistant was being characteristically meticulous. At this rate the queue would still be snaking through the building after curfew. He would have to put in an appearance himself.

3

Filtered by a far skylight, a watery wedge of autumn sun slid across the wall of the corridor. A tattered poster lay in its slant path: *Abzeichen des Ordnungsdientes*. Underneath a chart of ghetto police ranks and their insignia. All wore stars of David. Idly, Alicia's fingers sought her own star. Yellow. Cloth. They had trembled sewing it on. And Chaim's. Back home in Vienna. A world away. Time. Ahead of her the line of people stretched toward a door, scuffed wood, a half panel of grey frosted glass. Beyond, grey figures swam. Occasionally the door opened and the person at the head of the queue would slip through, invisibly summoned. She glanced behind her. Faces now, not backs. Pale. Ageing. The line straggled to the corridor stairs then dropped out of sight. But didn't stop there. She saw it now, as in a mirror, threading in reverse the way she had come, down the stairs, along another corridor and out into the street where children with rags wrapped round their feet, walked up and down holding out tin dishes daubed with 'homemade' chocolates, coiled and smeared brown like the droppings of birds, their high incomprehensible voices harsh as birds.

Her gaze moved back and rested on the figure directly behind her. Chaim was still squatting, chin in cupped hands, on the red and black carpet bag. In the carriage that first morning Alicia had produced veal (a nut rissole for Henryk the vegetarian), sauerkraut and soda. It was a picnic. Everyone still thought the journey would be short and so trusted to whatever food they had managed to pack. Chaim had been smiling then, a fifteen year old on an unexpected jaunt into the country. But then had come the change to windowless wagons, their floors strawed and evilly damp. Night and day had merged. The food ran out, the drink. Then Chaim had ceased to smile, his head leaning against her shoulder, bobbing to the lurch of the wagon. Near the heart of that long sleepless dream there had been the unexpected midnight halt. Pale underwater lights through cracks in the wagon's sides. Shouts. Bangs. Sharp unfamiliar words. Was this their destination? But the great sliding door stayed firmly shut. Then a louder cry. Accents they understood. Water for sale. Bread going cheap. A sudden rush to the barbed wire ventilation grilles. Children on their parents' shoulders. Wives on husbands'. She herself hoisted up by Henryk. The bottle of water and the loaf floating in front of the snowy slit. The sudden decision to rip off the pearls Oskar had given her on their engagement. The string of pale seeds slipping away like her husband had slipped away, slowly, through her fingers, down the years. (*You're to blame too,* Grandma had said. *You're the wife, Alicia. Wives must learn to satisfy their husbands.*) Then wrenched. As Oskar had been wrenched. A casualty of Kristallnacht. Swept into the gutter, to lie there among broken glass. Then Chaim ravening and gulping. *Not too fast you'll be sick.* And at last sleeping. The train moving again. Hours. Hours. Another halt. But no one standing up this time, no one believing. Then, like a molten rip in the darkness, the door grating back. Guards. Smoke of breath. *Raus. Raus.* The platform. Their bleary staggering forth. *Get in line.* The girl whose sister had died during the journey, weeping and weeping. Then, beyond the platform, a waste area. Giant thistles, rutted earth. Over which they must stagger, with their suitcases and their bundles, chivvied by kapos, towards bullet-pocked, crumbling walls. *Is this where we are to live mother?* The ruinous city within a city. Yes. This is where we are to live. Here.

Now, in one of the darker recesses of that city, in the first floor corridor leading to the Offices of Census and Registration, she watched her son, her young stranger, silent, wideawake, watchful. It was the mood she dreaded most of all. Silent. Picking at the *O.S.* engraved on a plaque stapled to the side of the carpet bag and inside all those useless garments packed in such haste; folded silks; the electroplated statuette of the Lion of St Mark given Oskar by his employees a year before he died; the copy of Chaim's pre-war exam results; useless, rushed, unwanted, loved. Beside him sat Grandma, though with more finality of despair, on the edge of the cardboard valise. At the Praterstern and in the carriage she, like Chaim, had borne up. Or at least hadn't complained overmuch. Then came the wagon and a long slow lapse into oblivion, waking only once to shout *My mask, they've taken it, my carnival mask.* Then sleep again or unconsciousness. And at last this blankeyed indifference. Stroking and stroking the long grey plait of hair she had always kept pinned up. (*My mask. Men like a good time. Who can blame him? I can.*) Her death near.

Uncle Henryk sat a little to one side of her mother. At the start of their journey Alicia had feared the worst. Two years of virtual concealment in her apartment had not made Henryk any more careful about his eccentricities. In the

6

goods shed at the Praterstern a clerk had been checking their papers.

—Your husband O. Schultz, he is dead?

He seemed disbelieving, as though even death might turn out to be some kind of semitic subterfuge, a ruse to avoid resettlement. She had wanted to cry. Then Henryk butted in.

—On Kristallnacht. My hens knew about it. I had a smallholding then, you see, outside town. The hens all went quiet that week. Wouldn't come out of the house. I said to Richard, my partner – he's only half-Jewish, Richard – well, I said . . .

With difficulty she had pushed Henryk back towards Chaim. 'Not quite right in the head'. 'Innocent'. 'Eccentric'. Once such terms might have evoked a smile. Now they carried terrible overtones. Then, out of nowhere, the Oberleutnant with the shaven skull. The butt of his riding crop pressed to poor Henryk's throat. But the officer was laughing.

—Look at those hands.—Turning them over like specimens. In the light.—Butcher's hands. He'll do the work of two. Out East.

To which she had almost replied *A gardener's actually*, in that free and easy assumption of social equality she had still not fully abandoned even after the years without Oskar, as if somewhere, inside her, the world hadn't changed; but bit her lip just in time, hustling Henryk off to where Chaim was waiting with valise and carpet bag, the one Oskar almost lost out of the gondola on the Grand Canal.

—Next.

A bald clerk stood in the office doorway. He ignored the squat redfaced man who pushed past him angrily and walked off down the corridor. *I am – was – a banker. In Cologne.* He had been in their wagon. Alicia smoothed down her dress and, motioning her family to wait, walked forward into the office.

He recognised her at once. Alicia Schultz. They had met in Vienna, seven, eight years ago. In a cafe on the Kärntner Strasse. She had been sitting at one of the outside tables, toying with a chocolate sponge and a coffee, alone. To this day he did not know why he had gone up and talked to her. Afterwards he told her it was the way she held her fork. *Your fingers said you were unhappy.*

Her husband was in the haberdashery business. She had a young son and a mother. The husband, Oskar Schultz, was often away on business. He owned three shops and wanted to branch out into lace. In fact, he was in Venice at that very moment, clinching a deal with one of the Murano factories. He sensed her unhappiness had something to do with this absence. Oskar, it transpired, did not travel alone. There was a secretary, a niece of one of the Italian factory managers. She interpreted for him. At least, that was how Oskar put it.

So their friendship began, that autumn of Josef's visit to Vienna. He was from the East he told her, near Cracow. After studying Theology and Philosophy at the university, he had lost his faith, abandoned his thesis on Jewish Messianic movements and switched to Law. Now he was in Alicia's home city in his capacity as a solicitor to disentangle the estate of a remote relative. No, he had not wanted to become a solicitor. His father had not wanted it either. He always carried the unfinished thesis with him. He might resurrect it sometime, this glowing, painful ember. Isaac Luria. Shabbateanism. Alicia had touched the back of his hand. Josef too was unhappy.

They went walking down avenues of Sweet Chestnut trees by the river. Fallen leaves lay matted on the banks of ice-curdled waters. *They're like birds' wings* she had hazarded, sweetly vague. *No, like fish. Look at the ribs. Herring perhaps. Is Oskar often away?* And she: *Yes often. Oh look at this one. It even has a sort of tail.* Smiling up at him. *And do you regret your loss of faith?* To which he replied slowly, as if after years of solitary brooding: *For my father's sake, yes. He was a believer as well as a doctor. But I regret the unfinished thesis more.* She, holding one of the dry brown papery leaves to her cheek. *So cold.* Then kissing him lightly on the ear. *Oskar took me to Venice once when Chaim was a baby. We were happy then. Now I think I would like to go with you.*

So it had begun. Or ended.

She did not recognise him at first. Or did not want to. Seven years ago they had met, then parted. She could not leave her family despite Oskar's persistent infidelities. Nor could Josef stay indefinitely in Vienna. Once his relative's estate had been cleared up he must return to his practice in the East. So time had driven them apart. The next year the passing of the Nuremburg laws made it even more unlikely that Josef would return from the East to see her as he had promised. Then had come the Anschluss and Kristallnacht, Oskar's body face down in the gutter, sprinkled with icing of glass from the smashed store window. The years that followed were a blur of deprivation and constriction: Chaim withdrawn and resentful, Grandma enfeebled, Uncle Henryk a new clumsy muttering presence in the apartment. If she could have received news of Josef she might have felt happier. But they had agreed it was wiser not to exchange addresses. And now after last week's resettlement papers and the midnight packing; after the station and the train and the siding; after this half ruined city within a city (*Wohngebiet der Juden betreten Verboten* said the signs facing outwards on an unseeing world), she had no use for memories. All that filled her mind was how to secure her little family a place to sleep, food to eat, and the work that would guarantee that food, that sleep. So that, as she stood in the cramped grimy office, echoing still to the imprecations of the recently dismissed ex-banker, the bald clerk hunched at his desk again, scribbling, lamenting, she did not even turn to look at the man who entered silently through the door at the side of the room, the door with its little metal plate engraved *Census and Registration Officer*. He was just another ghost, his haunting a series of half understood questions, commands, adjurations. *They* were elsewhere, but their will darkened and twisted the speech of those who served them.

—From Vienna, Yes. Four. A family. You want ID's?

Not what he might have been but what he had become. After the shock of memory came the collapse back into the present. Mirrored in her unseeing eyes rose a stubble-jawed, sag-fleshed bureaucrat, his suit worn at elbows and knees, a crumpled yellow star sewn clumsily above the breast pocket. Into that mirror crowded the years of self denial after they had agreed to part, the tedious work near Cracow, his father's death, still grieving for a son's scholastic failure and atheism. Then more recently came the invasion, the move from the provinces to the city, the months of uncertainty, the ghetto. Where he had found discipline in oblivion, oblivion in discipline. So that he had begun almost to enjoy the punishing privations of work for the Judenrat, overseen by the Chairman, watched shadowily by Schaefer. Until the guilts had come. For beneath every form he signed lay a pool of flattened, wasted faces. The bodies of those who had been shot at the wire or left to waste away in unvisited rooms fell stiffly to be stacked beside the mounds of census forms, ration cards, *scheins*. And he must see them, touch them, live with them. Then had followed weeks of darkness, where he hung between what he did and what he knew, helpless, riven. It had been Solomon who had shown him a way forward, a pallid gleam. *I heard from my brother* he said one afternoon when Josef had been staring at another report about the criminal smuggling of food into the ghetto. *In one of the ghettos they're compiling an unofficial record of events.* It had perhaps been an idle remark. Or perhaps a hint. But at that moment Josef's own secret archive was born. The guilt still swirled around him. Yet there in the secret room he and his clerk had constructed that very week out of the lumber cupboard at the back of his office, he might if not atone (that for him was too sacramental a word) then at least attempt some recompense, some witness. And now he stood before Alicia, deeply ashamed.

And when finally she recognised him she wished time would turn back. To see her there like that, in such a place. Yet she knew him. And suddenly all her desperation and anxiety streamed to coagulate round her old lover alone. Leaving the door half open she rushed forward. The clerk looked up, still muttering. She ignored him and held both Josef's hands to her lips in the old greeting. How frail they felt and cold. Yet he was still Josef. And – she had to be honest with herself – being Josef might help her, her family. So that, intermixed with the kinds of enquiry any two old friends might make of one another, rose darker forces. The need for shelter and food. Need. Need. The ghetto's slow devouring simmer. It had begun to work inside her already, a gelid flame feeding on the old love, threatening to engulf even the figure who stood before her now, miraculously reborn. Or brought back to life.

After the flurry of greetings Josef became anxious. Why should Oskar hang back with the other members of the family? Was he ill? Alicia sensed his unease and herself gestured to the corridor.

—They are out there. Yes. But not my husband. Kristallnacht. I never had your forwarding address Josef. You remember how we agreed. How could I write and tell you? And the times . . . you must realise . . .

Her words drained away into silence. But Josef felt only exhilaration, a sense of imminent ascent.

—And you never . . . ? I mean there was no one . . . ?

It was his turn to lapse into silence. To which she responded by shaking her head and smiling.

—And you? You are still alone?

—Do you remember Alicia, how we used to dream of visiting Venice together?

Immediately he regretted his remark. The people in the corridor were shifting and murmuring. Outside the wan sunlight had been washed away by drizzle. Autumn was here. But it was the wrong Autumn. They had met again. In the East. In a ghetto.

—If this is Russia where are the farms? Tell me that. And the animals? Henryk can look after the poultry. Is it Palestine?

Alicia turned back heavy-hearted to the open doorway. She wished Josef hadn't mentioned Venice. Not here, not now. Outside, Grandma was addressing the line of people behind her. Someone coughed. A baby cried. Was shushed. Grandma's voice crackled, wavering. Chaim looked the other way, embarrassed. Henryk was stumbling forward.

—No, little mother. We don't work. Only sleep.

Henryk's own mother had died during his birth. He was only Alicia's half uncle. There had been whispers of pre-natal oxygen starvation. Yet he could often take control of a situation.

—Sleep.—Grandma's echo was faintly interrogatory. She swayed a little but did not fall. Her father had been a cantor. And her father's father. That side of the family always had good posture even in defeat. Upright, she consented to be guided back into line. Henryk was starting to laugh to himself. Alicia pushed the door to.

13

—That room the Goldbergs were in—Josef was sorting papers on the desk. He looked up at his clerk. Alicia realised in a moment of wild relief that the Census Officer was not about to entrust this family to the mercies of an underling.

The stairs were slippery and unlighted. Alicia led the way with Chaim and the two bags. Below in the darkness she could hear Henryk puffing to assist Grandma.

—It's just like the steps to the synagogue gallery. Remember, little mother?

Grandma had been too weak that last year even for the short journey to her place of worship.

—I've always hated them. So steep.

—But you like the services, the talk. Remember how old Mrs Levin used to gossip about her sister's folks?

Henryk could be canny in his mild way. Their voices rose as if from some malodorous cave. Oracles.

—I do. And so would Alicia, if she'd only relax. But no. And now she says even the boy's bar mitzvah isn't necessary. I ask you. Necessary. That Oskar and his irreligion. If she . . .

There was a muffled thud followed by a long ribbon of tumbling. Alicia's heart leapt.

—Henryk.—She tried to whisper it. Out of consideration for the many unseen presences the tenement contained. The tumbling had ceased. Henryk was grunting more distantly.

—I'm getting them. Seven, eight . . .

Why had he dropped the potatoes? They had cost her the fox-head stole. And when the old man had shuffled away into the dusk she had discovered at least two rotten tubers. Why? A little spasm of misery overcame her. She gripped Chaim's arm.

—Which floor did Josef say?

But her son did not reply. He had seen Josef through the office doorway. He thought he knew who he was.

—I've put them back in the shirt. Now we're coming, aren't we little mother?

Chaim had gone forward with long bounding steps into the darkness above. He was invisible to her, coughing hollowly.

—He said the fourth. This is the fourth.

He had seen Josef. He knew.

Newly disinfected. Clean. A window. Josef would have accompanied them but—the pressure of work. He had smiled. Wanting to be understood, excused, absolved. At the time it had seemed unnecessary in any case. All she felt was gratitude, relief. Now her misery flickered tiny points of rage. Such power and such indifference. Newly disinfected. One autumn afternoon not long before Josef left Vienna for good, they were lying together on a slope under the pines. The weather had been unseasonably mild. When she rolled over he said *Look at all the needles stuck to your derrière*. And laughed, picking them off. *They leave little purple grooves. Look. Like a grid*. She laughed back. *How can I? They're behind me*. The sharp odour of resin wafted again through the dim stairwell. *Derrière*. It had seemed coy then, though she hadn't admitted it. And mannered. Now only he could decide where they should live and how. In this nameless place halfway between Germany and Russia. A stinking room in a rotting tenement. The pines swayed darkly across her eyes. Plumes of darkness. Disinfected. And yet she wasn't helpless. If he had allocated the room she had found it. And led her family there. Soon it would be her responsibility to feed them too. Responsible. She had not collapsed in a heap like that poor woman with the six children in the Praterstern. She was strong. And felt a renewed warmth and stillness. They had met again.

—Can you see the door Chaim? The one on the left Josef said.

From cracks and openings light seeped, voices.

Josef stood up in the room of the secret archive and switched off the light. The power would be cut soon. Along with all running water. Then there would be curfew. He must be back at his apartment before then. He glanced down at today's carbon. A chronicle of events, deliberately objective, without emotion. Time would understand, the countless eyes of futurity: the suicide; the shooting at the main gate (one of the child smugglers); the new arrivals from the West. He felt suddenly absurd, almost bogus. For him there was only one arrival, one event. Yet this could not be mentioned but had to be buried in the coded objectivity of chronicle. Reaching for his pen (the one father had given him after the subject for his thesis had been approved), he switched the light back on and went over to the wardrobe that served as safe and storehouse for the archives: their genizah. From a bottom shelf bearing the legend *Socks* he drew out a battered blackboarded and red-spined Minutes Book. Before the war it had belonged to the hellikot, the religious council that occupation had distorted into a Judenrat. Back at the second desk (the other was reserved for his own typewriter) he turned to the first clean page and wrote at the top in a strong cursive the date, followed by 'Seven days before Rosh Hashanah.' The pen shook for a moment in his hand. He began.

Chaim had found a slab of compressed coke under the big double bed. It would fuel the stove for now. Henryk had taken the pot from Oskar's bag and was bumping downstairs to the latrines for water. Josef had warned them about the nightly supply failures. It had been Henryk's idea to pack the saucepan. How she had cursed him back in Vienna. The delay. The danger. Now she sat at the little table watching Chaim blow on the flame through cupped fingers, while potato peelings screwed from her knife into the bowl on the floor.

—Uncle has foresight. If only he wouldn't talk to strangers, Germans.

Chaim nodded, puffing.

—He kept quiet in that office.

Alicia felt suddenly ashamed. Almost humble.

They ate in silence, quickly, Chaim and Henryk at the little table, Alicia by the stove on a three-legged stool and Grandma on the single divan near the window. Once the air was split by a fanfare of factory klaxons. Minutes later doors began banging throughout the tenement. There were footsteps, low voices. Then all fell silent. The family from Vienna went on eating, spooning the thin broth toward pale faces. It grew dim. Their single candle (another of Henryk's foresights) wavered against the uncurtained black of the window. Josef had warned her about curfew. She reached across to pinch its flame between finger and thumb. As if to mark the moment a far shot rang out. There was no aftermath. No footsteps. No cries. A shot. Then silence. The flame hissed its death against her wetted fingertips. The four hunched figures sat on in the twilight.

—That official. He seems a helpful man.

Henryk had stood up and was washing the four tin bowls (courtesy of the ghetto administration) in a tin bucket he had found in the latrine. That year Josef had been in Vienna, Henryk was still working his smallholding. They had never met. Still Alicia felt obliged to dissemble.

—He's an official that's all.

—But an old friend too. It's useful.

Henryk could be annoyingly matter-of-fact when he chose.

—Where do we pee? In the night?

Chaim was standing up. He still mourned his father. He thought he remembered being with his mother and Josef once. The three of them had visited St Stephen's. Father was away on business. He must have been six or seven. Even then he knew his parents were estranged. It had something to do with Venice.

—Little mother can't manage those stairs every night. And the latrine backs onto the street. There are patrols.

Swiftly yet with infinite slowness they rigged up a closet in the corner of the room furthest from the window. They used Henryk's tweed hunting jacket and a couple of the more threadbare blankets left behind by the previous

18

tenants. *Resettled East*, Josef had informed Alicia, his eyes straying from her to the clerk and back again. *In the summer.* The washing-up bucket was their only container. Dully she remembered the pot back home under Oskar's old bed, its china handle shaped like a cockerel's head. For years it had gathered dust, unused. Another pail. They would need another pail.

On the office staircase Josef ran smack into Schaefer. He was surprised, on the few occasions when they came into accidental physical contact, how soft the Amtsleiter's body was. Fish-soft, chill.

—You're late Rosenfeld. Work keeping you?

—The new arrivals Herr Schaefer. We only finished processing them an hour ago.

—You need to work harder then. And faster. An hour ago. Does it take you that long to clear up?

Josef always sensed that Schaefer had an intuition about the secret archive. Yet for some reason held off from discovering it for himself. The Amtsleiter began humming now, still blocking the stairs. Short and soft. A god. He looked at Josef with his soft smile.

—You know it?

—The Woodbird's Song.—This business of identification had become a sort of ritual between them. Josef dare not be flippant.

—The Woodbird's Song. Of course you know it. An educated man like you. What was the subject of your thesis again?

Schaefer sighed. At such moments his look could seem almost maternal. Yet murderous.

—My father christened me Siegfried after him, you know.

Josef did know. Yet clove to the ritual. As on so many previous occasions he felt poised at the edge of some deeper contact. From which he would not have flinched, despite himself. Schaefer's hand was on his shoulder. It lingered.

—You should hurry.

And withdrew. And lingered, a soft fat warm pressure on Josef's heart as he stumbled through the gathering dusk.

She was staying with Oskar in the Danieli. It was the first time, when Chaim was just a baby. But somehow Chaim had vanished. They sat together on the balcony drinking coffee. Between them lay a plate of truffles glowing on and off like underwater lights. Beyond, over the Lido, dark clouds were gathering. The waters of the Grand Canal began to churn. Above St Sulpice the sky flared a green lightning. Soon fat rain drops were ricocheting off the ranks of gondolas moored to their forest of black and white striped poles. Across the lagoon's troubled surface a traghetto came lurching. Its sides bore painted eyes. In its prow stood Josef, wearing a spiked helmet from the last war and the long flowing robes of a Torah prophet. In one hand he held up a black book, in the other a bucket. She felt a sharp burning pain in the pit of her stomach. Oskar had shot her. She woke with a full bladder.

St Stephen's. His mother was disappearing down the stairs

into the catacomb with Josef. He followed them. Dimly lit tunnels. Bones sorted and stacked behind wire grilles. *Mother where are you?* The verger. Hooded. Daddy? *Don't be afraid Chaim. It's history that's all. A long long time ago.*

First it is light. Then it is dark. Dark light for Alicia and Chaim and little mother and me. But not for Oskar. Lying in the gutter with the bits of broken glass on his back. Nor my hens. The barnvelders, the cochins. Such strange behaviour the week he was killed. So that Alicia needn't have come and told me. Because I saw the dark in the light in their eyes. And then they killed the hens. And Alicia took me away. Because killing is eating. And we have come here to be eaten. Through the hole which slides away home.

2

'She has come again, my angel out of the West. How long before she too falls? Three months since the last resettlement. Schaefer big with knowledge. Refusing to be delivered. Dare I pray this interval, this gestation lasts forever. I who, two years ago, cursed my race, my origins, for being rounded up and put to work in the ghetto administration rather than shot like the intellectuals at the university. Dare I pray the ghetto lasts forever, this husk of creation, this kelippah. Shall I hope that it too is part of some Divine plan, I who ceased to believe in anything Divine even before I had abandoned Luria. Oh I shall, if she . . .'

Swiftly, guiltily, Josef Rosenfeld stuffed the hellikot Minutes Book under a heap of census forms. He should never have taken it out of the archives room. Arranging his hands, one over the other, he looked up through horn-rimmed glasses. Mendel. How had he managed not to be picked up yet again? And still with more than a suggestion of beard. Even after last week's public shaving. And that clothing. What outfit *wouldn't* make Mendel look hasidic? *If I see another Torah prophet walking the streets of this community* . . . The Chairman's threat echoed in his mind. Yet here was Mendel, unreformed, unregenerate. Josef stood up.

Had this mystic lost even that last ounce of commonsense that might tell him what danger he was putting them all in? He had. But at least the office was empty. He might have a chance of bundling him off down the back stairs before anybody else noticed. He strode across to the tall pale figure in the black threadbare coat.

—How did you get in? Did Solomon see you?

But something in Mendel's eyes made Josef pause. It wasn't the usual gleam, half supplication, half fear which, as an official in the administration, Josef encountered countless times every day. It wasn't even Mendel's own more frequent self-patented look of a furious righteous indignation. It was a quieter more ambivalent gaze. Watchful. Amused even. Turning away in an attempt at once to shield and dismiss, Josef was suddenly flooded with the old memory of her sitting outside the cafe in the Kärntner Strasse. Sunlight settled on her dark head and lay trembling along the teeth of a green hair comb. Two pigeons flurried away as he approached. Her backless high heels were red. She toyed with a chocolate sponge, her fork cracking through the thin dark crust, to re-emerge smeared and sticky. The fork glittered. A crumb of sponge badged the thin rift between two of her upper front teeth. Damp, half masticated, dark. It fell on his cuff as they shook hands for the first time. He did not brush it away.

—Before the restoration of paradise men's hearts must be opened. Yours is opening now. I see it. Like a flower.

At these last words Mendel cupped his bony hands then splayed the fingers. Grey flesh-thin petals. Here was the flower. The bloom of paradise.

Again Josef surged indignation. He was trapped as always, held fascinated by this man's terrible gentleness. It had been no different at the very beginning, before the ghetto; three years ago, on the west side of the city outside the reformed synagogue that mysteriously (yet not so mysteriously) burnt down soon afterwards. Things hadn't seemed so bad then. There had been a few random killings, not all of them reported. A sudden influx of people from the nearby shtetls. But you could still move about freely, get a decent meal. Josef had been thinking about food that sunny summer morning Mendel appeared. He was waiting to cross the road opposite Karol's Restaurant (still open despite some harassment immediately after the occupation) when a shadow came between him and the sun. At first he had attempted to avoid eye contact. These provincial hasids could be a nuisance, especially if they'd been starving themselves. They were dangerous to be seen with too. You might end up together, yoked to a cart. Or worse. So he had veered discretely aside, only to be pursued by this dark eighteenth century figure who, as they reached Karol's, suddenly fumbled under his long coat and produced a mimeographed sheet of text. It was a synopsis of Josef's own unfinished thesis: *Shabbateanism. A socio-historical perspective. Lurianic and Messianic movements in Ashkenazi Poland.* How his father had glowed pride and pleasure. *You will be a great scholar, Josef, a great beacon of knowledge and belief.* But something had gone wrong: belief fading first, followed by the love of knowledge itself. *And so you have turned aside to secular law. You will be a solicitor perhaps, a mere functionary.* They were inside Karol's now. Incredibly he was sitting opposite this country cousin, meeting his eyes. How had he obtained the synopsis, through what subterfuge? Josef remembered depositing a copy in the university library all those years ago. But the likelihood of them granting access to a shabby rural hasid was infinitesimal. No matter. Mendel was discoursing now. The ten sefirot. The breaking of the vessels. Tikkun. Their restoration. These were not metaphors. Josef must understand. These things were true. The shattered fragments of God's light would be refashioned. Through prayer and action. In our time. It was as if he had met the person his father had wanted him to be, the person who had died with the thesis. He hardly tasted his gefilte fish.

So their friendship had begun. In those palmy unrestricted days Josef had had a decent set of rooms just off the Ringroad. He was even practising a little, drawing up the occasional Will or preparing a Deed of Settlement. Here Mendel would visit him (and it was a sign of his friend's power that Josef soon ceased to worry about informers) to discourse and argue over ersatz coffee into the night. Soon he began to look forward to these unannounced visits. Through Mendel he had begun to recapture some of the intensity of his early student days. His old immersion in messianism seemed once again a living thing. He even dug up the unfinished thesis from the bottom of his trunk and read it again with Mendel poring over his shoulder. The dust of learning that had finally buried his faith seemed riddled afresh with strange points of light. In time – he caught himself speculating – he might even come to believe. Then too, now Alicia was beyond reach, Mendel soothed his loneliness. Soon afterwards the ghetto had been established.

Their friendship now was thrown into harsher relief. While Josef became an administrator in the Judenrat, a trained solicitor entrusted by the Jewish council with the complex burden of statistics and census-taking, Mendel remained himself. He could not change. So that, what previously had seemed to his friend like an almost oriental vagueness, an unwillingness to name or describe, became now – in the dark slow underkingdom of the ghetto – a deep well of otherworldly strength. Which Josef could not draw on. While Mendel prayed and fasted and meditated as before, the ex-student of messianic movements plunged ever deeper into a swamp of facts, numbers, lists. Mendel's purity became almost transparent in that murky place, but Josef felt himself mired in a reality he could neither condone nor escape. His rulers were the Judenrat, the Chairman and, above both, Schaefer. At worst they had to be obeyed; at best placated. Mendel acknowledged nothing but the Ein Sof – the unpronounceable infinite One – along with its ten mysterious emanations. So while Josef grew more distrustful of himself the more he took care to satisfy his superiors, Mendel grew more defiant but less vulnerable. He defied his friend and intellectual adversary (the old midnight disputations were no longer possible); defied the ghetto police and the Chairman; and even, on one memorable occasion, defied Schaefer himself, refusing to cut his beard in the market square and earning from that profoundly unpredictable figure not a bullet in the back of the neck but a curt laugh. So he survived and rose up repeatedly in front of

Josef. To sermonise, prophesy, correct. Or simply to bless. As now.

—Like a flower. It is His love.

Mendel had moved into the middle of the room now. Dazedly Josef realised that he was going to have to work hard to eject his friend this time. He glanced out of the window. A thin pillar of sunlight appeared between two swift-moving grey clouds. And was expunged. Before the war this had been a suburb already sinking into decay. Now the ghetto hastened that subsidence. On every side buildings rose, their shells pocked with bullet holes, their stucco flaking and stained, their windows boarded, broken. The streets ran darkly beneath. Ravines. But dry. Suddenly Josef longed for water, a pond or a lake, an ornamental fountain. He felt a rush of tenderness for his strange friend, all the more disturbing for being mixed with the old tenderness for Alicia. When he turned back from the bleak window his eyes were full of tears. He spoke quietly.

—Where are you living now? You must remember to keep a low profile.

Mendel raised his head and stuck out his chin. It occurred to Josef that his friend had grown taller since they had been in the ghetto together. It was a troubling metamorphosis. And though he had that familiar hollow look of the perpetually hungry, he seemed somehow to wear it as an attribute rather than a mark of shame. Even the yellow star on his old coat looked as if it might have been designed from one of the symbols in an ancient kabbalistic drawing. Josef felt ill at ease. Almost afraid.

—They'll have you for the next selection if you don't stay

out of trouble. I can't intervene. Are you still at the leather factory?

Mendel shook his head.

—Not after the tefillin came back.

—Back?—Josef tried to put on an official air.

—From those who were resettled.—He paused.—East.

—Consignments aren't labelled. They could have come from anywhere.—Josef rolled his pen back and forth along the edge of the desk. Uncomfortably. His friend was breathing.

—I recognised one. Mordechai's. Who ran the Talmudic study group. Before you closed it down.

Josef tried to intervene. It had not been his department. But Mendel waved him aside.

—Now they are making them into shoes. I don't go there. It is blasphemy, not work.

—But without work you don't get vouchers. No vouchers no rations. Mendel be reasonable. I contrived that job for you.

Josef hoped he looked suitably indignant, hurt even. At least it disobliged him from confronting the disturbing question of whether such items as phylacteries did indeed return from those who had left the ghetto. And if so, why? But Mendel was smiling.

—Yes, it is beginning to happen. A little shard of His light in every heart. Oh to join them together. To remake the shattered vessel.

Then he was gone, by the back stairs as Josef had hoped. Busying himself with a plan to employ his awkward friend as a sort of office runner, a gatherer of information, Josef attempted to suppress the storm of emotions Mendel always aroused. Yet, as he sifted through his papers, he came again upon the ledger where his journal, as if unbidden, had begun to take shape. The language he had used there was as much Mendel's as his own. And today Mendel had seen through him to Alicia.

In the cold autumnal square two peoples converged, two currents. Behind improvised wooden stalls and trestles stood shawled women, patting with fingerless gloved fists pyramids of soiled potatoes, swedes, carrots. In front of the stalls drifted other women, furred, high-heeled, gripping handbags in which some last valuable glimmered. Occasionally a furred figure would dart forward and hold out what she had been hiding. Then the shawled double on the far side of her clotted necropolis of roots would spit or grimace, raise an eyebrow, a finger. No one understood each other. No one wanted to understand. Yet all needed to exchange: paste jewellery for turnips, turnips for lingerie. So the two currents swirled round each other, turbid yet distinct.

Alicia had joined the flow. She had found a feather boa in Oskar's carpet bag, coiled like a soft snake inside a second smaller saucepan. Now its uselessness might be turned to good account. For in this straitened, levelling place, what was essential to life could be acquired in exchange for the seemingly decorative or meretricious. She approached one of the stalls where a woman she had known vaguely back home was protesting with shrill urgency.

—It's worth all this. It's worth the whole damned ghetto. My grandfather made it.

She began to weep, in long irregular shudderings. Some new arrivals were like this, immediately overwhelmed and beaten. This one, Alicia realised, would never recover from the knowledge that a family heirloom, a slender gold ring set with sapphires, could not buy more than a few pounds of second rate potatoes. The fruits of rock glittered in her trembling hand, sharp, hard and inedible. She knew their real value yet she needed the fruits of earth.

—She'll give you this as well.

Alicia knew the peasant woman barely understood her. But tearing the silk wrap from the Viennese woman's head and shoulders she guessed that sight and touch would do service for words. The vegetable seller scrunched and twisted the delicate pastel-tinted veil between knobbled fingers.

—Thief. You took it from me. I only bought it last week. At the sales. You took it from me. Thief.

Alicia would have slapped her to stop the screaming. But she noticed that the whole of the woman's left cheek was scarlet with a port-wine stain. Back in Vienna this would have been concealed with powder. Here she had none left. It had been bartered already. So the scarf served as her shield. Until now.

—And the ring.

Stunned into naked submission the woman watched horrified as Alicia prised apart her clenched fingers, removed the ring and handed it across to the squinting stallholder.

—Now give her your best.

The stallholder understood her timbre if not her words.

Taking the woman's basket she poured in potatoes from a second pile hitherto concealed by folded sacking. Their milks showed through clots of soil. The woman was still crying.

—You took them and I've got these.

She was cursing and thanking Alicia in the same breath. But Alicia had turned away. Chaim had been nearby just a minute ago. Now he was gone. All her old protectiveness flooded back. Silent, resentful, but still her child. Then she saw.

From the far side of the square a street led away for some yards then melted into barbed wire. The ghetto perimeter. In front of the wire, on the ghetto side, stood a group of children. They were variously ragged, of different ages, heights. But in every one of them an emaciated intensity of posture had been transfigured by some mysterious energy. A light had visited each one in turn, making him forget for a moment who and where he was. As Alicia moved closer she could sense that this light had its source on the far side of the wire, the Aryan side. All the children were looking through the wire. Now she could hear things too: barrel-organ music, laughing whoops, high shouts of mock fear. And beneath it all a steady rhythmical hum as of a giant drum or wheel slowly revolving.

The fairground was busy even this early in the morning, swarming with adults and children who, however shabbily dressed, bore themselves with none of the hollowed-out finality of those on the ghetto side of the wire. These people were out to enjoy whatever meagre pleasures might be on offer, conscious that they had a right to do so, even though

31

their country was under occupation. So they threaded among the stalls, set up as if in innocent mockery of the dark vegetable barrows in the ghetto. Some bore nothing but trinkets, sweets, confectionaries. Others shadowed games of skill and co-ordination under garishly striped awnings. But at the centre of the waste patch lay the focus of the Fair and of the ghetto children's longing and hopelessness. A carousel whirled there, its platform set with battered wooden horses, cockerels, carriages. Light-bulbs flashed from the underside of its canopy, pale in the morning sun. To one side a steam-engine vibrated, its red wheels glimmering. The children on the carousel seemed oblivious of their haunted audience. They waved without seeing, crying out in self-contained and oblivious ecstasy. Disappeared and reappeared. The ghetto children watched. Though separated from the spectacle by ravines of suffering and knowledge, their very concentration made them almost a part of it. They too gasped and pistoned and waved. They were one with the mirage of the carousel. The veil of adult lies dissolved. They would cross the fence and join their brothers. Chaim was amongst the leaders. A good climber of trees. The ghetto policeman who, up until this moment, had been talking with two German guards outside a sentry box, took out his truncheon and moved forward.

The roundabout was still whirling when the strange western woman appeared from nowhere and leaped on the big boy who had tried to leg it over the fence. A stupid yeke who didn't know this was where the ghetto ended. She pulled him to the ground and lay on top of him panting. The children had all scattered before the policeman came over and pulled the two figures to their feet. He noted where they came from. He noted they had no work permits. Chaim was rubbing his shoulder, frightened but a bit of a hero. Alicia tried not to look too long into the guard's eyes. She remembered Josef mentioning work permits. Food, work, safety. Now she knew what she must do.

—You. Western woman. I might have had you shot.— He pointed to the German guard who stood nearby.

Alicia looked and did not look. Food. Work. Safety.

—You know what the penalty is.

Some of the children had slunk back. They were snickering. In an arc. Chaim made as if to swing at the nearest, who jumped away, calling.

—You have to dance.

The guard nodded, pointing the head of his truncheon towards the ground near Alicia's feet.

—That's right. Something lively. For old Schmoyl.

So in that cold place already hunching under the premature breath of winter, the perimeter fence soughing its low plaints of hollowness and distance, Alicia, the new arrival from the West, danced a tuneless, partnerless Strauss waltz for the emprisoning prisoned policeman. Chaim looked away in shame. She began to sweat, the sick warmth of September still lingering in the stricken air, despite the always encroaching cold. The children watched, grinning. The policeman stroked his chin.

—Hey Schmoyl, we've caught another one. Over here. Smuggling.

Schmoyl turned then, as if remembering something. Absentmindedly he waved his dancer away.

Work. Food. Safety.

Mendel was trying to dance. Round the disused well in the courtyard he moved, slowly at first then faster, but always shuffling somehow, always out of time, unable to establish a rhythm. He could see the village street, the ruts shining with water after the day's rain and Cohen with a bucket trailing his speckled brown scarf of hens towards the coops behind the blacksmith's. He could see the steep pitched shingled roof of the wooden synagogue set apart in the compound, its external gallery with carved balustrades and tall V-shaped support struts. He could see the grave-yard, overgrown with nettles and grasses, the headstones peeping through, the letters on their carved sacred book-spines brimming liquid pink from the after-blaze of sunset. And beyond it the field. They were dancing there now. It was Simhat Torah. The weeks of fasting were over. He moved towards them, his feet barely touching earth, and joined the festivities. Some were drinking, handing round the great wooden flagon with its ringed copper handles carved into shapes of cockerels' heads, the combs and wattles grooved golden. Some sat down to rest, mopping their sweaty brows with handkerchiefs that billowed like white birds in the gathering October dusk. Their faces were molten in the bonfire's unsteady glow. It would be thus until dawn. So he danced with his brothers, praising The One in his heart, longing for the time when the shattered vessels would be made whole. The fire collapsed upon itself, sending up long flickering ladders of sparks where Jacob's seventy two angels climbed, unveiling bright caves in which the ten angels of the sefirot danced, mirroring and mocking this poor earthly dance that was their offering. On the horizon, where the cauldron of the sun still simmered, clouds were piling up in long contused bars. No one noticed. The dance was all.

He shuffled on, in the dirty courtyard, trying to relive that time, to remake it. Always he failed. Heavy-hearted and light in the head, he circled the crumbling brick courses of the well like a child playing a game to make himself dizzy. But it was useless. He willed it thus. He whose name has seventy two syllables and is lost. Sadly, lost, he sat down on the well-rim and gazed into its dry shaft. A few feet down, from a fissure in the side of the shaft, a hart's-tongue fern raised crinkled leathery straps toward the pale sunlight. Profane life. Dark world. Useless. The ecstasy of the morning when he had stood in Josef's office seeing light, was gone. There would be no more Simhat Torahs. No more Sabbaths even. When had he last seen a candle? His tallit and tefillin had to remain hidden in his room, in the cavity under the floorboards beside his bed. Not even a candle. Darkness. The gross, yellow-scorched leaves of the fern flapped slightly in some unfelt breeze, tongueing grossly the black powdery brick. Black tongues of this world. Yet He willed it thus. He, whose name must be sought in all the scattered husks of His creation. He had decreed this darkness. And Mendel His servant must bow to His decree. For even in the driest well-shaft echoes of water lingered. A shard of light could be found, even on the filthiest corner. And in the office of Josef Rosenfeld, slave to the Kingdom of Ham, love itself was growing.

It had been on the windowsill. A small pool of condensation. The room was always cold even for the ghetto, as though the air had been impregnated with some arctic essence, some tincture of cellar and pit. A midge had strayed and foundered there, its shredded wings creased and folded, an exile from the excrement tip. And he had seen. A rainbow sleeping on the waters. Its iridescence quivered. It was a beam from His eye. And then, when he had turned back to the Census Officer, it had shone forth from him too. A dim reflection but unmistakeable. So he had gone, swiftly, with no words of parting, eager not to disturb the brightness of that place, the love growing. How long before it flooded out into the street and across the ghetto, over the perimeter fence and into the city, over the land and across the seas? Almost without realising it Mendel stood up and began dancing again. On and on he danced, the rhythm firm, the pattern whole while, from an upper storey window, two of whose broken panes were stuffed with crumpled up copies of the ghetto newspaper, a half starved young girl stared and stared. *Come away from the window Rachel you'll catch your death.*

Alicia turned the corner into the street where the Department of Registration, Census and Relocation half stood, half leaned against a neighbouring building's fire-blackened shell. People were gathered outside the front door, a bee-swarm thick and clinging. They had fastened onto something firm and unyielding in their midst. As she approached, the density of the swarm thinned a little, letting her sight penetrate to its magnetised, unstable core.

Here was what these desperate people swirled around and clung to and threatened to devour. A god in his chariot of fire. A prince in his golden carriage. An old man in a cart pulled by a grey nag with protruding ribs and charred eyes and driven by a flatcapped policeman wearing dark glasses.

—Mr Chairman we've been evicted . . .

—Mr Chairman. Isaac at the clothing factory. He doesn't understand. You see . . .

—Is it true about the postcards from the East? My Erika said . . .

So the swirling crowd drew close again, their cacophony of cries blurred and droning. So much that they wanted. So much they needed to know. So little they had. And at their centre, in his ice world, sat the god, his grey hair raked back in hard ridges from his temples, his monocle in place, his trilby poised. His eyes closed. So little they had. And less. His eyes were open. He was standing up. The dog-cart rocked.

—Listen to your protector.

Silence. A jingling ghetto coin stilled by a boot.

—Listen to the man who has made all this possible.—A vague sweep of the arm.—Who alone saved you from resettlement.

A cough. A sigh.—*My Erika . . .*—Stifled.

—Work and you live. Idle and you die. That is all. All.

And he was gone: the crowd parting to allow his unimpeded progress into the building, silent and limp, as though in shock, then suddenly recovering, surging forward, magnetised with renewed hope and misery, their voices raised and raised again.

37

—The postcards, the rations . . .

She waited on the pavement. His eyes had taken her in. She had seen murder there. And fear.

—Why did you come here?

Josef's voice made her shiver. She shifted uneasily on her hard office seat. It had been difficult enough reaching this inner sanctum, through the swarm of plaintiffs on the stairs and along the corridor. Thrown into confusion by the Chairman's sudden disappearance through a side door leading to the cellars, they were hostile to anyone who might try to pierce their humming, magnetised cloud of longing and expectation. Then, after the Chairman had reappeared and made for one of the subsidiary record offices (he often visited these lightning strikes on unsuspecting departments in the ghetto administration), the crowd had thinned to follow him and she found herself in front of Solomon, bald complaining Solomon. His goggle eyes and wheezed *Who are you?* incongruously reminded her of a translation of Lewis Carroll she had read as a little girl in Vienna. Then Josef had appeared and, brushing his clerkly caterpillar aside, led her upstairs. But even he seemed guarded.

—Why did you?

It was another gate before which another guardian stood, riddling, importunate. She almost said If you're going to ask damnfool questions like that then why did you overrule Solomon just as he was about to throw me out? But refrained. For beneath his tarnished ghetto armour, the Josef Rosenfeld she had known still lurked. Her reply was weary, rehearsed almost.

—Because you said you could find us work. More quickly than through the normal channels. Work is life the Chairman says. I just heard him. I want work for my family.

The tarnished guardian was tapping on a scuffed black and red ledger. He seemed suddenly diminished, older. The sound of the pen irritated her.

—I mean why here? Your memory is as long as mine. You remember what we did, felt . . . I . . .—The pen tap-tapped. Her head was aching. White mosaics, black.

—You think I chose? To be widowed. To live for three years on what little the Germans didn't confiscate. To have Henryk as a non-paying lodger. How could he pay? To have those deportation orders stuffed through the door one afternoon like some circular, some bill. To come here in those, those wagons. To come here.

She had stood up. The tap-tapping had ceased. She had begun to cry. He came round the desk and squatted beside her, one hand on her shoulder.

—I'm sorry.

She looked at him. He was frightened. Not – like the Chairman – of what he might do, but of what he might not do, or do too late, or do and then undo, in this place. He was reaching back to the desk for a sheet of paper.

—Would you look at this.

Dabbing her eyes she began to read aloud, hesitantly.

'Concerning the saluting of Germans in the ghetto.'

—What is it?—Her eyes were innocent. Too innocent. She lowered them.

—A Judenrat announcement. A wheel within a wheel.

Somebody, some tailor, forgot to take his cigarette out of his mouth when Schaefer walked past.—She raised her eyes to his. He loved her greyish swirls of pupils. Innocent. Not innocent. He stood up.—In other words a matter of life and death. And we, the Judenrat, are its machinery. I am part of that machinery, Alicia. If a tailor is executed for insolence my name is on the death warrant. If ten thousand people are resettled this winter I will have helped draw up the transport lists.

He stopped. He had said too much. Yet not enough.

—I thought *this* was where we were resettled to.—Her eyes betrayed a quiver of depths, a small vertigo, as if looking into the reflection of a mirror in a mirror. Their light guttered, recovered. He took the piece of paper from her.

—So did I, once. In the ghetto we work for our masters. Here,—he lowered his voice as if questioning his own right to speak—we work if you like for the war effort. All well and good. Or not.—He tapped the ledger again, dully with five fingers.—But the ghetto is not stable. People leave as well as arrive.

—Leave? Where?

He shrugged his shoulders.

—How should I know?

Then smiled.

—Perhaps I do. There are rumours at least. The point is, the ghetto is being gradually, inexorably reduced. And every so often, like last summer, there is a big shift, a big selection. This is not our terminus, whatever the Chairman says. We are in transit here. Alicia . . .—Here he reached across and took her hand.—When I asked you that question I was talking aloud. I'm sorry.

—You are part of something you think I should not know about.—Her eyes were clearer now, washed clear.—If you are part of it then I too . . .

—Alicia . . . ?

A sudden turmoil on the stairs outside drowned Josef's reply. Their hands separated. Running feet and shouts of *Mr Chairman* drew closer. The petitions were beginning. There was a bellowed silence and the door opened.

He wanted to talk about water. To start talking now. Then the words would carry him there into the heart of water. He imagined it as a crystal globe, expanding and contracting, everliving. Inside he would float with eyes closed. In the lens of water he would grow young again.

—Schaefer's on the rampage. It's that bloody saluting business. We must have accurate records.

Josef ran his fingers through his hair and glanced at where Alicia leant unknowingly against the entrance to the secret archive.

—If there's another resettlement . . .

—When?

—How should I know?

Water, he wanted to talk about water.

—Get your stenographer onto it.

Josef was nonplussed. Could the Chairman mean Alicia? He was looking at her approvingly.

—I shall want the east sector lists revised by tomorrow.

Alicia had moved instinctively from the filing cabinet.

—One of our westerners . . .

She nodded.

—Educated. And trained as a secretary. Yes?

Again she saw Oskar turning at the door on the eve of his last departure for Venice. *And why you want to work in an office god alone knows. Haven't you got enough to do at home with Grandma and the boy?*

—Those milkchurns down in the cellar. Do you need them?

Josef coughed, a little too loudly.

—They are useful for storage.

Why a woman in your position needs to work . . . She remembered turning to the mantelpiece and stroking Oskar's statuette of the Lion of St Mark. A symbol of power. And power's futility.

The king of the ghetto was leaving. She looked up at him and nodded, again, smiling.

Yes. I work here, in the administration.

The Chairman had been reclaimed by his unstable universe of supplicators and blasphemers. They were left alone.

—I can find you work elsewhere, in the hospital for example.—Josef was embarrassed at the evident insincerity in the voice. *I can but I won't.*

—No. This is what I want.

They were talking water. It was the water that rose and spun and fell in the Donaupark seven years ago. Flames and columns of swaying water, merging, splitting. The verdigris lips of lead dolphins were its source, lionheads rayed with sunlight, masks of gods. Her lips glowed cinnamon. She leant against the rim of a ribbed basin, her breasts nudged upwards and splayed by its scalloped edge. She let water trickle across the webs of her cool fingers. Cool water. Cool flesh. I am drowning in you.

—You know how it is between Oskar and me.

She was running the tip of a forefinger along the crinkled edge of Schaefer's communiqué. Her lips were cinnamon. Cool. Water.

—There can be no reconciliation. And yet I cannot leave him, or Chaim, or Grandma. You understand that, don't you Josef?

He did not understand. Only longed. Slowly she let him draw her away from the ripple and play of water. She let him hoop her waist with his arms, brush her lips with his.

—How did he know? About my training?

A rueful laugh.

—Oh he knows everything, the Chairman. He even knows about my milkchurns.

They said he had four eyes. That's how his death started. Outside the Kärntner Strasse shop where he'd been stocktaking. Four-eyes Schultz, the king of the yids. That was what they were chanting. But they were wrong. He only had one eye. Inside his trousers. The others were all false. Glass and light not eyes. Josef has four eyes and sometimes six and sometimes seventy two. They help him see round corners. They help him see time. But my hens could see time and what good did that do them?

3

Chaim was walking and he didn't know where. All the streets were the same, the squares and the courtyards. Ruinous, flaking, crisscrossed by hollow-eyed wraiths, locked into unknown trajectories of need and loss. There were no fountains. No parks where he could climb the plane trees or – since it was already autumn – throw sticks into the emerald hearts of sweet chestnut, then wait for the tumble and swish as their matted hairy brown shells fell about him. And there was no one to talk to. The children who had watched the carousel with him that first morning shunned him now as mad, someone dangerous to know, an outcast. The adults were all staring, blind strangers. Even his family seemed remote, stunned by their exile into routines of evasion. For Grandma this took the form of her own imminent death. She hardly seemed to notice they were not back at home, in the apartment. For Henryk evasion was nursing, performed with a gentle perfunctoriness which Chaim had witnessed before, when his great uncle massaged the engorged crop of a barnvelder cockerel or worked loose an impacted ball of earth from a cochin's claw. For his mother, after the humiliation of the dance, evasion could only be work. And something else her son could not quite articulate.

So he walked the streets looking at nothing, absorbing nothing, razing the ghetto to the ground and sowing the remains with tears. Then in its place he would rebuild Vienna, but without the old tensions and hostilities: the barbed remarks at school turning to pinches and kicks then finally, one afternoon in St Stephensplatz, a beating that left purple bruises on his rib cage. Afterwards his mother had withdrawn him from the grammar school for good and he had worked or pretended to work at home. But above all the Vienna in his mind contained his father. Gone were the straitened years without him, Henryk in the spare room, Grandma beginning to have her attacks. But gone too were those times before his father's so-called accident, when there had been silences at the dinner table and afterwards, when he was supposed to be asleep, long muffled raging arguments. In this dream city, constructed by Chaim as he passed the blank featureless tenements of the ghetto, his father never took off unannounced on business trips, his mother never went for long walks alone in the park, Grandma in her lucid moments never took him aside and tried to distract him. In this city no one looked askance at you in the street, no windows were boarded, no graffiti were daubed on the boards: *Go back to Palestine. Out. Go to Jerusalem.* In this city his father sat in his favourite chair as he had done during Chaim's early childhood, large, his dark beard closely clipped and smelling faintly of eau de Cologne. *Look, I can blow smoke rings through my ears* he said and sucked intently on a chewed grey meerschaum. Or he said *Look, this saved me in the war* and held out a battered silver cigarette case with a dent in its lid. *That bullet was*

*meant for my heart. Look at all the soldiers in the metal. They're
Prussians at Waterloo. One day you'll have this.*

Yet just as the ghetto seemed – for all its unreal frailty – to
possess supernatural powers of recovery, rising out of the
ashes of Chaim's hatred as diseased and mildewed and
hopeless as ever; so the dream city of Vienna where his
father was always home and his mother never self-pitying,
would suddenly be invaded by its darker lonelier double.
He could not erase his parents' estrangement. And once that
black flame had leapt back into life, Chaim found himself
circling yet again round the fact of his father's accident and
disappearance. If he could comprehend that, perhaps even
the mystery of this exile might become clearer.

He remembered how, the morning after, when he still
knew nothing, his mother had come to his bedroom and sat
on the edge of the bed. A thing she rarely did. She was
sobbing but something in the heave of her back, stiff
beneath a white chiffon blouse, told him that she was
watching herself, reining herself in. A bluebottle hummed
against the window. Afterwards Chaim found it in the sink,
sucking at the edge of a droplet of water. Its stubbly legs
rubbed against each other, obscenely slow and deliberate.
His father had been killed in a train crash on his way back
from Venice. He did not believe her. What was all that
shooting in the night? And that red glow on the skyline
downtown? His mother had murmured something about
festivities, unruly crowds, blasphemies. The fly buzzed.
Normally, she never used words like blasphemy. Then,
walking to the bakery that morning, he had seen the
boarded-up windows of his father's main store in the

Kärntner Strasse. White painted letters had been hurled across it; *Judenfrei*. In the gutter outside the bakery lay a crumpled sheet of paper. It had been ripped from an old copy of *Der Stürmer*. There was an illustration on one side: some ancient woodcut depicting four rabbis seated round a baby. The baby's body was pierced by straws which the rabbis sucked on. Underneath the modern caption ran: *A Passover Feast*. The manager of the bakery – a gentile – was nervous, offhand. He wanted his account settled, quickly. Then Chaim knew that his mother had lied about his father's death, just as she had lied about his business trips to Venice and elsewhere. And he knew too that, in some obscure way, these lies were mingled with the painted lies on the shattered shop fronts and the printed lies in the gutter. The funeral had been swift, almost perfunctory, as if the rabbi had one eye permanently looking over his shoulder. Then his mother had fetched Henryk, initially for six months but eventually for three years. Henryk too had stories about what happened the night of Oskar's disappearance which, though not lies, had more to do with hens than people. Gradually the disappearance became simply The Accident. His mother was not happy. But nor was she in deep mourning. This too Chaim took as another mendacity, a kind of trick. So that, when the resettlement papers came through, he was inclined to treat their contents as one more black fragment from the world of adult lies. His mother had cried packing. She had wondered whether to take the framed photograph of Oskar and then decided against it. The picture dated from the day of their engagement. Chaim sensed the resentment behind her sadness.

So his childhood had ended. He too had cried when his mother had told him there would be no room for Toni, the Rabbit, who had sat on his chest of drawers for years, dressed in a flowered satin waistcoat and green lederhosen. Yet he too found himself watching his tears, resenting them. Toni slumped sideways, his pink velvet ears flopping. Father was dead but unaccounted for. Buried but wrongly, standing up. They were travelling East, no one knew where exactly. The apartment must be locked, the rooms where he had lived for fifteen years curtained to gather dust. Toni slumped, his head turned away. Gone. Then the Praterstern. How he had loved it that day his father had taken him to look at the long distance trains. *Some go all the way to Russia. Look. You can sleep in them. Look. Little cubicles. With curtains.* Ten years later he wore the yellow star. Even the pigeons whirred mockingly overhead, in the steam-flecked girders. Henryk was spattered all down one shoulder. *That's good luck. He'll need it where he's going. No couchettes for them. Fourth class rolling stock.* Then the journey. The change into cattle trucks. Here. Lies. He was glad he had left Toni the Rabbit behind.

And now the ghetto flowed back to sprawl before him, an exile within exile. Briefly he touched the yellow badge sewn onto his lapel by his mother. How her hand had trembled. More than when his father disappeared. He could easily tear it off, hurl its light rag away. But it would make no difference. The star was indelible now. Like the ghetto. Like his father's absence. Yet it helped him see. He saw how the crowds swarmed round the horsedrawn vegetable carts when they creaked into the market square on alternate

Tuesdays; he saw the ragged children fighting in the dirt of the road for a few stray tubers that had fallen from the back of the cart; he saw how the workers would emerge slowly from their factories and workshops at midday to sit hunched in rows in the dim alleys, spooning sops; he saw tongues dully flicker across dry lips; he saw a man grab a grey loaf of bread from a woman in a ration queue and bolt it down in three gulps; he saw the man being beaten; he saw another man, tall, black-coated, dancing round a well. To his wonderment the face of this figure glowed. It was smiling, ecstatic even. But then the man turned away, his face shutting down like all faces in the ghetto. And Chaim continued on his solitary, aimless path.

They beckoned him into the courtyard. It was where the dancer had moved the other day. Round and round the wellhead. Unaware. But this was no ritual. They were both his age. They shifted nervously from foot to foot. They looked past him, vigilant.

—Was it you trying to climb the wire the other day? When they made the woman dance?—His accent was thick and eastern. But educated.—We could use you. You're agile.

—I'm better at trees. There aren't any trees. Here.

The boy had a sort of rag balaclava wound round his head. Almost a turban. His companion, shorter, tapping scratched wooden clogs, butted in.

—You can cross the wire at night. And you don't have to climb.

—What for?—Chaim felt the yellow weight in his heart stir a little and lighten.

—What we need.

—You mean . . .

—It's a sort of ghetto out there too.

The boy with the rag balaclava paused and smiled. His cheek was pitted with an old fury of acne. Chaim could see something grey crawling there. With expert fingers the boy picked off the louse and smeared it against the wellhead.

—Out there they want things from us same as we want things from them.

—Finestuffs for food,—the smaller one added.—It's bartering really.

—We can show you how you get across. At night.

The pale face that had watched Mendel from the upstairs room glanced briefly down at the shivering trio then faded into shadow.

Grandma was in the big bed. Ashen-faced, dry-lipped. Mother was still out working in the Census Department. Henryk had gone to the post office to try and send a card to Richard, his old companion on the smallholding. *I'm thirsty* Grandma said. He went to her.

They met at dusk by the old well. There was an excitement in breaking the curfew and being on the loose. A short underground route led from there to an unguarded sector of the wire under the wall of the hospital. They had cut a hole then disguised it with sow thistle. From this point it was a short crawl to the first houses, the contacts. The one with the rag balaclava was called Bernard. He would meet them there tonight. Bernard said: *At least we're doing something.*

They were crossing the Grand Canal in a traghetto. It was evening. The palaces flickered light from the oily water. They stood together hand in hand. Then the boatman stopped poling. He had Schaefer's face. He said: *Rosenfeld, did you know ghetto is a Venetian word?*

There were thousands. They passed by. Schaefer's voice said *They are gone. Look at those to come.* There were thousands. They passed by. Alicia passed by.

The water was warm and clear. They swam together, naked. Fringed with bubbles her breasts lifted and fell. He looked down. There beyond the floating weed of her pubic hair, between the pale tapering parsnip roots of thighs, a city lay. Green, open to the water above. Together they swam down to it. For years they lived in the submarine ghetto. When at last they were told to leave they cried.

Water, Henryk, water.

She was telling him about Henryk's attempt to post a card out of the ghetto. Her tone was gentle, concerned. In spite of his clumsy eccentricities she had grown to accept Henryk in the years after Oskar's death. He was at once the trusting child Chaim had long ceased to be and the faithful adult her husband would have scorned. She looked up in the gathering dusk. With her grey discs of eyes.

—It was the man he lived with in the Wienerwald before they burnt the smallholding down. He's only half-Jewish, lives under a false name somewhere. But they still correspond about fowl. Why couldn't he send the card?

On another occasion, earlier or later in their relationship, Josef might have dissembled. But now was neither too early nor too late. Her protective, bogus mothering of Henryk stung him to irrational jealousy. He went over to the office clock which was always, it seemed, ahead or behind.

—Only pre-printed cards can leave the ghetto now.

He tapped the glass face. Sighed.

—On whose order?

—Theirs. He was lifting the clock away from the wall. Its machinery suddenly fascinated.

—But you implement the order. You prevent Henryk from sending greetings to his old friend. He may not get another chance. Especially if we have to move again.

So she was angry. He hadn't wanted this. He let the clock bang back against the wall.

—And what are you doing? In your work here? With me? You prevent him too.

Desperately he had wanted not to upset her. And now his words echoed tinnily in the shabby room. Across the street the lights in Isaac's clothing factory had come on. They burnt all night above rows of workers making uniforms for the Eastern Front. He glanced back at Alicia. Her face had shut again, darkened. There would always be a part of her that would not yield. She would never stop blaming him for her presence in this place. It was this knowledge that decided him. Along with an almost impish desire to shock. Swiftly he crossed to the empty filing cabinet and began sliding it aside. She looked on, half in wonder, half in fear.

When she stepped through the narrow, irregularly cut doorway, she might have been entering a shrine to a power she had long since turned away from in despair.

The room of the secret archive breathed dust of gathered papers. She moved between the two desks, the old wardrobe where the files were kept and the lopsided bureau stuffed with virgin quires. She touched the two typewriters gently, as if they contained something Holy, some precious Scroll. Gently she ran her fingers along the spine of a folder. It might have been a rare rabbinical commentary. In that room she had become what she had long since ceased to be in the world outside: a believer. Her anger and fear evaporated. Josef followed her at a distance, willing her to understand what dark treasures this cell contained, longing for her to glimpse – as he had glimpsed – the hidden wealth of the submarine city. She moved like one who has woken in an ancient buried storehouse, packed with the accumulated hoards of centuries. That the trove here had been gleaned from oppression and misery, that the hidden nuggets and grains and gems were all shards of the black vessel of the ghetto, seemed for the moment not to matter. The preservation mattered, the recording, the witnessing. Locked away in words and numbers, every outrage and injustice had been saved here from oblivion. Nothing would be lost. All would come to light. This was a work of light. The husks of evil might lie scattered in all their opacity. But the work of transformation was beginning. Through words and numbers the evil would be redeemed, the shattered vessel made whole, its shell the essence of light.

And watching her – the woman he had loved and the woman he loved again – move through that monstrous tension of light and dark, like a beautiful grey-flecked mermaid among the drowned pillars of the dwellings of men Josef, for perhaps the first time since he had entered the ghetto, felt a bright uplifting weightlessness. As if duty and honour no longer clashed. As if what he did for the sake of expediency and what he performed out of compassion and the desire for justice needn't conflict. He had brought Alicia here with, he admitted to himself, a certain cunning of foresight, wanting her to realise the enormous strains under which he laboured day in, day out. Then at last she might pity him, a lawyer turned unwilling Atlas. But now it was as if he saw the archive afresh through her eyes. As so often before, in the old days in Vienna, he felt the tarnished world grow bright beneath her gaze.

Sloughed off, her already deteriorating and patched clothes lie coiled and folded between the two desks like dull brown hanks of sea-weed. He palps her remembered breasts, the large empurpled silken areolae, the left slightly larger than the right. She rises and falls above him, mouth half open, eyes closed, head tilted sideways. Her black hair wedges half her face in shadow. It is striped with grey. Once his gaze shifts from the blur of her pubic triangle to a mimeographed sheet that lies crumpled beside his cheek. She moans. *Potatoes are getting dearer.* She moans again but more throatily now as if the weight of all these words were pressing down on her. *It is not advisable to eat beetroot leaves because of the amounts of salicylic acid they contain.* His hands clench her buttocks, pushing her down. *If you must, be sure to boil well*. Her moans are cries now he is thrusting up. *Bread at 1.30 marks a kilo*. She trembles then shudders. *Bread beetroot potatoes*. In slow motion she collapses on his chest. Her hair, falling, tickles his cheeks, his nipples.

Later, rolling over to get dressed Josef found another sheet underneath him, its edge yellowed by a gout of semen that had escaped from his thick sausage-skin prophylactic. A memo about work permits. He smiled and showed it to her as she bent to draw up a stocking.

—I'll have to retype this. And find some work for Henryk.

At long last he had been able to purchase a candle again. It was the new work for Josef that had brought this miracle to pass, work that obliged him to break the Sabbath. He pondered this paradox, one hand cradling the cool wax column concealed under his overcoat, as he passed through the market to the Census Department. It was akin to that other conundrum: Josef's transformation through profane love. Yet hadn't Shabbatei Zevi himself committed many sayings and acts that were contrary to all sacred teaching? And didn't Isaac Luria teach that when Abba and Imma, the father and the mother, come together face to face the broken vessels would begin to be restored? In the last days there must be many darknesses, many mysteries. Josef and the woman had come together. What matter if their base union contained dregs of a world where Samael and Lilith ruled in corrupt glory? He had seen the light in Josef's face. What matter if, forced by demon and witchcraft, he broke with Holy Writ? Nervously he fingered his candle. At least

he could acknowledge the Sabbath even if he was con-
strained not to keep it. He saw himself tomorrow morning
in the high attic, lighting the candle and taking out tallit and
Torah. But first he would look in that commentary on the
Zohar. He wanted to check on the parzufim, the faces that
would remake the holy vessels of light. He repeated over
and over to himself: Abba, Imma, Samael, Lilith, Josef, the
woman, until a face stopped him. At the corner. The
policeman who often followed him. Striped suit. White
scarf. Dark glasses. Closing his mind he walked quickly on.
Yet this too must be a sign. They knew he had seen the
shards of God's light and were afraid. All round him the
voices of the ghetto rose like distant flood waters. The
messiah would be preceded by a great flood. This too was
written in the air.

She slid out of the office doorway. She was wrapped in
the shining garments dotted with points of light: God's
secret name. Her forehead glowed. It was the light of Moses
he himself had felt once or twice, radiating from the tefillin
of the forehead, after long fasting. The great restoration
was beginning. He would have bowed down then and there
if the policeman hadn't still been watching him. But he
could whisper. And bless.

She hurried past hoping he wouldn't try to follow. There
was someone, too, in the shadow of the arch opposite. That
policeman who had made her dance by the perimeter fence.
So the hasid was being watched. She quickened her pace. It
wouldn't do to be seen near such an outcast. And yet Josef
had found him employment connected with that very

office. And they were friends. Thinking of this and of how the hasid had whispered something about Lilith as she came out of the building she felt anger mixed, if she had cared to be candid, with jealousy. Walking down the stairs she had thought exclusively of Josef and their long lovemaking in the room of the secret archive. Now all was cold again. It was as if the ghetto were a maze of mirrors each of which dissolved into another when you looked. Josef and the hasid came from different worlds, different cultures and even – in a sense – different times. Yet they were friends and in the midst of the squalor and privations of the ghetto would quite happily sit for an hour swopping some obscure kabbalistic dialectic. How often had she come into the office and found them together. She felt at such times as though she were interrupting a consultation, part ritual, part seminar. Once she had found them hunched side by side over a chart drawn up in red ink. It consisted of two columns. On the left were the letters of the Hebrew alphabet. On the right their mystical meanings. *Qoph is light; Mem, death*, Josef muttered. Then Mendel was talking in his peculiar highpitched way about the garment of the sefirot. Josef looked up, his gaze blank. *Shin is* . . . Neither embarrassed nor excited to see her there. *Shin is Sacred Fire*. Muttering like someone bewitched. Bewitched by a zaddik from the shtetl. Was this man, poring credulously over a scroll of spells, the same man she had made love to half an hour since, that paragon of uprightness, reason and fine feeling? Even her parents would have been horrified, minutely, pedantically pious as they were. This was the ignorance of poverty. Yet Josef was not ignorant.

Nearing the tenement entrance she felt a rush of wet warmth inside her. Josef had done that. The man whom she had never thought to meet again after those few weeks in Vienna all those years ago. She smiled. She could not deny that she had wanted him, that she had exulted in the room of the secret archive. She remembered his face, turned on one side, the eyelids heavy, half closed. Such a delicate skull. What did it contain? He had been a scholar once, a historian of messianic movements amongst European Jewry. Perhaps it wasn't so strange he should be attracted to what amounted to a living relic of those times, a sort of petrified tree, memorial to the vast green luxuriance that had once swayed all round it. Mendel to him wasn't ignorant. Nor was he confused. In his talk the apocalyptic longings of generations of Ashkenazim still lived and breathed. He may not have read widely but he had brooded deeply over certain texts and redactions. He was a relic maybe, but valuable. So at least she thought Josef might feel, as she neared the ruinous comb that harboured her small family. She turned round. He had not followed her. Nor had Schmoyl, the white-scarfed policeman. Surely, if she were ever forced to choose between Mendel and his watcher she would cross to the hasid's side. Perhaps Josef was even braver than she had thought. And more subtly sensitive. Forgiving him she asked him to forgive her. Profane and earthly and expedient as they were, these few words, whispered in the dank hallway of the tenement, became the first prayer she had attempted since entering the ghetto.

Josef had sealed up the secret room by the time Mendel

blundered in. But he still hadn't hitched up his trousers properly. His shirt billowed gently from the open fly, a guilty ectoplasm.

—Forgive me. I see you've been exercising.

Josef stared incredulously at his friend then turned away. How much or how little did Mendel ever know? A fly button came away in his trembling fingers. He cursed.

—Even Shabbatei Zevi himself ate the fats of the sacrifice and called upon his followers to acknowledge the one who permits the forbidden.

—He turned Turk didn't he? So much for the messiah.

—There are mysteries in that too. But look.—Here Mendel fumbled in his overcoat.—Look what a miracle has come to pass. With this candle and my bit of glass I can meditate once again on the sefirot which, as Luria said, are like candles reflected in a mirror.

—Those old analogies. They have great beauty. And sadness. They speak of longing, not fulfilment.

In spite of himself Josef was being drawn into the hasid's orbit of narrow intensity. Then too he still felt the satin breeze of her breasts brushing his lips.

—Not just as analogies. I know now.—Mendel had placed the candle between them on the desk. His face seemed suddenly suffused with light, the last light of the day.—I saw her not ten minutes ago.—Then, touching the candle—I understood. You and she are the parzufim, Abba and Imma, the man and woman who must unite face to face.

With a supreme effort of will Josef tore himself away from Mendel's magnetic orbit.

—Were you followed?

Mendel ignored him.

—Tikkun is at hand. The broken vessels shall be restored. She . . .

Josef slumped into his accustomed chair. He felt a sudden supreme weariness. The last days. The last days. Mendel was being more accurate than he knew. There would be a resettlement soon. Then a lull, then . . . The ghetto would not survive another year. Afterwards there would be no broken vessels left to restore. Messianism had its limits. He looked up, shading his eyes.

—Did you get the information about the soup kitchens from Moyshe?

Mendel ignored him again, staring at the white stem as if it were coated with eyes. Josef licked his dry lips. The last days. What right had he to clasp an old love in his arms? Soon he would be responsible for sending more people out of the ghetto. Even she, the woman he had loved in the room of the secret archive. He wanted to vomit in self disgust.

—You must be married soon.

He started. It was as if his own voice had spoken, disembodied.

—She will be your bride of the Torah.

Again the far sound of water, the play of light. The old sense of weightlessness returned. So Mendel did know. Somehow.

The yellow star became a bird carrying him over the barbed wire perimeter. His father was there to meet him. He was lying on top of a pyramid of swedes. *Have you mother's jewels? I wasn't killed. She wanted me out of the way so she could meet Josef again. I went into early retirement in Venice. They have a ghetto there too. At the bottom of the Grand Canal. Visit me when you can. But bring a diving suit.*

They say no one can send letters now but it's not true. It's because I wanted to tell Richard about the hens. That frightened them. They know hens see time. They don't want us to see. They want us to think we live here forever. First there is dark then there is light. First you go in then you come out. Under St Stephen's in the tunnels there are different cages for different bones. They have to be kept apart. Otherwise they might all join up together again and walk.

4

They called him yeke or sometimes, after a particularly good haul, treecreeper. They met in the yard of the mad hasid but only briefly, in ones or twos. Their real hideout – what Bernard, the lousey boy with the rag balaclava liked to dignify as their centre of operations – lay elsewhere. Beyond the wellhead a slimy passage led into a further inner courtyard choked with debris: the remains of a sentry box that had mysteriously caught light on the first day of the summer resettlement; a roll of rust-eaten barbed wire; and – incongruously – two backless rotting chairs. Windows glared blankly down on this abandonment. They were all glassless, the rooms they had served gutted and uninhabitable. In one corner, part of the containing wall had tumbled into the yard revealing, at first floor level, a fireplace set into the chimney breast. But, since the floor had gone too, the fireplace merely hung there, floating between the ground and the sky, its charred mouth gulping at the foggy autumnal air. The entrance lay at the base of this collapsed wall. Half hidden by a heap of bricks that, in the perpetual scummed twilight of the little yard, glowed verdigris and ruby, a spiral of steps sank down into a tiny Area. At the far end was a hole, once the chute for the coal cellar that had served the suspended fireplace overhead. In winters before the occupation the windows had glowed here all evening with red, wavering shadows.

The gang met in the cellar. Letting himself down through the chute Chaim would come up against a barrier in the form of an old iron bedstead. A spring had to be plucked to alert whoever was keeping watch on the far side. Then there was a password – for days now the refrain of a popular ghetto song about the western arrivals: 'Es geyt a yeke mit a teke' – which Chaim always whispered with a certain amount of resentment. Then the bedstead would tilt allowing him through. Beyond, in a foetor of urine and soot, a single candle smoked, shadowing vaultings and archways that disappeared into some darker interior. The smugglers would be there, sitting on old packing cases, talking softly. Some – like Chaim – would have descended temporarily. Up above the tattered garments of their ghetto selves waited to be worn again. For them the excitement and tension of their task was a mere relief, a welcome forgetting. Afterwards they would return to their families and workplaces, their commitments. Others had given up any pretence of belonging to the already crepuscular world overhead. As if sensing that the shock waves of events on the surface would be less violent by the time they penetrated under the earth, they had gone underground completely. Ghosts the ghetto preferred to forget, they endured a troglodytic existence, nourished by the proceeds of their smuggling like the ancient spirits who lived on blood. Yet for them this existence was no escape. Already, across their pale prematurely shadowed faces, an icy conviction was beginning to spread. Down in these caves whose walls they stared at as if seeking for oracles, they had begun to realise that one day smuggling would lead to armed resistance. Almost in spite of themselves they were preparing to become freedom fighters.

As yet Chaim sensed little of all this. He was drunk on the illicitness of it all. He loved the password – even if it did make fun of his origin. He loved the way the boy with the balaclava raised his fist as he entered the cellar. He loved the silence and watchfulness as they prepared to enter the passageway that led up to the unguarded section of fence. He loved the sweaty proximity of his brothers in crime: the short one, the one who had been fat, Bernard. It was a camaraderie he had never tasted at the grammar school. It flattened out and simplified the jagged contours of the adult world he was forced to negotiate up above. And it challenged the authority of his mother and her fancyman, the Census Officer. He smuggled to resist them, to make them less real. In this dark place he was back in a world of childhood games, pacts, terrors. At every turning he met his father, smiling encouragement.

The first time had been terrifying. The long dank passage. The slimed gulley. There were noises too, a distant thunderous unrest. Bernard had whispered: *The Eastern Front. You can hear it better underground.* Then came the sudden numbing entrance into upper air, the lungs grateful for what in daylight would have seemed stagnant and secondhand. Ahead glimmered a patch of wasteground, sentried with stout bushes of sow-thistle that dragged at you as you passed, their hooked dead crowns fastening onto any available piece of clothing then burrowing in with their cargo of seed. Hours later you could still feel their prickly dryness against your skin. You were crawling now, Bernard ahead, the boy who had been fat on your left. The short one had gone on to unfasten the flap of netting and wire they had cut a couple of weeks before. Then one by one you would squirm through, the last, usually Bernard, taking care to rearrange and disguise the opening. Then more crawling, more thistles. Finally the first house, empty and ruinous as any in the ghetto. Strange how like the ghetto this place was. A black mirror image of your own detested world. And in the faces of the two men you met in the abandoned dyeworks the same look of misery and hollow need. As if your own desolation had spread outward to infect the entire universe. That first night it was kohlrabi. Bernard had the stolen goods wrapped in a ghetto poster. Scarves mainly and a pair of woman's slippers, gold with white buckles. Chaim remembered his mother wearing a similar pair in the apartment on the night of his father's disappearance. He repressed a brief surge of longing. His father was beside him now in this bare cell of a place, whispering: *Nostalgia is for the old who have no time.* He busied himself stuffing the green and purple roots with their upraised candelabra of leaf stems into the neck of a hessian sack. Soon there would be the long journey back, the pause at the fence (this was the moment when most smugglers were discovered and shot by the German criminal police), the satisfaction of returning to the dank cellar. Chaim shivered.

—She'll like these, one of the dealers said, pocketing the slippers.

Despite his father standing near, helping to hold the sack open, he thought: So did mother. Once.

It was Sabbath again. He had lit the candle the night before, drawing it slowly out of his pocket and kissing its white stem as though the wraiths of all the candles he had ever lit still burned there. The glow of the flame pooled across the slant ceiling of his attic and might have gone spilling out into the night had he not had the foresight to drape his coat across the window. So that what he lost in shivering he gained in the warm bath of devotion. Not that he had left the candle burning too long. After the preparatory Friday prayer and a few minutes' contemplation of the Ein Sof's presence throughout creation he had found it expedient to pinch out the flame. It was contrary to tradition but not to do so would be to invite discovery. Schmoyl, the Chairman's hanger-on and sometime driver, had been following him again today, longing to make an arrest yet fearful of the hasid's new status as messenger for the Department of Registration, Census and Relocation. Mendel enjoyed his persecutor's discomfort but knew he could not afford to provoke him too far. If he was taken who among the people would recognise the messiah? Who would be fit, prepared, pure? God's law was law but the times before tikkun made it impossible to cleave to the letter.

Now the candle was alight once more. In the raw chill of the dawn, so close to New Year, so far from restoration, in exile still, conscious of the heavy shards of evil lying everywhere about him, Mendel stood before this one fragile flame. The tallit was draped over his shoulders. His bible lay open at the Song of Songs. Last night he had seen the garment of the Torah, its brilliant raiment lit with even brighter stars. Each star was a letter. And together the letters made up the Tetragrammaton, the one unpronounceable Holy name. He pronounced it now as so many holy men had done before him, willing the last days to arrive. A sudden draught made the candle flame waver briefly, letting a veil of blue smoke escape from its tip. Suddenly beyond the veil he saw her face. She was the Queen of the Sabbath and she was a woman. Sacred and profane flowed together, into the one vessel.

—How beautiful are your sandalled feet, O royal daughter! Your curved thighs are like jewels fashioned by a master. Your navel is a round goblet, brim-full of wine. Your belly is a heap of wheat, ringed with lilies.

The candle flared afresh, a wet paleness in the cold air. He trembled, welcoming her, the Queen Sabbath.

—May your breasts be like clusters of grapes on the vine, . . .

His voice grew louder in spite of himself, so loud that he did not hear the old hag below shouting *I've fetched them* nor the tramp of boots on the stair, nor the first splintering sound of his door being kicked open.

—. . . the fragrance of your breath like apples, and your mouth . . .

—Bring them too, the phylacteries. They're evidence.

He had been standing for nearly six hours. The sun that had begun as a vague aura sliding round the lefthand bar of the cell window, was now a sickly yellow clot puddled in a dough of cloud between the middle and righthand bars. At first he had tried to continue his observances under his breath but the pain in his back and side from the beating coupled with the ache in his legs from the standing slowly blotted out all prayer, all meditation. Soon he could only think of remaining upright as the servants of Samael, who ruled this place, had commanded. Yet were they not his people too? Schmoyl, who had taken great delight in punching him until he vomited air, the big one with the pincers he was going to use 'later', even that servant of Lilith and all the other she-devils, the old bitch who had summoned his persecutors. His people, his responsibility. They had ripped his tallit in the attic, the one grandfather had worn in Warsaw and that father had taken on the journey through the Balkans to Jerusalem. His tefillin had been torn from their hiding place (how could he have forgotten to replace the floorboard?), then trampled in the hall of the gaol. His people: kelippot, shards of evil that must be purified and redeemed. He remembered how at the beginning of the occupation, after he had met Josef for the first time, he had seen a group of Rabbis being harnessed by soldiers to a cart. Some of them had known father. Some he himself had disputed with in the house of instruction. One had denounced him as a vain heretic who followed the discredited teachings of Nathan and other messianic prophets. Enemies and friends. His people. Yet he had not intervened. A small voice had bidden him turn aside, in silence. Today he had paid that debt. Or begun to. He was still afraid, still unworthy. But he had endured. The vessels were beginning to fill with light. Somewhere in the ghetto she smiled, spoke, was. He shuddered. There were voices out in the swabbed corridor, approaching. He did not want to die. They had made the Rabbis clean latrines with their beards. They had jammed a high pressure hose into their mouths. She was alive, the Sabbath queen, princess of the dusk. He could not die, not yet. Again he shuddered, his tired empty body shuddered. His spirit was elsewhere, in Glory. The sun oozed away beyond the window.

It was Alicia who learned first of Mendel's arrest. She had gone down to the gaol on office business. It was a place no one cared to visit. But Josef was buried in a new series of reports for Schaefer and Solomon had been taken sick. In the hall she had passed two guards joking about the mad mystic. Not much up top. Not much between his legs. And less still when Schmoyl finishes with him tonight. Then under the single metal chair she had noticed a flattened object, shiny, brownish, like a crushed carapace. She cradled the phylactery's scuffed emptiness in her palm. The cubicle partitions were crushed, the scrolls of sacred texts vanished. A week ago she would simply have put the object down again and gone about her legitimate business. But now, after the encounter in the doorway the previous evening, Mendel was not so easily dismissed. To leave him to his fate was to sacrifice a part of the man she loved. Worse, it would take something from her too, something she could neither fully understand nor acknowledge. So she gripped the phylactery tightly, half walking half running back to the Census Department, her official business forgotten. Pulsing in some mysterious space between her and Josef and Mendel the violated leather pouch hung, her dark star.

Josef laid his hand on Mendel's bony shoulder. He was not so much escorting as pushing his friend out of the station. Schmoyl and his juniors looked on from the desk, puzzled. Why risk so much for a mere village zaddik? But Josef was one of the privileged administration insiders, someone to be appealed to in time of crisis, a man who might save your hide and the hides of your family. It was an unspoken rule that you did not cross such people. And there would undoubtedly be another time.

Once they were clear of the station Josef let his grip relax. How light Mendel's frame felt, like the skeleton of a bird. As if all the hunger of the ghetto were somehow concentrated in him. Yet he was tough too. The ghetto had not eaten him away. Josef's anger at the weightless resilience of his friend returned.

—Haven't you learnt yet? Won't you ever?

Mendel looked back blankly, still shivering a little. He would not acknowledge any fault.

Angrily Josef strode on ahead. He knew his mood was not wholly centred on this one difficult companion. His thoughts returned irresistibly to Alicia, pale-faced, standing in his office. *You must bail him out Josef*, a strand of her hair straggling away from the chequered kerchief she wore for work, her hand automatically tucking it back in, brushing the down of a cheek he had thought lost to him forever a month ago. At that very moment, perhaps more clearly even than in the secret archive at dusk, he knew he loved her. And yet with that knowledge came a disturbance and a darkness that threatened to engulf him. It was as if the more clearly he saw her, the more meaningless his life became. What had he been doing these last two years? What did he intend to do? Registration work. Archive work. Why? He remembered back to the period of the summer resettlements, the daily exodus of two thousand people, young and old, healthy and sick, but always two thousand day after day, seemingly forever. Why? He had presided over it all, a blind mathematician, oblivious of meaning. He remembered watching from the doorway of the old hospital. The trucks were parked further up the street, dull green in the morning sun. Then the people came, carrying their bundles (which later that day would return to the ghetto minus their owners), trooping by, neither too slowly nor too fast, neither eager nor reluctant. Doing what they had been told to do, as he did what he was told to do, drawing up reports, calculating statistics. Why? Two thousand a day neither more nor less. Here a baby born in the ghetto, there an infant with a wooden ball. Here a young man with a limp, there an old prunefaced woman pushing a handcart. And he had watched them all, as if enjoying an official cavalcade, shirtsleeves rolled up, one hand shading his eyes against the sun.

That had been the summer. After ten days the exodus had ended as abruptly as it had begun. Twenty thousand people. Gone. And the space they had left, the wound in the body of the ghetto? Gone too. Covered over almost instantly by the skin of routine and labour. Twenty thousand people. As if they had never been. Why?

71

Later the odd postcard had arrived, addressed to a relation who had not received one of the yellow resettlement papers. It spoke of the East. Hard work. Good food. People read, passing the grubby card from hand to hand in the workshops and soup kitchens. Their eyes betrayed nothing. They did what they always did.

And now Mendel was dancing in the street: another believer in the incredible, the truth of false messages, mere words. What was there to choose between the man who believed he was about to be reunited with his resettled family somewhere East and the man who believed the messiah to be imminent? Even when his beloved's clothing returned to the ghetto he would believe. Even when the date of the coming passed by without incident he would go on praying and fasting

—Haven't you learnt? They pull out your beard. They beat you. They threaten worse. Haven't you?

—Why are you so sad?

You must bail him out. Had Alicia seen something in Mendel he could no longer see? Exasperatedly he let go of the tall man's shoulder.

—Do you ever worry about time?

—Time will end soon. Why worry?

—When I was a child I used to worry about it a lot. I tried to get rid of it. You know, in my head. By dividing it up. At first that's easy. Years go into months. Months into weeks. But when you arrive at seconds it grows more difficult. Pretty soon it becomes impossible. You can't get rid of time Mendel. It's always here. We live in it. We are time.

—But time will end.

—Only when we end.

—We have no ending. The vessels will be restored. We will be as stars in the garment of the Torah. She rescued me today. Blessed be she that comes. You were merely her messenger.

Then the knot of his anger and confusion seemed to unravel a little. Here was a man for whom the blind mathematics of the ghetto were as nothing. To him the relentless hierarchies of command and obedience simply didn't exist. He acknowledged different hierarchies, higher numbers. His systems flowered from prayer and meditation, not war and hatred. This was why Josef had protected his friend from persecution. He still felt a small flutter of excitement when Mendel came into the room. And now Alicia had felt it too. He had seen it in her pale face this morning. *You must bail him out.* She too had entered the hasid's strange penumbra, an unbeliever who needed, if not to believe, then at least to believe in another's belief. And now their love floated in the penumbra too. He turned back to Mendel with a shard of his love.

—I will ask her tonight.

Mendel was smiling. They had turned a corner and entered a large square. Before the occupation it had boasted a railed park with formal borders shaded by plane trees. In the centre water had gushed from a stone lionhead flanked by dolphins. Now the railings and the borders were gone. The trees had been felled, grubbed up and burnt. The fountain had turned into a tank for rainwater. The park was divided into furrowed plots. It was one of the ghetto's new vegetable allotments. People worked there, bending.

73

—You have been too long among the shards of things, figures, reports, papers. Look at these people. They are old. Yet they trust in the light. They know it grows as well as shrinks. That one especially, he knows.

Mendel pointed. One of the diggers had stopped for a moment and was leaning on his spade. Then, after waving at the hasid and the Census Officer, Henryk bent back to work.

'I have decided. Mendel is right. Who would have thought that a man sunk in the mysteries of Kabbala would see further than an ex-solicitor employed in the ghetto administration. It is my fate. We are bound together. All of us.'

She stood opposite him on the stale-smelling landing. Overhead a bare bulb hung on its frayed cord. It had been raining, a cold thin downpour that penetrated to the skin. Their footsteps showed black against the bare boards of the stairs. Below, on another landing, a man and woman argued monotonously, rhythmically, slamming and slamming a door. Because of her he had saved Mendel. Now she must be saved. He repeated his statement then looked away, boyishly gauche. He might have been carrying a bunch of roses in the hands clenched so tightly behind his back. He had flattened his thinning hair with water. His shirt was fresh. A suitor.

—The Chairman has undertaken to start wedding services again, directly after the New Year.

She looked down, neither pale nor flushed. She seemed suddenly remote, for all their time together.

—Grandma you know. She's very ill. It would be unseemly . . .—Her voice died away.

—I've tried to obtain extra rations but all my sources have dried up. It's this smuggling business. If they could be caught. If someone could explain to them. They're doing us all harm.

She looked up. Less remote now. No less unobtainable.

—I don't expect you to feed us. Anyway she's past help. She wants to die.

Desperately Josef cast round for something to make his words connect. He must draw her closer to him, this remote being, afloat in the wet twilight. The couple downstairs had gone inside now. Their argument rustled distantly, a surf.

—And you'd move. My apartment isn't spacious but compared to this . . .—He gestured vaguely.

—A marriage of convenience.—She sighed but not bitterly. She was teasing him a little.

—And it would solve resettlement at a stroke.

He put his hand on her shoulder. She did not flinch.

—There are rumours again. Reliable. It'll be the westerners next. Last in, first out. A portion anyway. But marriage to me . . .

Again his words fell between them, hollowed-out shells for the tide of light to take, as it receded into night. Yet Alicia seemed almost compliant beneath his gaze. His hand slid down to her waist. They had not met again so as to be sundered. Then the door opened. Chaim glanced from his mother to Josef then away. His underwater world was different from theirs. Last night they had smuggled horse meat and lard into the ghetto.

—Where are you going?

Chaim did not reply.

—Who are you going to see?

Again he kept silent. Josef coughed and ruffled the boy's head in what he hoped was a suitably paternal gesture. Chaim gave a muffled squeal and darted sideways. Then he was off down the stairs. Alicia stared after him as if a part of her had gone too.

—A move might help him out of this. A man about the place.

Now she was laughing. He felt hurt. She saw and drew his face down to hers.

—Poor Josef. So persistent. So reasonable.

—I came at the wrong time. I'm sorry.

He turned to go.

—But will the Chairman accept that I am widowed?

He had been sinking in darkness. Now all was light.

Today we dig tomorrow we don't. It's not like the soil back home but it'll have to do. Feeding ourselves to feed them. Two spits down. Fork the bottom over. Trenches. Mendel knows but he only sees light. Josef knows but doesn't want to know. Alicia knows but is beginning to think Mendel knows more. Chaim refuses to know. First it is light then it is dark. The first spit from the second trench goes to the bottom of the first. The second spit goes on top. Keep digging keep digging. For them all.

5

He was crawling across the wasteground on the far side of the perimeter fence. Tonight they had come to a section of wire several hundred yards further along from the original opening. One of the younger members of the organisation (as they liked to style themselves) had noticed a ghetto policeman hovering in that vicinity earlier in the day. They could not risk discovery. But now they were out again. Scratching himself on stones, feeling earth and ashes under his palms, Chaim experienced the usual exhilaration. Behind him his mother and Grandma, Henryk and Josef, Mendel and all the other ghetto inhabitants were trapped in dream or waking, at work or in bed. But he was outside and not trapped at all. Now if he chose he could go anywhere. Yet tonight he had met his mother and Josef on the stairs. He had known without their saying anything that they were going to be married. And this knowledge had sparked a painful conflict. Now more than ever he longed for his father. But a part of him was drawn just as fiercely the other way, towards the new life his mother was making for them all. So he crawled forward, free and not free, into the darkness that surrounded the ghetto.

Tonight too there was a different contact; a small ruddy-cheeked man with a clipped moustache. He seemed faintly military in his trenchcoat and boots. Bernard was extremely deferential.

—It was good of you to come.

He might have been at a party.

—How many?

The man with the moustache spoke quietly as if used to being obeyed. Bernard fumbled under his jacket.

—Six I think.

He drew out a leather belt strapped with gold watches. The man snapped his finger. A second figure emerged from the shadows holding something wrapped in an oily cloth. He balanced it across both upturned palms. Bernard stepped forward and unwrapped the cloth as if it held something sacred. There was a pause. Then he looked swiftly round at the moustached man.

—Only one. But I thought. And it's so old. Don't you have any semi-automatics?

The moustached man spat. He had long since pocketed the belt and the watches.

—You Jews want the earth. We bring what we can. We too are at war. Don't you want it?

Bernard was hastily wrapping the object up. He clutched it tightly. Chaim had never seen him so flustered.

—I didn't mean. That is I mean I'm sorry. But there will be more?

The moustached man shrugged.

—Depends what you have to give us.

—Yes of course I see. Of course.

And so in one night the child smugglers had graduated from potatoes to weapons. The object under the oily cloth was a bolt-action rifle dating from the last war. Bernard showed it to Chaim as they passed the lookout on the stairs of the empty house. Chaim noticed the lookout was carrying a mauser. He felt betrayed and frightened. Excitement had dissolved into pure terror. As they prepared to cross back to the fence, he spoke in a small voice.

—I thought we smuggled food.

Bernard grinned, his grey-green teeth faintly luminous in the dark. Disappointment had turned to pride. He was holding a real rifle.

—We still do. But there's a ZOB cell forming in the west sector. Bundists, Zionists and others.

Chaim shivered. Suddenly he longed for the warmth of his mother's bed. Again, he heard her talking to Josef on the stairs. That was love. That was peace. Not this cold nudity of weapons and darkness. Bernard was preparing to crawl. His voice, though low, seemed to possess a new authority. And a distance.

—Are we sheep for the slaughter?

Chaim did not reply.

Josef had intended to visit the Chairman at his office in the Judenrat the next day and there make a formal request on behalf of Alicia and himself; but the Chairman summoned him first. Outside the office a green Daimler purred. A crowd of ghetto children stood near, gazing. It was Schaefer's car. The stairs to the office were steep and always made him puff. Today, because of a sleepless night and the burden of his own mission, he had to pause more than once. On each occasion he heard two voices coming from inside the office, one dark and smooth, the other light and sharp. Sea and seabird. The Chairman was talking with the Amtsleiter. It was too late to turn back.

The door opened into veils of smoke. This too put him on his guard. For the odour belonged to none of the cheap adulterated tobaccoes imported into the ghetto: Brezawa, Rama, Drawa. This smoke had a sweetish, heavy aroma. You felt you might touch it, rolling the heavy blueness between finger and thumb. It was the Amtsleiter's smoke. Something important was about to happen.

He entered and out of the cave at the heart of all this swirling air, the Chairman advanced, hand outstretched. This too was strange, heavy with portent. For the Chairman rarely accorded his Census Officer the courtesy of a good-day. Still more rarely did he greet him by his first name, or put his hand on his shoulder, leading him into the room as into a gathering for cocktails. It was as if some covert shift had occurred in the ghetto's magnetic polarity. Everything was slightly out of true. A fissure had appeared in the fabric of things, seeping smoke. Although the Chairman seemed as bulky, well groomed and powerful as before he was diminished somehow. He wanted Josef to come between him and his guest. He wanted to shed some of the weight that had been placed upon him, suddenly and without warning by Schaefer. He had taken fright.

—Herr Schaefer requires some lists.—The Chairman coughed, waving his cigarette as if it might conjure paper from smoke.—The western arrivals. The east sector.—He crumpled. He was diminished.

Josef peered smartingly across at Schaefer. His eyes were

80

sea-blue, a bird's. His long legs crossed angularly, he perched at the edge of the Chairman's desk. He would not be staying long here, on this dunged green groyne. A bird of passage.

—The ghetto is becoming too large again.—His voice had something of a seabird's shrill importunacy.—There is too much surplus fat. Too many people without work permits.—He paused, drawing lengthily on his cigar. The Chairman moved to speak but the Amtsleiter cut him out.—Production is down, smuggling on the increase.

—We caught two last night Herr Schaefer.

Josef's heart beat harder. He had guessed where Chaim went in the evening.

—Two girls.—The Chairman was speaking rapidly, glad to be off the central subject.—Near the main gate. Only children Herr Schaefer. No threat.

Josef relaxed. But a new resolve had crept into his heart.

—Children or adults, they are all criminals. The ghetto needs rationalisation. I shall be downstairs. Don't keep me waiting.

Schaefer was making for the door. He had been a chemicals manufacturer before the SA and the war. He put great store by cost efficiency. His shoulder brushed against Josef's. He stopped.

—How is your tame hasid?

Josef looked away not wanting to meet the Amtsleiter's ambiguous smile.

—He's been warned.

—Does he talk much about the rituals, the disgusting rituals?

Josef felt the smoke closing in around him.

—The blood of children and babies. The dissections. —Schaefer's eyes betrayed the slightest quiver. He was excited. Josef's presence excited him.

—You should milk him for all he's worth. A tame hasid. You could put him in your thesis.

The Chairman was holding the door open. Josef tried to smile as if the conversation were quite normal. But the words had to be dragged from some obscure depth.

—Will there be resettlement papers, as before?

The Amtsleiter's eyes clouded for a moment. He was swimming up from a cave he frequently visited.

—Did I mention resettlement?

Josef could have dragged back the words and stuffed them into his mouth. Yet he knew that Schaefer had wanted him to say this. The Chairman coughed again, flustering forward.

—I'm sure it needn't come to that. The Amtsleiter merely wants to maximise efficiency. He . . .

The blow that swept across his mouth was hard and swift. The Chairman staggered back, dropping his cigarette, which rolled away, glowing, under the desk.

—I do what is necessary not what a yid wants me to do.

The gleam in his eyes faded. He was sliding a glove onto the hand that had struck out. It made a creaking sound. The Chairman had withdrawn a few feet, shaking. Schaefer turned back to Josef.

—Resettlement. Yes. But not yet.—Then with a sudden smile.—You look pale, Census Officer. Are you married?

Josef felt as though he and not the Chairman had been struck. He staggered in his head, fell.

—But you should be. To a nice little dusky princess.—Then Schaefer was on the stairs.—I want to see all the clothing workshops today. No exception. I'll be in the car.—His boots clattered away.

Still trembling the Chairman struggled into his overcoat. In a sudden blur of guilt Josef bent down and retrieved his cigarette. It had gone out. The Chairman looked quickly at Josef.

—Why say that?

Josef handed him the cigarette.

—He trapped me. He wanted to say it.—But Josef knew that he had trapped himself.

The Chairman was touching his swelling lower lip. His words sounded fat, as though in pain.—Haven't I done my best, always, my best? Negotiated and pleaded? I pleaded with him today. I demonstrated how some of the tailor-shops could be merged. I even suggested a new site for the leather factory, a larger workforce. Never mention resettlement Mr Rosenfeld. Not until they do.

Josef winced. Always beneath the Chairman's voice this undersong, this faint susurrus of power. As the Amtsleiter controlled him so he controlled those beneath him. What he did was for the best but it was also for his own self-aggrandisement. Yet just as Josef had to supply the census lists so he had to rely on the Chairman for all special favours. Without him he could not marry. The threat of resettlement might not be imminent but when it did come the families of administrators had automatic protection. Josef must make the Schultz family his own. As they walked down the stairs together he mentioned his private business. It was like dragging a buried vessel into the light – a green glass phial packed with scents long lost to the earth. He hated exposing it. He hated exposing himself. But he had no choice. Being as entangled as ever. And as helpless.

They were in Venice again, at the Hotel Danieli. Reflected light from the lagoon fluttered white contours across the ceiling of their first floor room. But everything had changed since that summer, when Chaim was just a baby and Oskar still faithful. The room had grown bigger. The windows were of stone, vaulted. They might be in the Ca d'Oro. Then she noticed that the window glass was broken here and there, the holes stuffed with old rags and paper. Dust grimed the floor, dust of the ghetto. And the sucking of waves around rotten seaweed-slimed groynes was also the slow wash of the nightshift returning from the workshops. It didn't matter. Both here and there she felt happy. In both times. Nothing had been escaped or lost. And in her arms lay Chaim, a suckling baby with the face of a fifteen year old man.

He was asleep. He had not rejected her. Carefully she took the nipple from his mouth. The lips went on closing and opening on a warm trickle of black. Black milk. The light was growing brighter. Two gondoliers argued down on the calle at the side of the hotel: they were new arrivals from Lublin on the floor above. Through a door veiled in mist Oskar came, wearing that red and black striped silk cravat he had affected in the first years of their marriage, but old as he would be when he lay in the gutter, his back sprinkled with glass shards from the smashed store window. He asked her if she'd like to go to Murano. To the glass and lace factories. It was an island in the Assembly Rooms Josef said. Where we are to be married. *Of course* she said to them both. *And look. Isn't it good? I'm feeding him black milk.* And they laughed, the two men, chucking oldyoung Chaim under the chin with different, superimposed fingers. And the baby who smuggled arms into the ghetto looked up, gurgling.

—What day is it?

The voice, tired and transparent dragged her from the place of two times, the city within cities.

—The first, mother. Rosh Hashanah has begun.

There was a sigh but no more words. She knew her mother was muttering a prayer of repentance. She could not join in. How long since she had prayed? Since before her marriage. Then she had been youthfully fierce in her rejection, a ferocity compounded by Oskar's cheerful secularism. Yet her parents had watched her, seeming, in their submissive puzzlement to imply that the story wasn't over. Then father had died and Oskar went away for the first time, alone, on business. She might have prayed then or later when Josef almost drew her away. Or when Oskar lay in the road. Or when they stood at the Praterstern, shivering. Yet she hadn't. And always the eyes of her parents, the one vanished, the other vanishing, watched and waited. She did not pray because she could not. And this inability was a sadness to her now. She rolled over and felt the cold empty sheet where her son should have slept. She could not even pray for him. It was time to be stirring.

Preparing porridge with the rye flakes that had just been issued she glanced at her mother. The cracked lips were still moving. An age-old piety. But passive. Almost unthinking. She thought again of Mendel and how she had come upon him in the square where Henryk worked on the allotments. He was playing ball with two urchins, throwing it high into the air and crying and laughing *catch it catch it*, his black coat billowing in the wintry wind, a scarecrow lifted out of some dark superstitious era. And yet there was power in him. His piety submitted to nothing. It was dynamic. His systems and visionary hierarchies were not born of passivity and acceptance. He reached out for things, took them, changed them. He did not wait for the world to come to him. That was why she had been possessed by the need to save him from the police. He was too important to be sacrificed.

Yet she could not pray. And as much as Mendel's light magnetised and ran through her she dared not yield to it. Soon she and Josef would be married. Then they would all move in with him, drawing closer to the ghetto than ever before, identifying with its life and fate. Watching the porridge suck and burst in soft creamy blisters, she knew her marriage was going to be a part of Mendel's world as well. In her dream of the two times he had been just visible in the veil of the doorway opposite the vaulted window, a smiling witness.

It was the tenth day of Repentance. For the tenth time he sat worshipping with the rest. The place of worship was both makeshift and inappropriate, being the vestry in the abandoned church of St Mary and All Saints. But even in his heart Mendel did not question this. Many ages had passed since he had stalked out of the leather factory, outraged at their abuse of sacred objects. He knew now what dark things hid the light. He had been to gaol. He had seen Alicia in the shadow of the doorway. The profane and the sacred could no longer be separated. Out of the broken shards would rise the restored vessels of light. That the ghetto's only surviving Torah scroll lay on a trestle table rather than in a sacred ark; that the shawled Rabbi wore a suit; that even the traditional division between male and female could not be observed; all these were signs of hope not despair. His stomach rumbled. Five days on water only. He felt a surge of pride but quickly quelled it. If only Josef hadn't noticed he was wearing the kittel on the first day of Repentance. *You'll be hauled in again. And next time I won't be able to save you.* It was just like Josef to use a sacred word in an earthly context. And that too was to be expected. The soiled surface of the kittel could not conceal the whiteness underneath. Again he felt himself soaring in whiteness and again he had to suppress his deeper desires. This was still a day of mourning. The shofars were sounding even if, during these dark times, their tekiah existed only in the memory. He lowered his head and concentrated on asking his unknown neighbours for forgiveness. He too was weak and full of blame.

She slipped in halfway through the service. It was growing dark and foggy outside. Light filtered greyly through a high narrow lancet, its glass long shattered. The candles in the seven branched candelabrum had been extinguished. The Rabbi stood before the trestle table where the scroll of the Torah lay. His congregation sat on canvas backed chairs, old pews, a vestment chest. There was a small bookcase near the door. In the past its shelves had contained Catholic hymnals. Now they were empty. She perched there. The place was cold and smelt of sweat. Yet she felt happy.

The Cantor had stepped forward. It was the one who had had him forcibly ejected from the study group two years before. *None of your messiah talk here. That's for workmen. We're educated here.* Now he began recounting the story of Jonah. Mendel listened, trying to imagine himself in the body of the whale which was the ghetto and all the evil the ghetto swallowed or disgorged. He lay in the rib-vaulted stomach, the sewer of sewers. Bile. Excrement. He called on the Ein Sof. He begged for forgiveness. A light appeared in the distance. He might be able to crawl that way.

The Cantor's story of Jonah was her childhood reborn. She remembered the great uncle who sat her on his knee and, while she played with his collar, pinching at the rough purplish fold of flesh that oozed over its starched creams, recounted the old myth. At the time she had wondered aloud why the whale didn't first make sure to chew Jonah up. Later she had asked her mother if whales really do swallow people. *Undoubtedly*, she replied, although she had never seen the sea. And now the whale had returned, only this time it was small and friendly, a fish leaping in a lagoon, fringed by white towers. Wading through the lagoon, hunting the fish, came giant Jonah, a goldplated Goliath with a harpoon. The sky was dark, a vaulted sewer. The harpoon turned into a rifle. The fish had Chaim's face.

When he saw her first he felt a sudden panic and anxiety. It was too soon. He was not ready. Not worthy. He bowed his head and tried to live inside the whale. But the vaulted prison was bathed in light. Her light.

The fish who was Chaim had gone. And the hunter with the deathshead tattooed on his wrist. She was in the middle of the sewer. Someone was coming towards her, rowing a boat through the slime. She could not see the boatman's face.

When he walked up to her he saw in a sudden spasm of pity that she was afraid. She swayed towards him as he swayed towards her. They were both trembling.

—Do not be afraid, he whispered.—Pinhas of Koretz said: *The kernel which is sown in earth must fall to pieces so that the ear of grain may sprout from it. In the husk of forgetting the power of memory grows. That is the power of redemption. On the day of destruction power lies at the bottom of the depths and grows.* Do not be afraid.

Why was he saying these things to her and her alone? The Cantor had stopped speaking. Some of the shawled women were swivelling round and tutting. But they were such beautiful words and she had felt so lost.

—Go on,—she whispered,—go on saying those things.

89

★

He had taken nothing but water since the beginning of Tishri. He was as light as a feather. Their hands lifted him up like the wind. *Princess of the dusk* he called as the Rabbi's two helpers manhandled him through the doorway into the nave. *I will come to you.* She was haloed in light now. It was the Shekkinah. God's presence in the material world. *I will come.*

6

They had hidden the blankets behind the archive wardrobe. That evening when she tugged them out and constructed, between the two desks, first a bed then a canopy, he smiled and said *Our Sukkah*, remembering the ritual arbours which he had seen in pious homes in his childhood. They were a precious memory to him, less for themselves, – although he had marvelled at the interweaving of leaves and cereal and branches, the mysterious suggestion available even to a young boy, of harvest brought into the home – than for their association with one particular trip he had been allowed to make with his father into the country round Cracow. And now, for Alicia's sake, this woman who had returned to him by chance, forced against her will across half a continent, he was prepared to use the memory for a pleasantry, guiding it down a fresh, faintly disrespectful channel. Kneeling in her slip to smooth the blanket she did not smile.

—Josef. Sacred things. Why do you always mock?

The old guilt returned. He saw again the little arched alcove where his father kept the Talmudic books along with a little volume of selected hasidic sayings. His father had just finished in the darkroom, a sheaf of photographs taken on their latest journey: children in a schul; a village zaddik who might have been Mendel; a vegetable seller holding up radishes, carrots. The life of the diaspora. His father was a social historian as well as a doctor. But above all he was a believer. *So you have a dry mind after all, Josef. A lawyer's mind.* It was the day he arrived home and announced his intention to abandon pure scholarship. His father behaved as if he had known all along. That was what galled the most. The sense of having been watched and pitied and despaired of in silence. And now fifteen years later his wife to be was reacting in the same way. *You never change Josef. I know you inside out.* Where had her piety come from? Why this sudden interest in the few public religious services the administration still allowed, the acquisition, through some unrevealed third party, of a battered bible printed in the last century. He had seen it in her room last night, stuffed under the pillow, open at Exodus. It was Mendel of course. She had been exposed to him as Josef had before her. But where she capitulated he resisted. Mendel's friendship provided him with a useful adversary. He was the whetstone on which to keep one's intellect sharp. Or so Josef liked to tell himself.

For even at his most self confident and disputatious, he knew how tired he had grown of not believing. Lying there under the hairy blanket, Alicia cold and withdrawn at his side (the room itself had begun to grow colder by the day), he saw again a little boy standing in the hall of the chief Rabbi's house in a village that had since been wiped off the map. One hand held his father's. The other clutched a small box that mimicked, or so he fervently hoped, the black case father carried, packed with equal quantities of medical and photographic equipment. The boy was looking upwards.

A gilt Hannukah lamp hung from the ceiling. Crowned by the ribbed valve of a golden shell, the lamp's central panel bore a double-doored shrine flanked by lion-headed colonna santa. Reflected in the shrine's latticed and fret-worked depths the afternoon light came down to him across the years as a condensation of harvest, the cornfields through which they had just passed absorbed and trans-figured in its liquid glow. Some ears from those very fields had been brought into the house and, bunched into slender yellow pillars, leant now on either side of the Sukkah. The roof was made of myrtle and willow branches plaited with barley stems. Beneath it stood four chairs and a table where the kiddush wine cup had been set. His father let him move closer. Carved in the cup's rosewood bowl was a repre-sentation of the very meal that would take place here later that day. Then he saw, in this room within a room, a still smaller world, as if two mirrors had been set facing one another, their mutual reflections receding back and inwards forever. Only when a parchment-thin hand passed, half breeze and half wing, across the crown of his head, did Josef look away from this ancient kingdom of reflections into the cold, breath-fogged air of the room of the secret archive. Behind him the Rabbi greeted his father. Before him Alicia was speaking.

—*We lack lemon and palm. But we can imagine them, no?*

—It's Chaim. You don't know how I worry. He's away half the night now. He hates me for Oskar's death. Blames me even. I don't know.

The past was gone. He had presided over its destruction. He opened his hand in the dark under the blanket and felt goosefleshed thigh. If Alicia was to be his wife, Chaim would be his son. His own father had given up on him once. He let his hand rest briefly on her pubic triangle. She flinched slightly.

—They shot two smugglers yesterday. They were barely adult. I saw them laid out near the overhead walkway. Chaim should be told.

Then she was turning into him, sobbing. Her knees had jackknifed upward. She was folded against herself. He knew they would not make love now. It would be curfew soon. And there was, too, this weariness. After two years in the ghetto he had thought himself innured to the daily erosions of living. He had believed himself strong in body as well as in mind. But recently conditions had taken a notable turn for the worse. The rations were dwindling and deteriorating. The supply of marmalade had ceased. The ersatz coffee quota had been cut. The rye flour bread made in the ghetto bakeries and distributed to all inhabitants now contained a proportion of chalk and other adulterates. As a good ghetto administrator he knew it was his duty to blame the smugglers. But as a man he guessed it was part of an overall policy. The Chairman might have averted disaster in the short term but eventually the Amtsleiter's rationalisations would lead to resettlement. A weakened man is a docile man. His father had said as much during his last illness. And if suitable rumours were spread about the superior diet in the East so much the better. Much later, after the last contingents had left the siding, the rations would mysteriously improve once more. Those who were left would be persuaded by their stomachs if not to forget, then at least to accept. Eat sleep work. No, they would not make love. The time for love was past. As Mendel said, darkness is deepest in the last days.

—He may listen to you. A man.

She still hadn't drawn her face away from his chest. He stroked her hair.

—Do boys of that age ever listen to their fathers?

Such weariness, such fear. As a ghetto administrator he could hardly afford to have a smuggler as a stepson. Yet wouldn't he have done the same at fifteen? What was the point of a secret archive when you could run out into the night and defy the very world that had been created to trap and destroy you? The little boy who still stood, rapt in front of the Sukkah knew nothing of such things. Yet perhaps his wonder was not so very far removed from the anguish and anger of a fatherless boy in a cellar.

The organisation was breaking up and Chaim did not care. He had never found his father on the far side of the wire. He had not even escaped the ghetto. He was still a member of his family, loving and resenting his mother, pitying Grandma, puzzling over Henryk. Yet if he must come to accept that he was no less trapped than they, he could not embrace passivity. He was no Mendel. He was not even attracted to the piety Mendel had recently begun to arouse in his mother. So he struggled and in struggling hurt only himself. Bernard said as much when they met one cold morning by chance in the market.

—It was no good, that old blunderbuss. The bolt was

faulty. But we used the parts. And there'll be others. Maybe even a light machine gun if we play our cards right.

Bernard's breath coiled through the coat rack they were using as a screen. Above them, from a broken downpipe, small icicles hung. The first of the winter. Chaim knew Bernard wanted him formally to join the underground. A great weariness possessed him. The icicles dripped dark greasy water.

—There aren't many of us left now.

It was meant to be a statement of defiance. A threat. He knew about the executions. And the defections. Many of the smugglers had been very young. They understood about stealing and bartering. They had been up to the same game on these same streets before the ghetto was founded. But guns and resistance were adult business. So they melted back, into the passageways and cellars, unattached as always, eternal wraiths of the city. Which left only youths like Bernard, a member of the anti-Zionist league even before the occupation, his whole being straining inexorably toward the light of commitment and action. Beside him Chaim felt pale, one of the ghosts of the cellars. He was shrinking away, back into darkness.

—You yekes.

Bernard spat. He had not used that name for weeks. Nor sung the song they had once used as a password. Its refrain reminded Chaim of a time that now seemed impossibly remote, almost innocent. Tears came to his eyes.

—You ought to find a job in the Census Department. Where your new dad works.

But he had already left that taunting voice far behind.

Clenched fists jammed tightly into his pockets he wandered unseeing through streets already tense with fear of the Amtsleiter's 'rationalisations'. He was alone again. And haunted. A year before his father died the Schultz family had made a second journey to Venice. Grandma was still fit enough to look after the apartment. Chaim guessed this visit was to be an attempt at reconciliation. It hadn't worked. The arguments in the hotel were as bad as they had been at home; his father spent long evenings on mysterious lone 'explorations' of the city. Once Chaim had stood with him on a calle near the Accademia. His father leant against an ochre wall whose bricks bubbled black slime. Above his head a lion mask grinned, its eyes weeping green tears. The canal slopped. The papers were full of rumours about Hitler's designs on Austria. Oskar said it was preposterous. There would never be another war. Not after Versailles. Mother was back at the hotel. Her eyes were red. How he hated his father at that moment. And hated himself for hating him. But he hated the lion mask most of all. Slowly the mask faded. Now it was a year later. His mother stood in the hallway of the apartment block in Vienna. Behind her head was a shelf on which a vase stood, stuck with the red-veined wafers of poinsettia. They fringed her hair like a headdress. He had been leaning against the gilt cage of the lift. The shaft gusted and howled. Warm wind flared across his mouth. He knew it had not been an accident. He knew that in some sense his mother blamed Oskar for his own death. If Chaim were to plunge through the concertina door he might find the answer. Now it was two months later. Uncle Henryk came into the living room in his old trenchcoat. His suitcase – Chaim would discover later – was stuffed with poultry manuals. His mother was not glad to see him. But as she said to her friend on the phone the next day: *What else can you do in times like these? He couldn't have stayed in the village. Not after the outrages. Poor man.* Sometimes Henryk would take Chaim aside and tell him that his chickens knew all about Oskar's death. *They want to eat us you see.* So the old ghosts and the old voices pursued Chaim through the ghetto.

—*Chaim, Chaim, do it with me.*

It was the girl whose face he had seen in the window. Tonight, for the first time in weeks, he would not go out to meet the others. Instead he lay awake in his mother's bed, hearing Henryk snore and Grandma moan. Then she came to him, flushed and naked. *Chaim, Chaim.* Soundlessly masturbating he heard Mendel muttering *Every pollution of semen gives birth to demons. Remember that Chaim* which only made him rub more furiously, her small silk breasts pressed suffocatingly close against his face. Finally he shuddered, turning away so as not to disturb his mother, already wakeful in case he disappear again. Feeling his own wetness on stomach and groin he thought of the demon he might have created – the body of his father with a lion mask head. All night it pursued him through the ghetto at the bottom of the canal. The girl looked on from a palace window, smiling into nothing.

The soup kitchen swarmed with workers taking their noon break. Steam smoked from the roped and clotted vats at the back of the room and hung in damp sheets above the heads of eaters. It smeared the windows and collected in opaque sticky drops on the stained ceiling. He had not wanted to come in here but his future stepfather had been insistent. It was as if he knew how completely this boy had managed to avoid most of the normalities of ghetto life. He had inhabited a crepuscular world where, despite privation and fear, you might at least believe in yourself. But Josef also seemed to have guessed that his stepson-to-be was growing weary of his half-lit, rootless existence. When he had accosted him on the pavement outside he had said *You look hungry. And not just for food.* After the disillusion of the day before Chaim had offered no resistance.

Now, while his mother's suitor threaded his way back to where women in stained overalls were ladling out the thin meat broth into tin bowls, Chaim waited and listened. All around him the people talked. Yet nothing they said demanded a reply. It was a low droned recitation, a black psalm of half facts and rumours, broken at intervals by rapt slurping. Swiftly and without logic the theme shifted from the price of cigarettes (twenty-five pfennigs each) to the eastern front; from the incident of the smugglers near the overhead walkway to the threat of rationalisation. Everyone spoke, no one listened. Steadily the black psalm grew more contrapuntal as more voices joined in, more circular as the themes began to mirror one another. It was the voice of the ghetto itself: full of significance yet meaningless; vibrant and without joy. Its whirlpool of sound tugged at Chaim's heart, begging him to join in, to become one with the dark chant of helplessness and decay. By the time Josef returned Chaim was already surrendering to the tuneless song of the ghetto's suffering.

And so, as administrator and former child-smuggler plunged into the whirl of sound, adding their own versions of the familiar subjects, Chaim hardly needed to be argued round. He knew that this hump-shouldered slightly balding forty year old sitting on the other side of the greasy table was not primarily concerned with him. He was an administrator who wanted to marry a woman he had known for a time before the war. Having hacked out a little clearing of privilege in his life he was not going to let a child who happened to be that woman's son set light to the surrounding thickets. But watching Josef as he ate and talked, a clear thread of soup streaking his greystubbled chin, Chaim felt no animosity. Bernard was still on the far side of the rack of coats, whistling the yeke song. The girl sat in the window smiling. *You are young like me* he heard her say. *Why die for a cause you don't believe in?*

—Work is the thing. I've spoken to your mother. There's a place in old Isaac's clothing factory. You must take it,— and here Josef's voice dropped,—especially now.

Chaim watched his future stepfather roll a pellet of the coarse rye bread back and forth across the ringed table. Slowly its grey grainy surface absorbed more and more of the invisible dirt of the soup kitchen and grew almost black. Chaim felt repelled and fascinated. Perhaps with Josef as his protector he might come to a better understanding of who he was. The clear cold excitement of action still ached somewhere deep inside him. But the underground theatre of tunnels and passwords could not satisfy it. Here in the upper world, surrounded by the drone of the ghetto, in workshop and street he might find another route to the freedom he craved. Again he saw the girl at the window. She was nodding to him now. Saying *Yes he's right, this Josef. Follow him for the moment.* And Chaim nodded too, drawing from the haggard administrator a rare smile before his face closed down as several petitioners shuffled forward to beg and complain. What he had meant by 'especially now' Chaim did not care to know yet. For the moment it was enough to accept Josef's offer.

'So he has accepted. As his mother did before him. I Josef am the lord of power and wisdom. Rubbish. I suspect there is more wisdom in Mendel's little finger, more power in Alicia's big toes which . . . but no matter. The old woman is dying. Let us hope she passes on before too long. It would be impossible to hide her if there was a resettlement. For the moment Schaefer seems content to toy with us. Longer shifts. Old Isaac's place double the capacity now, in that warehouse next to the church. Plus a clearout of the two prisons. Poor souls. These are our bargaining counters. And soon Alicia's family will be my family. Oh but I am weak and long for childhood or youth or those weeks in Vienna. Any time but now. These last days.'

The door was ajar. Through the crack seeped a low mumbling. He was reminded of the soup kitchen. But this sound was thinner, more mellifluous. It had a shape. On the inside of the righthand doorpost hung the mezuzah. His mother had nailed it up two days ago. There was a connection between that and the sound. Henryk's coat had disappeared too. He could just make out the empty hook on the wall opposite. If Henryk had gone someone else had come in, for his great uncle had grown increasingly misanthropic of late, vanishing to the Park allotments at the slightest hint of company. This new arrival was responsible for the sound. Or at least he orchestrated it. Chaim walked in. Grandma lay in the big bed, the one where he usually slept with his mother. On the near side knelt her daughter, head swathed not in a fringed prayer shawl (that would be blasphemous), but in a secular and seemly chequered scarf. On the far side, wrapped in his old, torn tallit, knelt Mendel. Slow, erosive and insistent, his chant rose and fell.

—She is Rachel, daughter of Rabbi ben Markowitz. Hear O Samael, angel of death. She is Rachel.

Chaim's eyes swum. He felt as if he had blundered into some country hovel. He knew no one here. Surely there should be chickens scratching nearby. The air was thick with the cinnamon smell from a glowing incense stick tilting from a vase at the foot of the bed. His grandmother's lips were blue. She breathed intermittently, in short, tight lunges. His mother heard him and turned. Her eyes were different. More distant, darker. He longed for Josef to come in.

—Who's Rachel? I don't know a Rachel.

Mendel looked up sharply. His mother motioned him to lower his voice.

—We're changing, I mean Mendel is changing it – her name. So that the angel thinks he's come to the wrong house. It's an old custom.

Mendel had finished his recitation. His bony hand lay on Grandma's arm, among the knobbled mounds of ganglia. He was swaying slightly, eyes closed. Chaim felt a spasm of anger. His grandmother was not called Rachel. They were trying to erase her.

—Witchcraft. What would Josef say?

His mother had her hand on his shoulder.

—Only a charm. And Josef says these zaddiks have great knowledge.—She turned to Mendel who was holding a piece of paper over Grandma's head, suspended from a string. The paper was covered in symbols: a Magen David, a crudely outlined female figure with the distended belly of a fertility goddess.

—Samael and Lilith. The dark lord and his bride.

—Does this holy fool have a charm to help us escape this place? That might help her.

His mother looked away.

—Perhaps. Perhaps he does.—Then quickly, as if in spite of herself,—Kneel with us Chaim, help us ward off this death.

He was no longer a smuggler. His father was dead and could not be reborn. He had seen the girl in the window. Josef was his protector. He worked turning clothes into blankets for the Eastern Front. So he knelt and said that yes this dying woman's name was Rachel.

Snow was falling. The Assembly Rooms were cold, invaded by the blue snowlight. She had no father to lead her in. Henryk might have been an acceptable substitute. But he was sitting up with Grandma who, after the name-changing ceremony, had seemed to rally a little. That left only Chaim. She felt pride at this. But feared the touch of his hand, its still smoulder of resentment. The death of his father and their arrival in the ghetto were for him part of the same adult nightmare. Though he had assumed the respectable disguise of a ghetto worker he did not relax. Yet if they hadn't come here she would not have met Josef again. Oskar had been a ghost to her even before his death. If only she could have made Chaim understand this. But it was impossible. Nor could she deny that her marriage to Josef was as much about pragmatism as affection. Would Chaim blame her for that too? She lowered her veil and walked forward beside her son into the chilly hall.

Mendel was making a song and dance again. Josef hadn't been at all happy about Alicia's suggestion that he invest his awkward friend with the title and role of groomsman. Now his doubts were being confirmed. Firstly there was the problem over the kittel. Mendel insisted it was essential. Gently, Josef reminded him of the impossibility of obtaining any ritual garments in the ghetto. Smiling, Mendel had pulled his coat apart. *You forget quickly for a man of law.* Josef was furious. Then fearful in case the kittel was noticed. As usual Mendel seemed indifferent to the constrictions they all lived under and, as usual, pride and guilt swamped Josef's heart. But the kittel was still unthinkable. Mendel would have to keep his coat firmly buttoned. Then almost immediately the groomsman had turned to the subject of ritual ablution. Josef was beside himself. There were other couples beside themselves getting married today. This was a ghetto in an occupied country. He was an administrator not a hasidic saint. Mendel looked hurt for a moment then suddenly seemed to forget everything they had just been arguing about. He was holding out his hands towards one of the vestibule's long sash windows. It was open slightly. The wind was blowing flakes of snow through the gap. One lay in Mendel's cupped palm.

—Look. Look.

—A snowflake Mendel.—Josef was impatient.

—The sefirot. See how they are linked to the one. Like a tree.

His long fingernail traced each spine to the ice core. Josef remembered the diagrams in the old Lurianic treatises. The paths between the vessels of light. The tree of emanations. Now Mendel had found them in a snowflake blown by chance through the window of the ghetto Assembly Rooms. The flake was beginning to melt, even in that chill air. Josef was at once abashed and calmed. He waited for his friend to accompany him into the hall.

It was the first time that he had witnessed the machinery of the ghetto organisation in action. Once he would have considered it another proof of adult mendacity and betrayal. But now, having listened to Josef and knelt beside his mother, he too belonged to the adult world. He shivered. Around them on the floor a chaos of snowy footprints trailed this way and that, indicative of the many marriage ceremonies that had already taken place. Their palimpsest of conflicting spoors suggested conflict rather than harmony. Most marriages here were desperate affairs, contracted out of a mixture of cunning, cynicism and pure despair. The Chairman sat at the far end of the hall behind a trestle table. He might have been trying to sell something. *Next* he bawled, turning from shifty stallholder to harassed clerk, presiding over some obscure application procedure. Chaim and his mother walked forward. It was like a judgement then, the two of them scrutinised by the grey-haired man with the purple lower lip. But this tableau too evaporated as the Chairman became an old family friend, asking Chaim about his work at Isaac's. He felt his mother leaning on his shoulder as once in the early ghetto days he had leant on hers. But time had moved on. Talking to the Chairman, dissembling the fact that he had ever been a child smuggler, he suddenly realised that he could no longer visualise the face of his father. His mother squeezed his arm. Josef and Mendel were behind them.

The blue cold light fell on the Chairman's swollen lip (he had had a nasty fall he said) and on the register where their names would be written and on the faded copy of the bible at its side. The double-branched electric candelabrum pulsed dimly. The Chairman began to recite the seven blessings in a dry perfunctory singsong.

St Mark's glowed and closed behind her. The mosaic was of two cockerels carrying a fox strapped to a stick. She would tell Oskar about it. He would laugh in their sea-rippled room. *Not too loud. You'll wake baby.*

You are betrothed to me with this ring in accordance with the Laws of Moses and Israel. It was not her hand shaking but Mendel's. He seemed to have passed from the trance of the snowflake sefirot to something more intense, less stable. Josef could feel acutely the Chairman's sulphurous unease. There was no one present from outside the ghetto. But rumours might spring up. Certainly Schmoyl, stationed at the Assembly Rooms entrance, had looked distinctly puzzled as their wedding party approached him along the slushy street. Yet Josef could not go back on his word. He had done this for Alicia's sake. Also he could not deny a certain pride at the way this solitary had singled him out. Schaefer had shown him just how fragile his world was. *Are you married? You should be.* Now he looked at Mendel as a traveller might watch a kestrel hanging in air over road or railway line.

He remembered the Talmud story about the bride and the bridegroom. He would tell them, the beautiful white cold stars of the snow floating now past the high window of the hall. They would see then that this was no profane union but a sign of tikkun, the restoration to come, the end of exile. Even the Chairman would see.

—There was once a man who pledged his faith to a maiden beautiful and true. For a time all passed pleasantly and the maiden lived in happiness. But the man was called from her side, he left her: long she waited but he did not return. Friends pitied her and rivals mocked her. Tauntingly they pointed at her and said 'He has left thee. He will never come back.' The maiden sought her chamber and read in secret the letters which her lover had written to her, letters in which he promised to be forever faithful, forever true. Weeping she read them but they brought comfort to her heart. She dried her eyes and wept no longer. A joyous day dawned for her. The man she loved returned. And when he learned that others had doubted and asked her how she had preserved her faith she showed his letters to him, declaring her eternal trust.

He was dancing, as David had danced before the Ark of the Lord. He had the letters in his hand, the Torah.

His father would not come back. The girl would.

Oskar would never return. Josef would.

She had returned, after years in exile.

The snow fell upward into heaven.

Messiah!

The blow struck Mendel full in the face and sent him sprawling back across the scratched wet parquet floor. The opened bible went slithering under the table, a wounded bird. His glasses fell in front of Alicia. Schmoyl had come running in from the porch. His truncheon was out. He waited for a sign from the Chairman who stood, both hands resting palm downwards on the table, breathing heavily. His purple lip glowed. The incomplete electric menorah lay on its side, flickering. Josef was helping Mendel up. Chaim stooped down to retrieve the bent spectacle frame. Mendel was smiling, pointing to a piece of broken lens that had become embedded in his hand.

—We had no wine glass to break. But this is one of its fragments. The broken vessels shall be restored.

With a slow heavy movement the Chairman waved Schmoyl away. He had been a believer once. *Next* he called, though with a considerably weakened voice.

The following day Grandma died. Snow was falling again, settling in thick quilts on the roofs of poorly heated tenements. The street below ran brown-grey with sullied drifts of snow. People hurried past, hunched up against the air's milling whiteness. Grandma, supported by Josef and Alicia heaved sideways and up. It was her last breath. Henryk stood at the foot of the bed, his hand on Chaim's shoulder, murmuring *little mother, O little mother.* Mendel was on the far side reciting the Kaddish.

The following day she was wheeled on the back of a handcart to the cemetery. Henryk dug the grave. Snow wafted into the trench as he dug.

There are bones in this soil. Soon there will be more. When I reach the catacombs.

7

Spring had entered the ghetto. Its misty wraith drifted through the barbed wire of the perimeter fence and under the boarded overhead walkway that had been built to connect two sectors divided by an Aryan street. It drifted past the Department of Registration, Census and Relocation where Josef Rosenfeld sat, forehead in hand, worrying about the Amtsleiter's new demands for lists of workers; and past the adjacent window framing the head and shoulders of Alicia Rosenfeld who, trying to work, constantly found her famished thoughts wandering from bread queue to soup kitchen, accompanied by the accusatory, resentful ghosts of Grandma and Oskar. It drifted into the Park allotments where Henryk bent, rolling wrinkled beads of radish seeds between finger and thumb, letting them drop one by one into the steaming furrow; and to where, in his slant-roofed garret, Mendel sat, having just run another errand for Josef, a prayer book in hand, meditating on the wars of God that would precede the millennium. It drifted down a water-runneled street where a young man and a girl walked hand in hand through black slabs of shadow to an inner courtyard.

—Spring comes so late here. In Vienna . . .

—Vienna, where is this Vienna you always talk about?

—The girl on Chaim's arm laughed. She seemed both young and old. Old because of what she wore: wooden clogs intended for feet a size larger than her own; a bulky fawn wool jacket and beneath it soiled and patched blue dungarees. Her youth lay in the body these garments obscured. Glimpsed at wrist or throat it seemed thin and vulnerable. But in the face these two conflicting pressures came together and merged. Dark socketed eyes flickered above lips still mobile and generous. Cheeks still furred with a girlish down rose to meet a forehead tense with lines. It was as if part of this person had gone missing and what remained had knitted together to disguise the void as best it could. She laughed again, questioningly.

—Vienna? I don't know. Dreamland.

Chaim disengaged himself from her arm and kicked at a rust-eaten tin that had once contained some inferior brand of sausage. It richocheted hollowly round the yard.

—Have you the bread?

She patted her oversize jacket.

—We can eat in a minute. Kiss me first.

He came to her and ran his tongue round the inside of her mouth. It was furred and dry. Her breath smelt. He loved her. Then it was her turn to pull away. He felt the brittle body in his arms go tense and hard.

—Not here. Not now. We have to get back. Old Isaac. . .

—Old Isaac's only forty five. And he's up at the office. They're preparing some list or other, Josef says.

He paused. Then nuzzled her left ear lobe.

—Just one feel.

She sighed, glanced quickly behind her and unbuttoned her coat. Swiftly he slipped his hand down the waist of her dungarees until it encountered hair and wetness. She moaned faintly, her lips parted. Over the scarf that turbanned her head, he read a ripped poster pasted to the grimy wall she leant against:

'Do not believe in German lies. Do not believe the lies of the Eldest of the Jews. Resettlement is . . .' But the rest of the text was torn away. His hand went limp in her warm furred darkness. She looked up at him quizzically, then half twisted round. Her face when it swivelled back was pale and sad. Old.

—But you believe, don't you? Now Josef Rosenfeld is your father.

Chaim slid his hand out of her dungarees. The air felt cold against it. He would sniff the fingertips later, longingly.

—I told you never to call him that. Stepfather. Stepfather.

He backed away, disengaging his left hand from her shoulder.

—My brothers-in-arms. Or they could have been. Do you think Bernard is involved?

She smiled but said nothing, buttoning up her coat.

—They were trying to smuggle in arms and ammunition last year. What a flop. And there are other ways.

—Of smuggling in weapons?—Chaim knew by her voice that she wanted to provoke.

—To resist I mean. To be free.

—That Mendel. He gives me the creeps.

—Only because he mutters under his breath. Mother says . . .—Immediately he regretted this tack.

—You westerners are all the same. You either love us or hate us.

Chaim winced. When he spoke his voice sounded young, unbroken.

—Rachel.

—Not me and you. I don't mean that. But Mendel. You don't, you can't understand. To us he's just a beggar, a charlatan. He preys on all of you.

Chaim touched her cotton scarf. It was printed with a design of white fish against a brown rippling background. He felt bottomless thirst.

—And what about my stepfather? He's from the East.

She lowered his hand but held on to it.

—An educated man. He's friendly with Mendel I know. But for him Mendel is a sort of case-study, a throwback. And anyway your stepfather is trapped.

—What's so terrible about the Census Department? It isn't the prison.—Instinctively Chaim sensed what was coming. Her words were fast, almost garbled.

—You came here last September. What happened before that? In the summer? Resettlement. Yes. And how do you think they organise the selections? By the *scheins*, the workcards? Yes. But how do they separate the sheep from the goats? They need information. Lists. Census lists. Lists of workers. My brother was on one. He was too ill to work. And now at this very moment your stepfather is drawing up more lists. Trapped did I say? Condemned.

Chaim looked away, abashed. For him a part of Rachel would always smile down in the dusk from a dark upper storey window. He had not meant to upset her. Yet her righteous anger found no echo in his heart. Since the marriage, since Grandma's death, since becoming part of the ghetto workforce, he had felt numb about everything except her. Indeed if it hadn't been for Josef and the work at Isaac's he might never have met her. How then should he blame this place? Just as his mother had found her old lover, so he had found Rachel. The old rootless days with Bernard receded into dream. Again he tried to touch her fish-rippling scarf, thirsty for contact, for the coiled black hair underneath. She turned and ripped at the wall where the poster hung. Her nails came away bloody.

—Look at it. The one word that matters has been lost. The word everyone should know.

She was sitting with her back to the door when he walked in. Light flooded the room, its bright walls, its furniture. There were mirrors on either side of her, she the candle, the stem of flame glowing between, infinitely reflected. And before her the window, seeding flesh with light, casting her light out on the world. Oh glass, oh brightness, oh world. The creation reforming, the shattered fragments restored. He had seen them in the Park allotments, hoeing the blessed earth, its crumbs sifted and sown, raining light. And the worms segmented with light, glistening when a blade sliced through them, reknitting again. And the buildings leaning their warm mirrors down to catch the breath of the warm earth. And the barbed wire hung with beads of light, long tzitzit of pure whiteness, spinning, suspended.

She turned in her chair but did not speak. *The World is a wedding* he muttered, walking over to her. She took his hand. The single tiny diamond on her wedding ring exploded in countless sharp-rayed facets. Each sought each until the diamond grew whole again. He said so quietly, trusting to the truth of revelation. She nodded, smiling.

It made her smile to hear him say diamond when anyone could see it was just a bit of paste jewellery. The only precious stone she had left was the diamond on the engagement ring Oskar had given her. And that she kept hidden in a sewn up pocket on the inside of her best blouse. For emergency, not sentiment. Still, if Mendel wanted to believe Josef's ring was precious he could. Because it was. She smiled again to herself. Spring was here and she was living with her new husband and Chaim and Henryk in unlooked-for luxury. His apartment consisted of three rooms. It had a separate kitchen. Riches untold. Diamonds. And so many possibilities. The rumours at the office today about the Eastern Front. The Russians were advancing. And Chaim. The smuggling and vice long forgotten. The work at old Isaac's. Rachel. Even Henryk was happy on his allotment. And the food had improved since the threat of a winter resettlement had faded. They were even going to bake matzoh for Passover. It was official. And now Mendel. He had come upon her in a dream of surfaces and reflections. Just to sit here at noon (she had returned for a file Josef needed), to savour the potential of new life, new hope. She smiled again at the stooping black-coated figure. His glasses were taped and bent. His boots flapped at the toes. Yet for her he was that newness and hope. He had taught her the strength of prayer. Through him she had begun to believe.

—Will it be long Mendel?

Her voice sounded sleepy with warmth and light. She was still inside the dream.

—Not long Mrs Rosenfeld.

He had chosen her new surname deliberately. The marriage was a pact between them, a symbol of their mutual faith.

—And now you have come. How did you know I would be here?

The question was too rich and heavy with warmth to need reply. For answer he held up his hand. He was clutching something. Its streaked leaves were tattered and limp. But the bulbous purple phial of petals was intact. And within, the saffron sparks, the sepals, burning.

—Henryk gave it me. There used to be municipal flower beds in the Park. For you.

The stem bled milk onto her hand. The bulb had been left behind in the earth. It would not flower again. But that too seemed right, a reason for hope. The last days. When she looked up again Mendel had gone.

Josef pushed the file away and rubbed at his armpit, the shirt dark with sweat. There was something terrible in the fact that she had had to fetch it for him. His angel of life turning into a messenger of death. Not that she knew. Not yet. But tomorrow that file would squat in the middle of the Chairman's desk. Each member of the twelve man council would have looked at it in turn. Each would have studied the report he had drawn up on its contents. Schaefer had had enough of rationalisation and increased productivity. The ghetto was too big. He remembered back to the interview last winter when he had inadvisedly mentioned resettlement and the Chairman, trying to intervene, had been struck. There was a coolness still between them, compounded by the incident at the wedding. Yet he no longer felt guilt. Resettlement was inevitable. Only its time scale remained conjectural. No one believed the ghetto would last forever. No one except perhaps the Chairman. Tomorrow the ghost of the file would float out of the Judenrat to hang over the streets and houses. Its contents would drip blackness. Inside floated the names of all those most likely to be selected.

Then suddenly he was laughing. Hadn't he made sure his family would be spared? Even Mendel, so distrusted by the Chairman, so loved by Alicia, even he would not be selected. And the girl Chaim seemed interested in. All now had useful employment, were vital to the ghetto's existence. All, when the day came, would receive the yellow permits that guaranteed non-deportation. And in the case of his wife, stepson and Henryk there was now the added protection of being a ghetto official's relative. He had done right that day he talked with the Chairman and Schaefer. But the laughter could not last, despite the warm breath of spring billowing through the open window. The ghetto couldn't last. After this resettlement would come another. And after that another. The ground on which they stood was being eroded day by day. In the end not even a Census Officer's family would escape. He pushed the file away and took out the old red and black Minutes book.

'Last night. Walking through the ghetto after dark. A

thing impossible in real life. Everywhere people revelling, running out of doors in masks, their clothes garish and fantastic: pantaloons, crinolines, harlequin suits. Canals not streets. Bright constellations overhead. Achingly sharp. Then A. In a gold fluted dress that swept the cobbles (cobbles? there are none here) and a satin mask with silvery cat's whiskers. How young we were, dancing in and out of pillars hung not with ghetto newspapers but flags, multi-coloured. Then along the narrow sides of canals, over slender arched bridges, past moored gondolas heavy with yellow and lime fruit of lanterns. Chaim and his girl, M and H – I saw them all dancing as we danced, smiling. Then the gunshot. A sort of flare above the dome of St Sulpice which was also the ruined tower of St Mary and All Saints. Everybody running. A long drawn-out squeal as of a blade across china and all of them sliding, tilting back into some night behind the pillars, a darkness that magnetised and repelled. The gondolas were gone, the canals were long wet trenches in the earth, newly dug. Somewhere too, fires, the smell of burning. Yet we did not run. Slowly, almost meditatively, she and I danced on (which is remarkable considering I don't dance at all), the air cold, clouding our breath, icicles hanging from pediments, shrouds of snow folded on steps leading to a railway station where . . .'

She had come into the office and seen him writing.

—It is time to go now. Mendel will come for the Passover meal.

She seemed exalted. It was his dream again. Had she seen the diary? No. Nor the tear that quivered at his eye's corner. A secret deeper than any hidden archive. His ledger of time.

And tomorrow, Passover. The eve of the resettlement. Schaefer's time. They would be celebrating, Alicia in her new found faith, Mendel in his ancient kabbalistic mists, while everywhere people prepared to carry their belongings to the trucks (no march to the siding this time; efficiency was paramount). Time and timing. He laughed again and kissed his wife with dry whispering lips. He had lost weight since the winter.

Mendel thinks the world is coming to an end. And it is but not for everybody. Alicia thinks so too. That was why he took the crocus. It won't grow again I said but he didn't listen. This soil is poor. Potatoes I said. They help to improve soil. You could sprout some of the ration. But all they want is cabbage, rutabaga. They've had enough of potatoes. But I'm growing them anyway. Some eggs would be nice. My poor barnvelders. The cochins too. They don't like animals here either. Those two cows that got through the wire from the old gipsy camp the other day. They disappeared in minutes. It was a wonder people said. It wasn't. It was horrible. And the knives weren't sharp enough. Night of the long knives. Why do you want to be a vegetarian little mother said. Don't you appreciate God's creation. And the way they kill the chicken in the ritual. Swinging it round the head. Oskar knew. That time they visited and we had a fondue. Pity there's no meat in it, he said winking over Alicia's head. It was a joke between us. Not that he didn't eat flesh. He thought you needed meat for it. Which he did plenty of. Poor Alicia. And now we're here and there's hardly any meat at all. Oskar would have laughed. Chaim misses him. And now he's met the girl in the clothing place it's worse somehow because he wants to believe in Josef but can't and Alicia and

Mendel are always bent over that bible, the one with all the commentaries. I just look at my fancy fowl book. Because we're all chickens here. And they want to eat us. To get rid of their own pain because their bodies are all swollen with meat of war. Oskar fought in the last war. Alicia remembered it that day the deportation orders came through. Doesn't that make a difference she said. Not now I said. That's why they say we kill babies for Passover. It's to numb their own pain. That's why they say like vermin. *Because then they don't feel anything. It's not like the last time at all. Then we were on the same side. Now there's just a barbed fence and us. Alone. And Mendel doesn't understand. And Josef doesn't and Alicia doesn't. Maybe Chaim will one day. But not yet.*

8

The smoke hung heavy once more in the air of the Chairman's office. It was cheap smoke, from cheap ghetto tobacco. Schaefer was absent; yet he hovered behind every word and gesture, behind every glance from the twelve men who sat in a semicircle facing the Eldest, the saviour of children, the ghetto's king.

—Passover,—muttered the head of public works.

—Just Schaefer's little joke,—whispered the director of ghetto schools.

—That's as many as last year,—Josef mused under his breath.

But the Chairman had heard. He still held a grudge against his Census Officer. His loss of control at the wedding was just as much Josef's fault as the incident with the Amtsleiter. He would not forget.

—Yes. Twenty thousand Mr Rosenfeld. Including the westerners. All of them.

Josef started. This was not what he had expected at all. But the Chairman was smiling, eyes closed. He had felt the effect of his words. He savoured it a moment longer.

—That was what Schaefer wanted. But you of all people Mr Rosenfeld should know I do not give in easily. This resettlement might already have occurred if it hadn't been for my scheme to increase ghetto productivity and lower costs. Since the winter we have worked harder and eaten less. But no one has left the ghetto involuntarily.

The hospital manager leant across to the head of public works.

—Except the dead and there's hardly been a shortage of them.

The Chairman heard but ignored the interpolation.

—As I said, these deportations were slated for the winter. Some of you,—here he opened his eyes wide and glared at Josef—some of you even seemed willing to countenance such a disaster at the time. But I wasn't. Nor am I today. Schaefer takes some persuading I can tell you. But I am a good haggler.—Here he glanced at Abram the little chief of police who had been a dealer in rugs from Kurdestan before the war. A few of the others laughed.—I talked about our undeniable productivity drive. Our record on law and order.

—If you except the underground.—Abram had been nettled by the Chairman's refusal to authorise a sweep of the semi-official youth groups. The Chairman drew himself up.

—With the result that the number has been halved. Not twenty thousand, gentlemen, but ten thousand. Over a period of thirty days.

There was a stir. Abram looked round at the other council members.

—That was Schaefer's original target. The other figure was a bluff. They never concede anything.

The hospital manager waved his hand for the chief of

police to be quiet. He had lost an elderly relative in the last resettlement. He wanted some facts.

—And how are the selections to be made? By *scheins*?

The Chairman shook his head.

—The Amtsleiter feels that was too inefficient. There were many who slipped the net. No. Exemption permits. They have been issued to this office. Now we must distribute them among the heads of the four sectors. Those who are not exempt must be listed.

Here he turned to Josef.

—I have your latest figures Mr Rosenfeld. The lists of exemptions, to be returned here this afternoon,—he paused to look at the four sector overseers—will be checked off against them.

Josef's mouth was dry. He longed for water, to plunge into water.

—And administrators, officials? Are their families doubly exempt?

The Chairman eyed Josef. He despised the Census Officer's adoption of the Viennese family almost as much as his friendship with the hasid. Yet something in Josef made him recoil from out and out hostility. It was as if the Census Officer's transparent awareness of ambiguity and compromise drew them together. Where others acted out of selfishness and fear, Josef and his superior mixed expediency and morality in equal doses. Both were tainted. Hence the violence of one and the melancholy of the other. At that moment, the Chairman felt this affinity with painful acuteness. He grew almost tender.

—Administrators such as yourself will have special

permits. They will include three additional family members. You have three close relations.

Through tears Josef nodded. He would make sure both Mendel and Rachel received an ordinary permit.

On the street outside Josef's head reeled sickly so that he was forced to lean against the Judenrat wall, eyes closed. When Chaim had been involved with the child smugglers he had argued strongly for law and order. Yet today he had been involved in a process of anarchic destruction. There was no substance now, only form. He had left the file behind him with the Chairman. Alicia had touched it. Corruption. His briefcase felt weightless now. Opening his eyes he found himself staring straight at the excrement wagon. A huge slopping drum on wheels, it was attended by half a dozen, shoving, heaving men. All would die of typhus. The rusted cylinder creaked slowly past. Long after it was gone Josef kept his hand pressed tight to mouth and nose.

Rachel had handed him the letter as they trailed back weary and famished from Isaac's factory. Fatigue and hunger were made worse by the knowledge that no ration would be generous enough, no sleep too long. At first he had thought it was one of her strange whims, like the time she had given him a folded piece of paper on which she had imprinted the lipsticked outline of her mouth. There it floated, pouting up at him, fuller than in life, the pouches and clefts outlined in fluorescent crimson. Where had she obtained the lipstick? he asked himself. Then more urgently: why didn't she barter it for rations? But at last a languid happiness had seeped over him. He was content simply to place his real lips, cracked and dry as they were, against the dream vision she had created out of paper and lipstick. The imprint felt sticky and faintly powdery. It smelt too – a tart almost sexual odour. He had carried the feel and smell around with him all that evening. The next morning, in the factory yard, he had given her a lock of his hair. But that had been weeks ago. Now neither of them had the inclination to engage in the traditional playfulness of young lovers. It was as if an arid flame had been kindled in their bodies, consuming all passion, humour and desire. Work eat sleep. Work eat sleep. They parted at the entrance to the tenement where she lived, sharing two rooms with a couple who had been moved in after her brother's deportation: a woman too ill to work and her husband, some low functionary in the police department. Once she had told Chaim how this man was always trying to touch her up under the guise of an avuncular tickle. For a moment he had visualised the scene with aching clarity; its terror, its squalor. Then the darkness had come down again. Now he no longer cared to imagine Rachel's hidden life. It was enough to be together when they were. They kissed, peremptorily. People were shoving to get past. The letter lay unopened in Chaim's pocket.

Even when he opened it at last, sitting on the bed in the room he shared with Henryk, he still partly hoped it might contain some love token or private symbol. A brief memory of her smell carried round for days on unwashed fingertips rose up again to torment and taunt. Then faded. It was growing dark. His great uncle still toiled down at the

Park allotments. Josef and his mother were working late, sifting through the resettlement exemptions that had been issued to the Census Department. There would be one for Rachel, Josef had assured him. The letter glimmered before him. It was printed.

The great deportation will begin on Passover. We are preparing. Resettlement means death. Join us. Do not believe the Nazi lies. Nor the lies of the Judenrat. Resettlement means death. ZOB.

It was in the same style as the poster on the yard wall. But underneath something had been added. A handwritten note, hastily scrawled.

'Treecreeper. Join us. The bearer knows. B.'

Chaim sat for a long time with the letter in front of him. Bernard. A ghost returned from the cellars and the sewers to haunt and tempt. The print dissolved in the darkness. But Bernard's handwriting seemed bolder, less erasable. Chaim had entrusted himself to the ghetto administration, to Josef and the life of compromise. He knew the underground was not ready. They were still desperately short of armaments. Join us. Why? To shoot and to be shot? To risk the lives of his mother and Henryk and Josef? Rachel was the bearer. She knew Bernard. She wanted him to join. He picked up the letter and crumpled it in his hand. Not yet. Or yet.

His mother was fussing round the table. She was still visibly relieved every time she found Chaim safe at home, as though she had never quite believed in his change of heart. She placed a small waxed paper parcel in front of her.

—I've managed to get extra bread. Matzoh. They're

baking it for Passover. It's a new concession. 1.30 marks a kilo. You always liked it when you were little. And herring. But there . . .—and here she sighed in that irritating way, suggestive of resigned acceptance—this will have to do. And the noodles. Where are you going?

He had stood up. It was difficult to decide which he hated the most, her happy passivity or these sudden lurches into blind panic.

—Nowhere. I just thought I'd stand up.

Trapped he sat down again. Even Henryk's indifferent rambling would be a relief. Suddenly he remembered the crumpled letter.

—Look at this.

He smoothed it out on the table in front of her. She fumbled for her reading glasses.

—Chaim. After all Josef has told you. These are hot-heads, anarchists, I don't know.

Again he repressed an urge to run to the door.

—Resettlement means death. Look. It says so.

She took off her glasses and folded them. Her eyes were milky.

—How do they know. How? Anyway we have exemption papers. Rachel too.

Her face was rapt. But blank. A holy look.

—And the ZOB is outlawed. You'd better destroy that.

It was Josef. He had entered the room on soundless feet. He placed a yellow card beside the crumpled letter.

—For Rachel. See she gets it tomorrow.

If she hasn't already joined Bernard, Chaim thought bitterly. Suddenly he felt hopelessly entangled by the decisions he had had to make. He began to sob. The old hunger had hold of him. Josef put his head on his stepson's shoulder.

—All we can do is wait and work behind the scenes.

—And pray for deliverance.

His mother was kneeling by the storage cupboard to put away the dry wafers of matzoh. Its door was netted with a wire ventilation grille. Another prison. She looked up.

—Since you've both got nothing better to do you can help me sweep this room.—Then, at Chaim's and his stepfather's evident incomprehension—For Passover. The room must be swept of all leavened food.

Passover. Deliverance. Join us. Exemption. So many words. So many meanings. So many prisons. And Chaim was too tired and hungry to care. He crossed the room to fetch the handbrush from behind the stove. Returning with it he could not suppress a wan smile. He and his parents were about to sweep away a thing that didn't exist. No crumb of food was ever left to decay on the floor of a ghetto room.

So far the concert had been a success. The quartet, made up of two violinists from Warsaw, a viola from the ghetto and a western cellist had given creditable accounts of an early Mendelssohn and the second Rasoumovsky. After the interval they were due to be joined by a pianist from Cracow for a rendition of the late Brahms quintet. Now in the abandoned church of St Mary and All Saints, its pulpit still intact, its shattered rose window still shadowing the chancel with glowing fragments of an alien messiah and his disciples, the ghetto audience sat on canvas chairs and backless pews, murmuring again their black psalm of suffering and complaint. Soon the Chairman would be making his long awaited eve of resettlement speech.

Alicia sat to the side near a wall plaque that commemorated the pious life of an eighteenth century Lithuanian Merchant – a dealer in herbs and spices and – more importantly – a convert to the Christian faith. She was alone this evening, one of the first on which the light had been sufficient to allow for a public event to be held before curfew. She was alone and sad, having argued with Josef about Chaim.

—It's the girl,—he had said, after Chaim had left the room, announcing he must see Rachel.—It's the girl trying to turn him. I don't know why I went to all the trouble of obtaining the extra exemption card. Lying about that clerk who died a week ago. I don't know why.

She too had had her struggle with the knowledge that Chaim put Rachel before anyone. But she was his mother. She was allowed to be jealous. What business had Josef with such emotions?

—She's good for him and you know it. Kept him working. Kept him out of trouble. Those hooligans.—She looked down at the top of Josef's balding head. It was flaking here and there, enflamed.

—There are worse. Real outlaws. The ZOB. He'll have us all deported.

It was no use. Ever since the news of resettlement her husband had been edgy and ill at ease. She could understand his concern for his family. Even with work and the additional privilege of being related to a top administrator, none of them would be wholly safe until the last train had left the siding. There were always mistakes, sacrifices as well as reprieves. Some were left behind who had been certain to go; some who seemed safe were taken. But Josef's concern seemed to bleed out of this narrow channel and cover the whole community. Why such disinterestedness? He who only acted as a go-between, a messenger behind besieged walls. Yet she had encountered this mood before. It had ancient roots. Once, in the old days, they had met secretly in a gallery of the Kunsthistorischesmuseum. She was bursting to tell him of her complete loss of faith. It promised somehow to draw her closer to him. They were standing in front of Breughel's *Tower of Babel*. Distractedly he mentioned the political situation, the rich Jews fleeing abroad, the rumours of new, punitive race laws in Germany. She nodded. *Even Oskar's beginning to talk about Switzerland*. Then his explosion: *What about those who will never be able to flee? Those here and back home in the East?* She had guessed his passion was fuelled by a corrosive guilt. He felt powerless, pointing to the picture. *There they are. The ones who can't flee. See. The slaves. Building the tower. Too small to be individuals*. She had peered wonderingly. So much distance. So much detail. *But it fell, didn't it? It was destroyed?* And he, smiling again, never angry for long. *It fell on the slaves*.

How young she had been then, and easily cowed. But tonight in this alien place, still groping towards a faith more ancient than anything she had rejected in the West, she felt surer of herself. Again the slow movement of the Rasoumovsky floated through her mind. What had

Beethoven said? 'A weeping willow over my brother's grave.' A beautiful vision. To mourn and bear witness. Josef was a go-between who envied alike those who acted and those who prayed. She loved his moral bravery yet sensed it was doomed. Soon he would have to choose. It was her duty as his wife to show him the right way, as Mendel had shown it to her. She murmured the Kiddush ha-Shem to herself, feeling faint from lack of food. Then the Chairman strode in front of the derelict altar.

The Chairman's bodyguards were eyeing him suspiciously. There were four of them standing near the nave pillars closest to the porch. In pinstriped suit and spats Schmoyl leant against the oolitic swirl of polished marble, swinging a policeman's truncheon. Another ran knuckledusters round the dog-toothed arch of a blocked doorway. A third sharpened a knife on a worn font bowl. Mendel's distrust of all places concerned with Christian worship merged with a griping physical fear. He wanted to go back to his room and pray. Yet he had been doing just that continuously these last few days before Passover and still nothing had changed, no sign had been given. The shattered fragments lay everywhere, lightless. Now, in this echoing cave, more threatening for its hopeless dereliction (one section of the ribbed vaulting had collapsed to be replaced by grey tarpaulin sheeting whose many tears revealed an even greyer sky), Mendel heard the voice of the Chairman, explaining, justifying, exhorting. He moved forward a little, watched intently, insolently by Schmoyl, and peered round a pillar. She was there. He had to go through with it. He had to tell her. Once again he saw Josef standing in his room, distracted, trembling. *It is my doing. I am a murderer as surely as if I had lifted up my own hand. Ten thousand. And everyone could be me or you, Alicia, Chaim. What hope Mendel, what hope?* And he who had longed for the last days could say: Nothing. He had no hope to offer. Josef and Alicia had been married. The resettlement was about to begin. Some would be saved and some would not. But it was all profane and dark and broken. The divine stayed hidden, apart. *Prayer* was all he had muttered, *We must pray.* And so Josef had gone away unappeased. And now he was here to say to Alicia *The light is hidden. The world is profane. We cannot be saved.*

The Chairman's voice droned on. Samael's Voice. Dark. Banal. He was playing with figures, rearranging them. Surely now, at this utter depth of pitchblackness, there would be a blast of shofars, a great wind. But nothing. It had been thirty thousand. Now it was ten. Nothing nothing. Oh utter silence of the hidden Word, the light dwelling apart and shrouded forever. When would the vessels be restored? Blame me then, let me take on my shoulders the suffering and iniquity of this place where a voice says nothing and means the soul, where numbers swallow the chosen and the chosen are cast out. Let my exile be the cornerstone of our redemption.

'How the gold was tarnished, the finest gold debased! How the sacred gems were strewn about at every street corner!'

—What's he saying?

—He's kneeling.

It was the fall of Jerusalem again. He lamented with the prophet:

'Then their faces turned blacker than soot; none could recognise them in the streets. Their skin shrivelled on their bones, it became as dry as wood . . .'

—The Chairman's finished. You're not applauding.

—Kneeling.

—Growing a beard again.

He looked into the faces of Samael's host. They were created from fire and air. They met their Lord in dark places of smoke and violation. They copulated with human beings. They made more demons.

His smile crumpled.

It was her. The demons were melting away, back to the ruinous places, the temples of bone in Sitra ahra.

Her. You didn't cross the wife of the Census man. Not when your own family might be on the line. There would be other opportunities to deal with this one.

A last kick.

Her face was grey, hovering over him. She dabbed the corner of his mouth with a scented handkerchief. No hope, no hope.

—You must keep out of sight. Even though you do have a permit.

The light hidden. The Divine hidden. 'Strewn about at every street corner.'

—Faith, Mendel. We are in exile but not forgotten.

She had to think of something, convince him to keep a low profile.

She was the Queen of the Sabbath. She wore the garment of light, a million stars, words. Faith. Even when he writhed in darkness.

—You will stay with us the first night of Pesach? Josef thinks it would be safest.

Faith. Her smile. It reminded the demons of their own mortality.

She had tried to comfort him as she would try to comfort Josef. Like her Mendel could despair. She hadn't expected that.

The second visit to Venice she had again gone into St Mark's alone. It was after a particularly savage argument when her husband had accused her of frigidity. Then he had stormed out, taking a pale Chaim with him. Despairingly, nostalgically she had sought the blue-gold glooms of the Duomo. If only Josef could have been with her. Thinking of him in the cold East she paused in the narthex, looking up. The mosaic above her depicted a panting Noah trying to wrestle two reluctant lions into his boat. In another panel he was trying just as hard to wrestle them out again. She smiled. The flood waters had subsided.

9

Although it was still light outside the room had already been darkened. At first Chaim had attributed this to a now familiar ghetto caution. Just as ablutions had to be conducted in darkness, so an evening feast like the seder would have to begin before curfew, in case the candles were seen from outside. But as he hung up his cap on the nail and moved towards the screened-off kitchen to wash, he sensed a watchfulness in the three seated adults as if, by closing the curtains and lighting the wicks so soon, they had hoped to draw him more swiftly to the table. He stopped and looked from his mother to Mendel to Josef. Each of them seemed possessed by a tense expectation. For Mendel this centred on the fact of Passover. He was celebrating tonight with the woman who had shown him the way forward. For Josef it had to do with a feeling of power and helplessness. He could not prevent the resettlements. Yet he had saved his family. For that alone he was prepared to go through with a ritual he only half acknowledged. For Alicia tonight was a celebration of her love for Josef, of her family's deliverance and of her growing sense of religious awe. So Chaim stood before them, feeling none of these things, unsettled. Alicia was fingering the tablecloth. It was white and fresh.

—Do you remember this?

Chaim came closer. Lace. Swirls and rosettes. A lagoon of white. He did not remember. Or did not want to.

—I bought it in Venice. At Murano. When your father was alive.—She coughed, almost embarrassed.—I, I thought it looked nice.

Chaim felt a pang of misery. He glanced swiftly from his mother to Josef. How could she be so obtuse, so unfeeling? But no reciprocal light shone in Josef's eyes. He too accepted the tablecloth as a meaningless survival from some unknowable time. It was as if the past of the Schultz family no longer had any reality beyond their present incarnation as Rosenfelds. That at least seemed to be what Josef and his mother wanted him to believe. The lace tablecloth and Venice and his father were all in the ghetto now, changed by it, drained of substance, dry shells. Josef touched a wine bottle set in the middle of the white sea.

—And I found this. Elderberry. I had it stored in the cupboard. Mendel wasn't allowed his Passover wine ration.

—Is Henryk here?

Mendel stirred uneasily.

—I think not. He is still earthing potatoes.

He looked at Alicia.

—Shall we begin the Haggadah?

Alicia turned round to Chaim.

—Rachel? Did you give her our invitation?

Chaim looked away evasively. He could not tell them yet about the day at Isaac's. He wanted them to think well of her. But tonight she would not be coming.

—You gave her the permit at least?

Josef's voice sounded official.

—Yes. That is, she took it.—Again he was flooded by misery.

—She gave you that note. The ZOB note.

Josef's official voice grew strained. Alicia put a restraining hand on his arm.

—You said we would be finished before curfew. That Josef would accompany her back to her room?

—This Haggadah is too dark for me. Shall we start again?

Alicia and Josef looked blankly at Mendel who began to laugh.

—So many questions without answers. Surely the youngest son of the house should initiate the questions. Chaim, we must discuss the Exodus.

—The resettlements you mean.

Josef stirred with anger but now it was Mendel's turn to pacify.

—The Exodus of which tomorrow's events will be a dim reminder.

Chaim glanced again from one face to the next. He was struck with a sudden sense of transience. That was why the present felt so emprisoned. It would soon end. Dimly he remembered some of the instruction he had received for the bar mitzvah that had never been. The actual ceremony had been indefinitely postponed after his father's disappearance. He looked at Mendel and smiled.

—Why is this night different from all other nights?

Now the adults were smiling too. Against all the odds their youngest had joined in the seder. They felt pride in him. Mendel composed himself to answer.

★

137

Some minutes later, Chaim was able to interpolate another question.

—Why were wells important for Isaac, Moses and Jacob?

Mendel's response was almost automatic.

—They all met their wives by the well.

—And what were the names of their wives?

He was triumphant. Alicia clapped her hands with girlish enthusiasm.

—I know. Let me. Rebeccah, Zipporah and . . . and Rachel.

Rachel. Yes. So she was present at the meal after all.

That morning they had met at the usual corner. Before they joined the slow crowd streaming down the street he handed her the yellow permit.

—Josef said to give you this personally. You're invited to the seder meal too.

She looked at the card distantly.

—I may not need one.

Chaim stopped still. People cursed and budged to get by.

—Nor will you. You've read the letter. We can go there tonight. Bernard expects us.

—Rachel?

But she was walking on. He should have expected this. Yet he still felt stunned by her determination. And afraid. A part of him remained loyal to his mother and Josef. He caught up with her.

—My stepfather moved heaven and earth to obtain that permit. You can't just say you won't need it.

She looked at him coldly.

—I'll keep it for now.

So the estrangement had begun.

When noon came Isaac's workers sat drinking their soup in the factory yard, making a circle round the ruined plinth of a vanished statue. All carried permits, the ones who had not received them having gone into hiding. There was an inscription on one side of the plinth. It read 'Memory', 'War', 'Died'. The rest had been obliterated and no one now knew who this hero might have been. It was rumoured that his eroded Glory had been dragged here from the Park allotments in order to block up an entrance to the sewers much favoured at night by the underground. Now it made a pleasant resting place, having absorbed the heat of the morning air.

—Is this cabbage?

Chaim held his tin spoon up so that some of the cloudy glutinous liquid could dollop back into the bowl. Rachel was sitting at a pointed distance. They had not spoken again. Moses Zuckerman examined the spoon with mock-myopic reverence.

—On purely subjective grounds I would hazard the opinion that this liquid has at some not too distant date entered the vicinity of a root of the brassica family; to wit the swede.

Chaim tried to laugh. Moses had been a brilliant literature student before the war. Now he was a curiosity.

—They can have me.

At first no one responded to the third voice. It was so thin and slight it seemed barely a voice at all. The territorial song of the robin on the warehouse roof seemed louder, more insistent. But Rachel had heard. She stood up and walked over to where a very pale fair-haired girl sat a little apart from the rest on a lump of stone that had sheared away from the unknown warrior's plinth. She squatted in front of her.

—What is it dear?

—They can have me.

The slight girl looked up. She would have had freckles in happier times. And plaits. Someone had cut her hair short in crude jagged wedges.

—I've applied.

Chaim turned to study her. It was the Brendel girl. One of a large family down in the south sector, an area notorious for thieving and violence. Now she looked from him to Rachel with stony beseeching eyes. After all she had suffered (half her family had gone in the previous resettlement, then her father had starved to death during the winter), she seemed still willing to aspire to a maidenly bashfulness.

—It's easy you know.—Her voice grew more confident. She looked around.—You just turn up at the Judenrat and ask to have your name put on one of the lists. Then you're simply allocated a day, an assembly point. They're using trucks this time. To take us to the train. For greater speed and efficiency.

Moses was examining a flea he had just caught, pressing its shiny brown carapace between the nails of thumb and forefinger. It cracked, spurting blood.

—Methinks they are cunning these officials. Cunning as foxes. Trucks gadzooks. Plush.

—Shut up Moses.— Chaim turned to the girl.—But you're a worker. You have an exemption permit.

—Not any more. I handed it in for someone else to use. Anyway they want workers. For this new labour camp we're being sent to.

Rachel tapped one wooden clog on the other.

—It's always east of here. But we never know exactly where.

—But I've seen a map. My brother—(this was her only surviving relative in the ghetto)—had a map from someone who left the ghetto and came back. It's a real camp. They've plenty to eat apparently. They work for it of course.

Moses snorted and rubbed his hand on his jacket.

—That's why they'll take workers. And they can have me. Oh yes.

Then the Brendel girl was weeping, her head on Rachel's shoulder. Caviare would not help her now. Chaim realised with a little flutter of sadness that she might not even last until the day of her resettlement. She had the final blank look of those waiting for death.

As they formed two lines to go back into the factory, the one on the left to the looms, the one on the right to the sorting department, Chaim found himself opposite Rachel. He was desperate.

—Why didn't you tell her?

—What?—She did not look in his eyes.

—Resettlement means death.

He knew she had wanted to. But Rachel too had many inner struggles to surmount. She gazed at the factory wall tearfully.

141

—Because you refused to come with me. Without you I haven't the strength.

—You will come to the seder meal then. Josef said he would see you safely home.

Rachel looked away, her face hardening.

—No Chaim, no. I am not a part of your family. Not yet. But thank Josef for me. And tell him about the Brendel girl.

The Haggadah was over. The meal, noodles, matzoh and wine had been finished. Even Henryk was here now. Chaim knew his parents resented Rachel's absence: Alicia because it was an affront to her; Josef because he distrusted her involvement with the ZOB. Yet any pride he might have felt at her independence was crushed by anxiety. He had managed to forget this during the ritual questions and answers. And the meal had been more substantial than usual, blocking out thought. Now in the emptiness after eating he could not forget. Would she come to work tomorrow? Would she decide she did have the strength and go to Bernard after all? He might have rushed out then and there if Josef hadn't suddenly stood up and began reciting one of the old medieval Passover lyrics. It was a carefree drinking song. The mood at the table would not lift.

—Give me the cup that puts sorrow to flight, and let me have my share in the river of delights.

The noise drowned out the rest of the ancient Hebrew verse. Instantly all five participants in the seder ceremony stiffened. It was gunfire, one shot after another, at random intervals, drawing closer. Alicia put her hand on Chaim's arm. Josef reached across the table to extinguish the candles.

One red stem fell and rolled on the white lace, spooring a coagulated wax. The shots sounded closer now, perhaps just a block away, underpinned by another less familiar noise, the drone of a petrol engine. All vehicles in the ghetto were pulled by horses or humans. This was a car. From the world beyond the barbed wire. Josef stood up.

—Be careful Josef.

Chaim detached his mother's clenched hand from his sleeve and went to stand behind his stepfather who already had the curtains twitched back an inch. The street was black and fathomless, the sky overcast. Suddenly from the corner of a nearby tenement, two beams of headlights launched themselves like a pair of yellow calipers into the night. Slanting upwards, they climbed to roof level then guttered, their bright rods severed by darkness. Next they swung round and down, two divergent blades of light sweeping past blacked out windows and flicking into the blind sockets of courtyards. Just as it seemed these hot swords must have no root in anything, no cause beyond their own automatic compulsion to comb and rake and penetrate, the car, whose engine all five people in the little room had heard as a visitation from another world, squealed round the corner of the tenement and came lurching along the street, now in the middle, now to one side, its black windows wound down on blackness.

—They're shooting from the car.

—It's a Daimler. A Coupé.—Chaim might have been reading a cigarette card. He could not help but be boyishly impressed. He barely felt the pressure of Josef's hand.

—Get back from the window. They're shooting.

As if in answer a volley of shots rang out, one bullet seeming to ricochet off the very wall of the room. Chaim thought of Rachel in her own tenement. Would she too be crouching like him, wondering about tomorrow? Or had she already thrown in her lot with Bernard? If so he would find her. He suppressed a sob.

—That sound. Listen.

Mendel had stood up, pale and tall, a witness to ancient pogroms. Josef crept back on his knees to the window and peeped under the curtain.

—They've got a megaphone. One of them's singing through a megaphone.

A slurred voice rose heavily on the warm night air. It hung there, as if willing someone to turn on a light, to come out onto the street, exposed.

—*Hoho! Hoho! Hahei!*

Schmiede, mein hammer, ein hartes Schwert!

Hoho! Hahei! Hahei! Hoho!

Der frohen Funken wie freu' ich mich . . .

—It's them.—Alicia gripped Chaim convulsively.—It's starting.

—Not yet. This is just a show. For our benefit. Listen.

—*Durch Glut und Hammer glückt' es mir;*

Mit starken Schlägen streckt' ich dich . . .

—Not a bad tenor. For a member of the SA.

—*Heiaho! Heiaho! Heiahohoho! Heiah!*

Again the voice rose. The silence seemed to irritate and affront it. There was another shot and the car moved on. Josef moved away from the window and picked up the candle. Henryk was hunched in a corner.

—They're frightened of tomorrow too.

—Lord, how much longer will this separation make me a homeless fugitive? The fires of wandering are ablaze, and I am ready for the stake.

The car had long since left the ghetto. Mendel stood before the door of Josef's apartment reciting the Passover Song. Josef stood beside Chaim. Alicia was on one side of the door. Henryk on the other.

—My Love for you, O my beautiful daughter, is broader than the sea. I shall take you back to Me, . . .

Josef was whispering.

—I am doing this for your mother's sake.

Chaim nodded. The separation of which Mendel sang was his exile from Rachel's arms. He bit his lip.

—She must stay here after tonight. It will be safer. I'll speak to your mother.

Chaim looked up at his stepfather in gratitude. He still had need of him.

—All of you who mocked me yesterday in the hour of my peril, and in the day of my distress – my Beloved has truly taken me back . . . I shall proudly declare: 'My husband loves me now and for all time.'

Mendel paused, then raised his arms.

—Welcome Elijah.

Alicia opened the door. For a moment all were assailed by the dank sweet air of the stairwell. Then Henryk quickly pushed the door shut again and bolted it. Mendel hoped that Elijah's ghost had entered in that brief space of time. He proceeded to pronounce the curse on all enemies and tormentors.

The night grew cloudier, more still. Pinned to the wall of the ghetto police station the flag of the Star of David rippled and tugged in a faint breeze. To one side a loose window hinge scraped in response. Down in the Park allotments faint green rows of unthinned seedlings glimmered against damp soil. A rat slithered past. Down a nearby gutter a child's wooden ball began its last hesitant journey towards a storm drain. At the perimeter fence, where a sentry coughed in his box, glad that on this night at least the child smugglers were inactive, a fragment of paper twisted, skewered. It still bore the letters ZOB.

She was a little girl. Daddy's girl. The steps led down to water. It swirled. Daddy gone. She was walking through the water. It wasn't wet and made her feel numb. Ahead rose Henryk's bulk. His face was blue. He was standing up in the swirls. He wore something on his face. A mask. *Not enough air. Like when I was born.* Daddy gone.

He was in the Chairman's office. The Chairman was his old tutor at the university. He stood naked behind his desk. *Black milk will help you pass the exam of life.* He was twisting and twisting something in his hand. A rag doll stained with gentian violet.

The Chairman was God. In his right hand he held a pair of

broken glasses. In his left a phial of mauve smoke. *Choose. These to be restored. Or this to be broken. Choose.*

The wagon interior was decorated with a dolphin frieze. Rachel came towards him. She was naked. She drew something out from between her legs. *For you Chaim because you didn't go with me.* A violet sugar cube. When he crushed it between his teeth water poured into the wagon.

He was running round and round the coop. They wanted to eat him for seder. The coop was full of feathers. Blue feathers. Water purled in the darkness.

The first of fifteen mornings. Soon now the first of many queues, crowds, the rolled-up bundles, clothing, bread, the creased ghetto notes, trucks and shots, dogs, truncheons, hiding places in lofts, cellars, walls, discoveries, cries, doors banging, people running, the crowds, the queues, dew on the wire, blood, silence.

The yellow permit holders also had their troubles. For the duration of the resettlement the Amtsleiter had ordered all night shift work to be suspended. In that way the authorities would know where everybody was supposed to be at any given time. So the exempted workers' main morning task over the next two weeks would be to get to the safety of the workplace before the deportations began. Even then there was danger. The ghetto police held many grudges. And if the quotas weren't met from day to day, their own families were at risk. There would be kapos, too, conscripted from outside the ghetto. Even, it was rumoured, a scattering of the SS. Neither of these elements could be trusted to exempt anyone, permit or not. Once in factory or shop the workers would stay as long as possible, making sure by a system of lookouts that the deportation was over before they left for home. In the Rosenfeld apartment, Josef was the first up. Normally he would have gone with Alicia to the Census Department but today they had three charges who couldn't be allowed to wander the streets alone. After Elijah had been invited into the room the night before it had been agreed that, while Josef made sure Chaim got to Isaac's safely, Alicia would take Mendel and Henryk direct to the office. Once there, Mendel could be put to work on some marginal business out of sight of any prying eyes, while Henryk might sit in the cellar. Josef went over to Chaim and shook him. Mendel was stirring on his blanket by the cold stove. There was a grumbling of engines outside. The first trucks were being driven into the ghetto.

Josef propelled Chaim into the quicksilver stream of workers. No one wanted to linger today. Or look up from the peculiarly interesting pattern of slabs along the street. Chaim's stomach churned. Would she be at their usual meeting place? Josef glanced at him quickly and guessed wrongly what he was thinking.

—Don't be afraid. I'm with you.

She was not there. Chaim fought against the current and fetched up beside an archway. Josef struggled desperately to his side.

—What are you doing? We can't linger.

—Rachel, I . . .—he was dumb with misery.

—She'll be at the factory by now. Tell her to come home
with you.

—But we always meet . . .

It was no good. They were swept along again, unable to
argue let alone talk. Still this gulf between them, ignorance
and mistrust. Josef was kindly but distracted, Chaim
possessed by conflicting desires. So they reached Isaac's and
parted.

She was still not there. After checking with the girls in the
sorting department (no, Rachel wasn't in yet) he had
returned to their meeting place alone. There was still time.
The stream of workers had dwindled to a ragged trickle.
Some were almost running. Then someone bumped into
him.

—Cease to linger, Oh pensive one. Even now the
chariots pursue us.

—Moses, have you seen Rachel?

—No. But be swift. He's come. He's come. He's here.
He's here.

Chaim watched the humped figure run off down a now
almost deserted street. He would have to go to her room.
He ran off under the archway and along an evil-smelling
passage that led, he knew, to her tenement. Turning a
corner he almost knocked the slight figure over. He had to
help her pick up her small bundle. It was tied with a purple
hair ribbon.

—I've left. The filthy bastard.—She grimaced.—He
knows his wife is too ill to notice.

—But where will you go?

She didn't reply. He knew she was thinking of Bernard and the underground. Despair. Then a thought, small but tenacious. If she had been absolutely determined to join his erstwhile companions she could have gone last night. She needn't have turned up for work at all. She needn't have seen him. He glanced at her face, floating its pale moon in the darkness of the passage. She had wanted to see him. She still needed his presence.

—I'll carry it for you.

Later, during the lunch break, he would suggest she come home with him.

—We must be quick.

Her adjuration was like an acceptance. He almost laughed. But stifled it.

—The trucks are in that direction.

The policeman had been leaning out of sight beside a pillar that had once contained an arched niche for a statue of the Virgin Mary. An old woman would place lobelias there every spring. Today the niche was plastered over with resettlement announcements.

—I see you've got your belongings packed. Nice ribbons too.

Chaim gripped the bundle more tightly to stop himself from shaking.

—We have permits. We work at Isaac's.

The policeman moved forward. He had a sick child.

—Aren't you Josef Rosenfeld's son?

—Yes. And this is his adopted daughter.

Still the policeman seemed undecided. He was about to

speak when a volley of screams burst from the passage they had just left. A man staggered into the street and vomited. He collapsed as a woman rushed out after him.

—He's swallowed it. Veronal. He's swallowed the whole bottle. And we have permits. Yes we do.

Chaim and Rachel exchanged glances and slipped away.

Shame. He who had longed for the last days, who had walked between Alicia and Henryk through the swarming silent streets, reciting under his breath the Kiddush ha-Shem, who had arrived at the Census Department with the light of tikkun streaming from his forehead; he was afraid. Sitting at Josef's desk, copying memoranda into this big black and red Minutes book (why had half of its pages been torn out?) he could not keep his hand from trembling. His neck felt sweaty. His stomach cramped. Where was the light now? He did not want to die. He wanted to be beside Alicia, a woman, profane, corrupt but living. Where was the light? Engines thrummed. *Elijah be with me.* He put down his pen. There had been a flash in the courtyard under the window. A tiny splinter of light.

He should be down in the cellar where he'd been once before and found that torn-up book under the old milkchurns in the corner. A good mulch that had made. Lots of pages. Some with pictures. There was one where all the people had heads of chickens. The churns were still there but nothing else was hidden under them, he'd looked. Josef had promised to bring him something to eat later. But until then there was nothing to do. He'd even forgotten the poultry manual. Then he'd noticed the trowel by the stopcock. Its handle was half rotted away. But the blade was fine. Lucky he had those left-over radish seeds. That yellow permit made a good seed packet. Just fold it once, pour them in and twist. There was a tub in the yard under Josef's window. No one had seen him yet. He could fetch the earth from that patch across the road where the warehouse had burned down. He knew he wasn't supposed to but radishes germinate in fourteen days. They'd be up to mark the end of the resettlement. Josef would appreciate that.

The trowel had driven its splinter of light deep into Mendel's heart. Now he was out of the window and clambering along the urinal roof.

He'd left the radish seeds in their twisted yellow packet on the rim of the tub. Now he wanted to go and fetch the earth. But that mad Mendel was saying 'No stay here I'll fetch it for you look I've got a bucket' wherever did he find that in the urinal maybe but he wasn't going to be put off and grabbed the bucket only Mendel pulled it away again so he grabbed it again and this time Mendel didn't struggle he just let him have it with a sort of milky shrug and a sigh.

By the direction of the sound they had started in the south sector. He must go upstairs and check Mendel. Alicia was already on her way to the cellar with some bread and water. Then Solomon came in.

—It's worse than we expected.

—What? They want more than the quota?

—No. They can't find enough to fill the trucks. Herr Schaefer blames our police. He's drafted in more of his own men. They're picking up anybody and everybody.

—I've heard there are some good dugouts in the west of the ghetto. Don't say I said so.

Solomon nodded then mopped his bald head with a monogrammed silk handkerchief. Josef applied himself with hallucinatory exactitude to the question of what this fragment of fabric would fetch on the black market. He was hesitating between five kilos of matzoh and forty cigarettes when the corner of a black coat slid unnoticed past the window.

Alicia found the cellar door open. She ran back to Solomon's office. Josef had gone upstairs. Solomon was looking out of the window.

—What are those two silly bastards doing? Wait a minute. It's them.

He turned to find Alicia in the room.

—It's them Mrs Rosenfeld.

He banged on the glass.

—Come inside. Quickly.

Upstairs the Minutes book lay open on the floor. Lucky he'd remembered to tear out the diary entries and hide them in the secret archive. Not that there was any time for writing now. The page Mendel had been using rustled in the breeze from the window. Wide open. He ran across and leant out. He shouted at the two struggling figures. Too late.

What was that banging and who were all these people? They were telling him to put the bucket down. And where was Mendel? And

why was Josef shouting? They were ignoring Josef. They were
pulling him into the street. Away.

In the temple with the corrugated roof he was frightened
again they were so close and they made such a noise until he
saw the fly it was the fly he'd seen on Josef's windowsill all
those centuries ago only now it was golden an angel of light
dancing on the altar of the One.

—That's one more. Lucky he didn't have a permit.
—There were two. This one's friend. Abandoned you
has he?
—He was too quick. We've no time.
—Schaefer's berserk.
—And drunk.
—Did you see the black coat? A zaddik.
—They can make themselves invisible I've heard.
—And fly.

Josef stopped shouting the moment he realised Mendel had
got away. Henryk was being dragged towards the street. It
took three of them. He found Mendel in the urinal,
crouching over the trough, laughing, pointing to a bluebottle spinning in the stinking yellow fosse.

When Josef came to lure him away from the temple that had
been rebuilt by Henryk from the shards of light he had
begun to dance. Why was Josef shouting? Henryk was the
messiah's precursor. He knew now. But Josef didn't know.
He just shouted. Then Alicia was there. And she was

shouting too. Only more softly. About the window. And why if you were out there didn't you try to save him. Which was ridiculous. Because Henryk had helped to save them. With the shard of light he held in his hand. For he had raised the shard of light against the demons who are made from fire and air and fly or become invisible at will. He would conquer them with it.

They weren't very strong but there were lots of them. They wanted meat. And the hencoop was on wheels. It moved too, in a wobbling roaring sort of way. And it was full of hens. A little girl in a pigtail sat next to him, her skin soft as feathers. She saw the trowel and asked for it so he gave it her to play with wondering whether anyone else would plant the radish seeds and why Mendel had suddenly disappeared saying The Lord is my Shepherd.

10

When he saw his stepfather run past the factory yard he stood up, spilling some of his soup over Rachel. The very fact that Josef was running implied an extraordinary state of affairs. No one in the ghetto ever expended more energy than they had to. Chaim was immediately possessed by the need for an explanation.

—I'll be back for the afternoon shift. Don't leave this evening without me.

—The Brendel girl's gone. Moses saw her.

Rachel was still cool. And ambivalent. The bundle she carried beside her might not necessarily be destined for the Rosenfeld apartment.

—I did. Bearding the lion in his den. Not the lion of Judah I hasten to add. Don't you do it Chaim.

Behind Moses' artificial floridity there flowered a genuine feeling. Chaim nodded.

—Be careful.

Glancing back he saw Moses lean over to lay claim to his unfinished food. Rachel had turned her face away. Still cool. Yet the encounter with the policeman by the derelict shrine had undoubtedly shaken her.

He knew and did not want to know the direction Josef had

taken. The street led to the siding just outside the ghetto, locally known as the Spur. All the trucks would be converging there, with the morning's haul. By the time he caught up, his stepfather had covered more than half the distance. He was shaking and pale but seemed to accept his stepson's presence without complaint. Chaim felt a momentary pride. He was no longer such a child.

—We take the shortcut. The overhead walkway. Avoid guards. At the gate.—Josef was breathing in short shallow gasps. He told Chaim what had happened

—Why did mother ever trust that zaddik?—Chaim felt a sharp pity for his gentle rambling half uncle. Rather Mendel than him. But Josef wasn't in agreement.

—Doing his best. Henryk the fool. At grave risk. And strong too. Mendel tried. Might both have been taken.

So Josef had already begun to reinterpret the painful scene in the Census Department yard. Meanwhile they were running on, with longer, more urgent strides. Chaim's stomach knotted and cramped. When they reached the walkway he was obliged to squat beside a low wall and relieve himself. His excrement steamed its green pool. Josef was already clattering up the rickety wooden steps.

—But what if they try to take us?—Chaim shouted, hitching up his dungarees and running onto the bridge. There was no one about. It seemed safe to shout. Josef did not answer. Could it be that this man, so willing to work inside a corrupt regime, had more innate bravery than the most reckless freedom fighter? The walkway was deserted too. Nobody wanted to be seen anywhere near the Spur, that malebolge of deportation. Their feet thudded dully on the slatted floor. They walked now to get their breath, hands on sides. Through the barbed wire flanks of the walkway you could see across the city to a low ridge of pineclad hills. The Front was beyond. Russia.

—The first transport won't have left yet.

—How do you know?

—Because I'm on the council.—Josef's panting voice hovered between pride and guilt.—The first train leaves this afternoon. The second tomorrow at dawn. And so on for the next two weeks. We'll have a completely crime-free community. Paradise on earth.

Chaim put his hand on his stepfather's arm.

—But why did they take Henryk?

The wind was snuffling round the wooden slats, keening through the ranked strands of barbed wire. A low note and a high. In unison. Yet off-key. People would force the wire apart sometimes. Jump.

—I told you. He had one of his damned ideas. Mendel almost killed himself trying to save him. We should have locked the cellar.

Josef could not give the answer Chaim had wanted. Chaim was not certain he could have given it himself. They reached the steps on the far side of the bridge and clattered down.

There were twelve carriages in all. The ones behind the engine and at the rear would accommodate the guards. They were first class passenger coaches, green, gleaming, upholstered. In between lay ten goods wagons. These had no windows, only ventilation grilles set high up in the wooden sides and crisscrossed with barbed wire. The sliding wooden doors in the sides of the wagons were all open. From each door curled a dull segmented snake of people, its body tapering listlessly away through the siding yard. All around was movement, noise. Ghetto police and a few SS guards stalked up and down, flicking at the odd back with a whip or pushing a straggler into line. The engine steamed and vibrated, its fire flaring now and then, a starved orange maw. On the pediment of the freight office, the swastika flag snapped and flickered at its slant pole. But the ten listless serpents, unmoving and silent, dominated the scene. It was as though a series of flat images had been transferred onto a living backdrop. Time itself seemed absent. Or else this was time: a distillation of seconds and years into one poisonous all-enveloping globule. Nothing it seemed could release that scene from its own stasis. Except a word.

For Chaim the word was *Henryk*, bellowed out by the man at his side. For the columns of people who began their slow trudge into the black maws of the wagons it was the Hauptsturmführer's softer *Schnell*. The two noises had simply coincided. Now Chaim saw that what had looked like an amorphous mass of humanity was in fact many cells of uniqueness: old and young, the sick on stretchers, families, solitaries. This was no workforce. No labour camp in the East awaited these ghost segments. Resettlement means death. And here the dying had begun.

—He has a yellow permit. And a proof of identity. He is a family member. An administrator's family member.

The guard was threatening but respectful. The time had not yet come when terror would make him treat ghetto officials as abominably as he treated the old and the ill today. His family was safe at work. The bowed columns consisted of strangers, enemies. He disappeared to fetch the Commandant.

—You must take this matter up with the Judenrat. I cannot help.

—But Herr Schaefer promised.—Josef's voice was suddenly small and petulant. Like a child's, Chaim thought.

—Amtsleiter Schaefer does not promise. Not to Jews. I have work to do.

The Commandant turned away, leaving a resinous wake of aftershave on the air. Then they saw Henryk. He was just about to climb up the ramp into the front wagon. He was holding the hand of a small girl in pigtails.

Josef was about to leap forward. The Commandant had turned again, eyeing him suspiciously. Some of the people at the back of Henryk's column, recognising a genuine ghetto administrator, had begun pleading with him. At least three pairs of hands scrabbled at his jacket. A woman moaned. *My son is back at the leather works. He does not know.* An old man wept. *I've lost all my money. I changed it into deutschmarks and now they've taken it off me. Thieves.* Josef struggled to move forward along the column. The Commandment stirred.

Chaim saw he would have to do something. He hesitated. Any wrong move now and they would both be inside the wagon with Henryk. Over the heads of victims and oppressors he shouted.

—Mother. Remember mother.

It was the first time he had spoken to Josef as if he were

his father. The first time he had publicly acknowledged their love for each other. Sensing rather than hearing the words Josef seemed to lose some of his desperate momentum. At the same moment, magnetised by the darkness beyond the train's sliding doors, the winding columns shuffled forward again. The scrabbling hands melted from Josef's body. The voices receded. The Commandant swivelled on his heel shouting *Raus* to a pair of loitering ghetto police. Like a patient coming round from anaesthetic Josef smiled weakly at Chaim. Henryk had disappeared.

On the way out of the yard they passed a loose pyramid of abandoned bedding, suitcases, pots and pans tied together with string. Here lay everything the first consignment of deportees had attempted to take with them out of the ghetto. Some kapos were loading up a cart. All would be taken back for processing inside the perimeter fence, more raw material for the rank ghetto factories. There was a glitter amongst this wrack and spillage, still warm from human contact. Chaim glanced at it and passed on unseeing: the blade of a trowel.

They sat together in the office, waiting for Josef to return. The afternoon light had yellowed, thinning the scratched walls to parchment. In the distance a shot echoed. The day's second selection was beginning. These unfortunates would have to wait all night at the Spur. Footsteps of someone running past in the street clicked faintly. Ceased. There was a shout. Then silence again. Alicia looked at Mendel through swollen eyes.

—Why?—It had become her last and only word.

Mendel made a dismissive gesture and stood up. He disliked this interrogation by a woman. Yet perhaps, he wondered with a sudden delight, even this was necessary. Her profanity and worldliness, her willingness to lie with Josef even in the midst of the last days, were these also not rungs on the ladder? Only thus could he ascend to the place where she stood in heavenly splendour. And now Henryk had been chosen. The temple was about to be rebuilt. He drew himself up to his full height, a movement which always seemed to emphasise his terminal emaciation. He hovered over her, a black winged thing.

—When the devouring flames seize upon the cedar shall not the lowly hyssop fear and tremble? When anglers draw the great Leviathan from his mighty deeps what hope has the fish of the shallow pond? Mourn for those who are left. He has entered into the eternal rest while we are bowed with sorrow.

Another shot rang out. The weak sunlight lay still on the wall.

—But they're to be resettled. Josef says he's seen the maps.

He gazed at her in a sudden access of love. Even her innocence must be a part of the divine purpose. And even now he was not altogether detached from the things of this world.

She began to busy herself tidying up the office. She picked up the black and red Minutes book. Some of the pages had been ripped out, one imperfectly. It was a journal of some sorts. She glanced guiltily at the words, his words. *My angel from the West*. She felt terribly tired. It was partly true. She was from the West. But Mendel was from somewhere else.

★

It had begun to rain, a fine tepid spring shower, as they headed back for the Judenrat. Josef felt profoundly weary. As if he had been running for hours. He could not bear to think of Henryk walking slowly up the ramp into the windowless wagon; still less of Alicia's face when he finally returned to the office. And he regretted having allowed Chaim to tag along. It couldn't be healthy for the boy, not only to witness such things in themselves but also (and here he felt a twinge of irritation) to confront the real powerlessness of ghetto officialdom. He was glad when the Judenrat building came in sight. Here at least he might be able to salvage some dignity.

A van came lurching round the corner, splashing through potholes filled with muddy water.

—They're late for the transport.

Chaim glanced incredulously at his stepfather. Did he mean to make it sound like a holiday outing? Then all at once he felt a sharp blow in the small of his back. It was not strong enough to fell him but it took his breath away. There was dust of brick and mortar in the air and on his jacket sleeve. A ricocheting noise too, of bullets. Almost simultaneously the truck swerved, crashed headlong into a handcart piled high with young beetroot, the first of this year's summer crop, then careered on into the side of a roofless stable. The bonnet was crumpled, the windscreen smeared with blood of beetroot. Inside the driver slumped over the wheel. The human cargo in the back were shouting and banging to be let out. Josef put his arm round Chaim's shoulder. He was drawing him back.

—Quick. Before they fire again.

But Chaim would not be bundled away so quickly. He was peering past the van, its spinning front wheel and its wailing cursing occupants, to a nearby third storey window.

—I saw him,—he whispered.

The ghetto police had arrived. They were dragging out the deportees, some of whom had sustained cuts and bruises. The driver they left for dead. It was the living dead that concerned them. These they chivvied into a shivering bunch in the middle of the road. Now one policeman was touching the windscreen's splintered impact point. Another glanced along the street. Josef felt rising panic. If they were seen the least they could expect would be interrogation as witnesses. Desperately he half-dragged half-pushed his suddenly catatonic stepson into the shadow of an archway.

It had been Bernard. He was convinced. The same balaclava. The slightly drooping left eye. Rachel had not lied. They were acquiring weapons, real ones, semi-automatics. His turmoil intensified. Here he was, having failed to prevent a close relative being spirited away from the ghetto in a cattle wagon while this Bernard, whom he had once accused of playing at life, had managed to prevent, however temporarily, a whole truckful of people from reaching the Spur. He had even put paid to one of the hateful kapos. The face at the window had gone now. A detachment was moving slowly along the street, banging on doors with truncheons, shouting.

—There'll be retribution for this.—His stepfather's face was pale in the dank light.—More deaths.

—Of the body yes. Not the spirit.

—You sound like your despised Mendel.

How pale Josef's face had become, a green deep sea fish, oozing phosphorus.

—Mendel wants martyrdom.

—And doesn't he, whoever he is, up in that stable loft with a gun?

A fish out of deep caverns, to whom light was alien.

A new truck had driven up. The people were being loaded on. They were in double shock. Resettlement. A crash. They went meekly. As the new driver revved up there was a faint whistle from the direction of the Spur.

—They'll have to wait with the next selection now. A whole night down at the yard. Your freedom fighter did that.

—And we let Henryk be taken.

Josef did not answer. But he seemed to have forgotten about the Judenrat. They made a detour, avoiding the scene of the crime, or heroic act. The rain lessened.

Mendel was moaning, flat out on the floor of the office. Josef stood astride him, panting.

—Stop,—Alicia begged in a small voice,—stop now.

Josef lurched sideways, kicking the red and black Minutes book (*my angel*) under the desk. His knuckles ached. But he could have started all over again, pummeling his friend.

—Are we sunk to their level after all?

—The Chairman guaranteed exemption for all council members and their families.—Josef turned back to the

prone black form.—He never counted on cracked zaddiks.—
He staggered to the door.—Perhaps they should have taken
you too.—Then he was gone. Slowly Alicia unwound
herself and tiptoed over to the moaning form by the desk.

—I'm sorry.

Mendel's cheek glowed with the outline of four furious
knuckles. But he was smiling. Alicia did not know whether
to give thanks or despair.

Dusk deepened. She was alone in the Rosenfeld apartment. Mendel had refused her offer of a floor for the next
two weeks. After Josef's unforgiveable attack he had
seemed more than usually calm. Josef was supposed to be
returning with Chaim. But he had disappeared in such a
rage that she doubted he would remember. Another five
minutes and she must go to Isaac's herself. No more
passivity, even though she still felt deeply involved with
Mendel's ancient vision. If she had acted a little more
decisively she might have been able to save Henryk. The
minutes ticked by. She would have to go. Then the
knocking began. At first she thought with a wild spasm
that they had come for her. Josef and Chaim had already
been picked up. The whole family would be taken. Then
she told herself it was too late: the afternoon selection was
already over, the trucks parked back down at the siding,
the dawn deportees huddled in the freight shed. In any case
the knocking was too gentle, if insistent. But she kept the
chain on as Josef had advised. In the dim well of the
landing Rachel looked paler than ever. She was carrying a
bundle tied up with purple ribbons.

—May I?—Her humility was a surprise to Alicia. And a suspicion.

—Chaim?—She hardly dared listen.

—With Josef. I said I wanted to go on ahead.

Alicia's relief allowed her to ask Rachel inside. She sensed but dreaded what was coming. So soon after Henryk's disappearance. This girl who had enthralled her son. Rachel did not want to sit down. She leaned over and touched Alicia's bible, a battered rabbinical edition from the last century. It lacked some of the Psalms.

—Not your kind of reading matter I suppose.—Alicia hoped she sounded suitably distant. Rachel's eyes were pools under the visor of her hood. It was raining again.

—My grandfather worked in the hasidic library near the reformed synagogue. You should have seen some of the books they had there. Great leather-bound tablets of manuscripts. Like slabs. With gold and silver buckles. And scrolls. Huge yellow cylinders wound round wooden spindles with carved medallions at either end. Beautifully illustrated some of the bibles were. There was one picture he showed me – I must have been very young – where all the human beings had chicken heads. They were at a banquet. The Coming Age he called it. You weren't allowed to show the human form in those days. Blasphemous I suppose.

Alicia listened half-doubting what she heard. Was this quiet seemingly pious girl the firebrand who had wanted to lure her son into the underground?

—They will have told you about Henryk.

—Yes. Chaim went with Mr Rosenfeld.

Alicia started. This girl could still be a dark messenger.

—To the Spur?

They had all been mad that day. It was time for reason, order, peace. Rachel was touching the bible again. She spoke in a sudden flurry of syllables, her cheeks burning.

—Chaim thinks I ought to stay here while the resettlement is on. So does his father. I mean stepfather. Mrs Rosenfeld?

Alicia was looking at the mezuzah by the door. She thought she had heard a movement.

—What happened to the library?

Rachel sighed. In this grey light she seemed older than Mendel, more rooted.

—They took out the volumes in great armfuls and burnt them in the square. Then they set light to the building. The fire lasted a day and a night. Mrs Rosenfeld?

Alicia knew what she had to say. Henryk's absence had left a space. Josef could sleep with Chaim. She felt a sudden rush of maternal solicitude and embraced the pale ill-clad figure. There was an indefinable aroma about her. Sweetish. Stale. She did not resist the embrace; nor did she fully accept it. Something in her still fought.

—It was a shame. All those books.

—But they can't burn words. The words are like light. Indestructible.

—I know someone who says the whole of the creation is a word. A single unpronounceable word. When the messiah comes we will be able to pronounce it.

—May I interrupt this theological debate?

Chaim had been waiting outside. He had wanted to see if

his mother would accept Rachel in solitude, uninfluenced by his presence.

—Josef has gone to Mendel.

He kissed his mother on the forehead and laid a hand gently on Rachel's shoulder. She had trusted in him at last.

How he managed to get back to his attic room he never knew. Nor for how long he lay on the straw mattress, shallowly dreaming. Henryk with a cockerel's head digging digging. Alicia naked and bound to a sort of hoop. Josef with the body of a goat sidling up to Alicia. It was all terrible and dark and mixed in with the shadows of ghetto policemen and truncheons and trucks. Yet it had to be thus. When the knocking started he was convinced they had come back. The ones who had taken Henryk. Yet he wore his tallit to open the door and felt no fear. This day had taught him much wisdom.

—Blessed be he that comes.

—Blessed be the present. You shouldn't wear that. Until you know who it is.

—It matters not.

Josef grunted and pushed past almost collapsing onto the straw mattress. He groaned as if he were the injured man. Mendel approached him wondering.

—You are in pain?

—Josef touched his breast.

—Only here. I've brought you these. He fumbled in his coat and drew out matzoh and a phial. He tapped the glass.

—Arnica. My mother used to swear by it for bruising. I've had some tucked away for years at the office.

He put the bread and the bottle down on the mattress. His need for forgiveness was greater than Mendel could guess.

Chaim slept fitfully beside his stepfather. Sometimes he dreamed of Rachel in the next room. So near so far. Once Henryk appeared at the window piloting a Great War biplane. There was a legend written on its fuselage in black gothic capitals: Greetings from the ghetto of Venice.

First it is light then it is dark. He didn't mind the thirst but he'd appreciate a bit more space. Cooped up like chickens. The little girl had fallen asleep on his lap. Her name was Tanya. Pity about the trowel. Still, they'd be getting tools soon. If only the straw wasn't so damp.

11

Summer returned to the ghetto, its warmth making people shiver in anticipation of the colds to come; its aridity clogging throats with a memory of rain. In his absence Henryk's plot flourished. Taken over by an elderly relative of Solomon's, its greens and yellows flickered their lit fuses in the Park allotments. Runner beans were just beginning to send their first clockwise-winding tendrils towards a sturdy rack of wooden batons; lettuces clenched and thickened, their wrinkled hearts pearled with dew; already yellowing and dying back for lack of moisture, potato haulms sprawled raggedly across trenches. The ground was poor, so that some of the plots could boast little more than a few sparse rows of turnip or beet. But because of some knack or mystery of husbandry, Henryk's old plot flourished. In fact his successor had little to do, other than tend, water and harvest. When Solomon's relative called at the apartment to present Alicia with a basket of produce (this was strictly illegal but he was grateful for the job security) he often spoke as though Henryk still possessed the plot, having just undertaken a journey on some important business. At first Alicia found this fiction upsetting but as the events of that year's Passover silted to the back of her mind, she too began to pretend, saying *Is he putting any endive in this year?* or *How is Henryk coping with the carrot fly?* for all the world as though they lived on some secluded country estate.

Josef would pass the allotments on his way back from the office. The curfew had been relaxed in May, not for the benefit of the inhabitants but so that the administration could organise longer shifts for the much depleted work-force. Josef himself often worked late these days, spending long periods alone, away from Alicia and the family. The solitude was healing. During the resettlement too much had happened too quickly for them to be at peace with one another for long. There would have to be a period of readjustment. And always behind everything was the fact that he was an official as well as an ordinary inhabitant. The rift that divided him and his adopted family would not easily be bridged however much they loved one another. So on these dry warm evenings when, hearing the voices of children playing in a sunshadowed yard, you might almost forgive yourself for believing in a world without war, Josef strolled past the Park allotments. Beyond the wire netting that protected the plots from pilfering, a green fresh life glowed and multiplied. Henryk's absence had almost become a comfort. It freed Josef to concentrate on those who still survived.

Rachel passed but did not see the allotments. At the beginning of June she had been moved from Isaac's main factory to a subsidiary sorting department set up in the abandoned Catholic church where Mendel and Alicia had heard the story of Jonah and the concert had been held. St

Mary and All Saints was now a warehouse for the bedding and pillows that had been salvaged from apartments abandoned in the last resettlement. The white mounds rose almost to the clerestory and quite obliterated pulpit and altar. Rachel was allergic to feathers. All day she worked with continuously itching, streaming eyes and nostrils, sorting and repacking and always – when an official came in sight – wiping the clear mucous discharge from cheeks and lips. To be weak was to be out of work, a fate not worth contemplating. By the end of the day she would return home with red-rimmed eyes that had wept a thousand emotionless tears and a dress sodden from sleeve to armpit with the efflux of a condition that merged helplessness and fear.

Home now was the Rosenfeld apartment. Her temporary private permit had been indefinitely and silently extended. This was Alicia's doing. She who had felt resentment and mistrust at first, slowly came to love this frail sneezing creature who needed a constant supply of handkerchiefs dipped in essence of lavender or balsam. There had been many changes. Weakened by illness, hunger and fatigue, Rachel no longer thought much about the underground. The encounter with the policeman on the first day of the resettlement had assumed a nightmarish talismanic significance for her. It was as if the threat of deportation had become confused in her mind with the withdrawal of love, so that she would wake in the night and cling crying to Alicia. *Don't let them take me* she said and sometimes *Don't let him take them*, mixing the traumatic end of her own family with more recent troubles. Chaim too was distant with her

173

now, not only because of his ambivalent attraction to Bernard and the ZOB, an attraction which, when Rachel had been well, he had done his utmost to suppress; but also because he distrusted the new-found closeness between his girl and his mother. It was like a maternal jealousy in reverse.

Sensing this filial distrust, confused herself about the role Mendel had played in Henryk's disappearance, increasingly cut off from Josef, Alicia naturally turned to the figure in the household who needed her most. One incident encapsulated that new love. She had been out. Solomon's relative came to the door and Rachel answered, diffidently, for even in this quiet interim she feared things. In his hand lay a giant beetroot dripping juice. *The biggest this year. Before the war Henryk would have won a prize.* But for Rachel he was the policeman again saying *I see you've come prepared.* When Alicia returned from the ration queue she found the old man trying to fan Rachel back to consciousness on the sofa. She knew then that the girl's fate was bound up with that of her family.

Mendel still worked for Josef, still prayed in his attic, still fasted. He had not forgotten the beating. He had not forgotten Henryk. But after the elation and the light of that spring morning darkness had flooded back again. The broken shards were everywhere, more tefillin and tallits returning to the ghetto, more random shootings on the street. The temple had not begun to be rebuilt. Who indeed was there to rebuild it? Not Alicia who, though she still held within herself the potential of all the ages, turned more and more nowadays in a sort of quiescent rapture of suffering to Rachel, the former girl revolutionary; not Josef who since the office beating, had never been able to look Mendel fully in the eye, as though he feared to see his own shards of darkness reflected there; not Chaim who was young and untried and watchful; not – and this, if he was honest with himself, fell with the hardest blow – not Mendel either. For nowadays he no longer knew what God wanted him to do. Shavuot was long past and the divine force still remained withdrawn as before. Even trance brought him no nearer to an unveiling. Only once when he passed the Park allotments and heard Henryk speak out of a hairy green-veined marrow leaf did he feel a slight shift towards the light. But Henryk's words *Their words are our ash* yielded only further darkness.

So the summer wore on and the ghetto waited.

Light slanted down in thick pillars onto the long tables, the hunched forms of workers, the grey and greywhite bundles being untied at one end of the gallery. Chaim was sitting next to Moses. The clothing was being passed along in great folded masses, like undersea growths of padded weed or coral. Sweat hung in the air. The sweat of those who had worn what was now being sorted.

—Do they go naked in that place? Are they as Adam Kadmon, the first man?—Moses blinked. He was growing more and more shortsighted.

—What do we have to do?—This was the department of Isaac's where Rachel used to work. Chaim preferred the looms. But there had been many changes since the spring. Fewer workshops were in operation.

—Do, do? Why, remove the badge of our race. The magic star. The Magen David. You have a receptacle.

There was a bucket beside Chaim's chair. Moses had already stacked a pile of men's overcoats in front of him. He was tearing off the dingy yellow six-pointed pieces of cloth with practised swiftness. He had been at this job a fortnight longer. Chaim stared at his pile.

—Are they given new clothes then?—He had meant to sound ironic. Yet his voice betrayed a simpler need to believe. Like Rachel he was tired.

—Uniforms my boy, most probably uniforms. I say, what's in here?

Moses was feeling along the lining of a jacket.

—Quickly,—he hissed, abandoning his habitual orotundity,—Isaac's coming past. There's something in here. We need a sharp edge.

—The edge of the table?

—That'll do. It's sewn into the lining. Might be a watch, jewellery.

Moses was rubbing the shiny lining of the old tweed hunting jacket rhythmically and fast along the ragged edge of the work bench. Chaim felt suddenly afraid. There was a short ripping sound and something metallic chinked onto the floor. Moses put a foot over it as Isaac walked past. The two boys continued tearing off yellow stars.

—What is it then?—Chaim asked when the coast was clear.

Moses bent down and retrieved the object. He glanced down at his hand and whistled.

—Show it me.

—A silver cigarette case. Look. I say. Who found it?

Chaim had snatched the case from Moses and was holding it up to the light. There was the dent his father had often shown him. *The bullet passed clean through my bible but stopped at this lid. Otherwise I was a goner. At Verdun it happened. In 'sixteen. I would have been nineteen.* He sat beside his father on the chaise longue, fingering the case, its engraved picture of Prussian hussars charging at the Battle of Waterloo.

—Let me see the coat it came from. Quick.

Deftly his fingers ran up the lapels and along the shoulder pads. He felt its weight and lifted its shiny interior to his nostrils. It was Henryk's. He must have found the cigarette case after he had come to live with them back home in Vienna. And sewn it into the lining.

—By the waters of Babylon I sat down and wept. This is not Babylon. Or is it?

Chaim swept his face with the hand that held his father's memento. He felt the cold of the metal against his cheek.

—If he let this go he can't be in a labour camp.

—But my dear friend what use have they for cigarette cases? Perhaps he hoped it might get back to you. Or perhaps he just forgot.

—Father always said it would go to me eventually. After my bar mitzvah. Henryk was keeping it for me. I know he was.

Moses was looking bewildered and even more short-sighted than usual.

—Well and now you have it. Look we've got to finish this pile by twelve. Old Isaac said.

—Damn Isaac. Bernard was right. And Rachel. Oh father how I miss you.

So Chaim worked on through his tears which were for many things and many people. The cigarette case lay wrapped in a handkerchief in his own jacket pocket.

As Chaim wept over his discovery Siegfried Schaefer was walking into Solomon's office, demanding to see Josef. Upstairs the Census Officer had imprudently taken one of the files out of the secret archive and was working on it at his desk. He just had time to thrust it under another folder before the clerk ushered the Amtsleiter into the room. Schaefer walked straight to the window from which Alicia had watched Henryk being dragged away. He brushed the hidden file. Josef went cold.

—You people are taking up too much room, do you know that? There are too many empty buildings. The Chairman says this office keeps the detailed maps, the street plans. Is that so?

Josef nodded, struck dumb by the proximity of his enemy to the secret archive. Yet if he could have spoken he would have asked: Why? Why do you always come personally to me rather than have the Chairman send over an underling? It is as if you want to see me yourself. Or perhaps he would not have asked.

—Too many places of refuge.

Josef struggled back to confront the figure before him. The Amtsleiter's remark was a lumbering coded signal.

He knew more about the underground than he let on.

—Very few shirk nowadays Herr Schaefer.

He pushed the file surreptitiously deep under its camouflage and glanced at the Amtsleiter. He was flustered beneath his haughty exterior. During the spring resettlements he had behaved like a savage. Now there was something soft about him, a fungus that Josef did not care to contemplate for long, battening on suppressed violence. It roused pity in him and another vulnerable feeling he could not quite define. For some reason he was reminded of Reuben, the bully at the academy. After two years of torment he had eventually sidled up to Josef one wet afternoon in the dormitory and begged to sleep with him. He had his thumb in his mouth and dribbled. He intimated that he would gladly swop the thumb for something else. A big soft infant with sub-adult desires. He looked again at Schaefer.

—What are you looking at? Where are the maps?

—I'll get my wife. I mean my secretary.

—Ah, so you took my advice.

This might have been said in a spirit of friendly male camaraderie but the Amtsleiter's voice was shrill with tension. He was looking past the Census officer and sweating. Josef remembered how Reuben had looked when he was still scared of him, just before a particularly savage beating.

—Your shoelace is undone.

Swiftly Josef ducked to the ground, his heart beating. He was a thirteen year old again, desperate to please. But the space under the desk was too cramped. He swung up and round and put his shoe on the side of the desk. Schaefer darted forward. His hand was on the shoe. He was stroking it through his glove, long rhythmical strokes. His eyes met Josef's. He smiled.

The cigarette case lay in the middle of the table, glinting in the light of the solitary candle. They all stared. Mendel's disquisition on the meaning of Sinai, requested by Alicia despite or because of all her recent disillusionments and listened to in respectful but restless silence by Josef, had ceased. Chaim could hear Rachel moving and sneezing in the kitchen beyond the partition. Josef reached across and held the case to the light as Chaim had done.

—Where did you say you found this?

Chaim explained again.

—It's true, isn't it mother? About the war and how I was to have it. Henryk was keeping it for me.

Alicia's eyes were wet. She was no longer the confident princess of the seder meal. She could not bear this reminder of the past. And of Henryk too. His last day in the ghetto. Mendel had moved over to the window. He dreaded the repetition of the old anger. Chaim had been prepared for all this, hardening himself to his mother's sadness and to Mendel's disquiet. But he had not expected Josef to be so indifferent. His stepfather simply pushed the momentous object back across the table and returned to his original remark.

—Shall I tell you what happened at the office today?

For Alicia and Mendel this was a welcome diversion. Chaim's hands closed convulsively over the silver case.

Ever since the abortive attempt to rescue Henryk he had been looking for some common ground between himself and his stepfather. He had wanted to draw closer to this man at once so upright yet so compromised. The relic had seemed to offer a pretext. Handing over this fragment from his previous existence Chaim felt he was passing on a responsibility. The new father should inherit what the old had so mysteriously discarded. In that slab of cold silver the truth of the ghetto lay waiting to be revealed. And shared. Chaim and his stepfather could share it. But Josef had shirked the responsibility. All he could do was talk about the Department.

—He was there again. Our eerie master. He wants maps. Here he looked at Alicia, who nodded.

—They're planning to reorganise the ghetto again. To make it more compact. That means another resettlement. I shall have to work harder than ever this time. If disaster is to be avoided.

So Chaim understood. Once more his stepfather had chosen the way of pragmatism and half truth. No amount of work, however convoluted, would put off the day when all their clothes and possessions would find their way back into the ghetto, there to be sorted and altered, sent out again and distributed. And meanwhile where would they be? He stroked the bullet dent on the case. Henryk had sent word after all. He must learn to interpret the message.

Rachel found him by the Park allotments. They gazed through the wire at the ranks of green growth. Her eyes were red and irritated. She embraced him. No physical passion could ignite between two such fatigued and wasted bodies. But there might be animal warmth. So they clung to one another, not understanding how each had changed, not wanting to understand.

—Do you think I should go to Bernard?

Her face was in his hands. He compressed it slightly. The skin puckered slackly. There was a caked milky film on her lips.

—Your father fought on the western front. That was his cigarette case.

He nodded.

—Then go. But take his case with you.

So Henryk talked to them too, in the evening light from the flickering green of the leaves.

Why were they stopping now? First there is dark then there is light. The dark slides back and the light slides forward. Better for you if you didn't wake up my little chookchook my feathered fledgling. Better for me if you never opened your all seeing eyes again.

12

Az. The weather dryer than ever. She longed for light summer clothes, silks, cottons, diaphanous stuffs. All she had were the remnants of last year's autumnal and winter wardrobe, packed in tremulous haste, a thousand miles away, before exile. So she made do, stripping the lining from one of her two remaining wool jackets (the fur had long since been bartered); cutting up an old wrap of Grandma's to make blouses. Then at least she could walk out into the dusty streets, those ravines that had once funnelled a cutting wind but now lay trapped in stillness – and feel a memory of summer on her skin. She had aged. Not as in normal times, slowly, imperceptibly, but in great bounds, many strata of wrinkles gathering at an eyelid overnight, an achilles tendon suddenly splaying blue deltas of broken veins. These symptoms bound her more closely to the ghetto that had caused them; and prepared her for release. So she walked the streets, searching for lost summer.

Rachel was often at her side. Sensing but not admitting that the next resettlement might be the last, Josef was increasingly preoccupied with the survival of the secret archive. Chaim remained as distant as ever, Mendel as distracted. But Rachel had become a charge. Someone to be accompanied to and from work; to be nagged about eating; inspected for head- and body-lice; to be chest-rubbed at night with tincture of balsam obtained at great expense by Josef from the ghetto hospital. For Rachel seemed to be growing weaker by the day; she had already been reported by her works manager for malingering; her lungs were bad now as well as her throat. Still she carried on, asserting an independence from her adoptive mother with a strength that astonished Alicia. So that when the older woman told her something of the old life in the West, Rachel countered with her own unassailable memories of Vilna. She could not be absorbed into her chosen family; but then perhaps Alicia and her son had never themselves become a part of Josef's world.

At first Alicia thought that the commotion outside St Mary's had something to do with the overturned cart of potatoes. A crowd had formed, many grovelling on all fours and using every available pocket and fold to salt away one or two of the precious tubers. There were police too, beating the thieves who seemed oblivious of their raining blows. But this whole scene was merely marginal, a tremor caused by an epicentre some yards away. Here, outside a cafe, a blue BMW had drawn up. The boot was open and several young SS officers were removing and poring over a variety of unfamiliar objects: metallic poles, black boxes, coils of flex. Meanwhile other officers were accosting passers by, ushering them with threats towards the cafe door. It was the resistance of one of these unwilling participants in whatever rite of black magic the officers were about to initiate which had upset the potato cart. He had run towards it in panic and now lay slumped across one of its wheels, a bullet through his neck. Alicia's instinct told her to run too. There was an alley beside the church. She pushed Rachel towards it. But too late. A young officer with acne had caught sight of them. His gesture was unmistakeable. They too must enter the cafe. Alicia moved, Rachel beside her, in a numb dream. The resettlement had begun, the one Josef was always talking about, the final clearance. She tried reciting the Kiddush ha-Shem as Mendel had taught her but the words would not come. Then she thought: but why the cafe? Were they intending to burn it down? She had heard of such things. Then why the complication of equipment, which even now was disappearing into the cafe interior? She squeezed her adopted daughter's arm, as much for her own reassurance as for Rachel's.

For the ghetto the cafe was a large one. A vault of low tables, a long wooden counter, the greasy-walled kitchen. There were barrels ranked along the foot of one wall, empty nowadays. Framed engravings of impossibly peaceful cities were interspersed with administrative announcements about ration cards, food distribution points. Usually the cafe would be deserted at this hour, the owner, a former hotelier with criminal connections, bawling out his two waiters for not polishing the glasses properly. Today he and his staff were nowhere to be seen. Tipped off in advance, they had all escaped ignominiously through the kitchen window. Beneath the nicotine-brown ceiling however the activity was intense. Tables and chairs had been rearranged in a semicircle. Beyond lay a clear space and then a battery of arc-lights, tripods, cameras. One officer was fussing over two vases of hothouse flowers on the central table: spotted trumpets of lilies, anthuriums with spathes like red wax plates, a mauve foam of hibiscus, all unimaginably, achingly exotic. In front of the table another officer was unrolling a pink silk Kashan rug, its stylised squares and fronds representing the tree of life flowering in the earthly paradise. In one corner a stack of crates wafted delicious and almost forgotten food smells: pineapple, chicken, paprika. A third officer, napkin on arm, was setting places. The cutlery gleamed real silver. The wine goblets were superior Venetian glass.

The swarthy officer ushered Rachel and Alicia through the door.

—She can be the rich yid's tart,—he shouted across to a thin man with a riding crop. The thin man nodded.

—What about the skinny bitch?

—Give her an overall. We need another servant.

Now they were shoved still deeper into the cafe beyond the eating area to where an officer smoking a cheroot stood beside the mounds of clothes. He looked at Alicia and rummaged in one of the piles. Then he stood up, holding out a silver fox fur.

—Bet you've never worn anything like this. Now's your chance. Strut about.

There were backless highheeled shoes, gold lamé dresses, fine shawls. Alicia was forced to strip down to her patched underwear in front of the grinning cheroot smoker. Out of the corner of her eye she glimpsed Rachel struggling into a shrunken soiled blue coat of the kind the fecal workers wore. Lastly came the makeup. This was greasepaint, inexpertly and contemptuously daubed by the cheroot smoker. There was no mirror.

—What about the jewellery?—someone called.

The officer took a small inlaid ebony case out of his jacket pocket. Flicked open it revealed drop-earrings set with rubies and a necklace of seed pearls on a bed of cotton wool.

—Don't get any ideas. We know exactly what you're wearing.

—Is she ready yet?—the riding crop shouted, adjusting an arc-light.

—Just doing the hair. My, it's thick.

Alicia tried to smile through tears of humiliation and rage. Someone muttered *They'll be shaving it off soon enough* but she had no time to decode the allusion. Rough hands were propelling her forward into the glare of the arc-lights. Waiting for her there stood an equally unwilling actor, a tall man dressed in a linen suit, panama and spats. He raised his eyes as she came close.

—Queen of the ghetto. And I'm the King. For a day.

It was Mendel.

So the charade began. The Viennese frau and the hasidic Kabbalist out for a night on the town. They were made to sit at the central table and hold up glasses already filled to the brim with Krug. An unbroached jeroboam was placed between them. The camera clicked. The glasses were taken away and set, still brimming and afizz, on the table. Then, in slow succession, their plates were stacked with and emptied of smoked salmon, caviare, breast of chicken, trifle. Each time the camera clicked. Each time they were forced to hold the cutlery as if about to eat. And each time eating was forbidden. Finally a cake was brought on. It had been shaped like a Tablet of the Law, the sponge copy of the Commandments supported on either side by two white-iced Lions of Judah. Mendel was obliged to stand over it with a knife as if about to cut a slice for his mistress.

After the stills the movie pictures. For these three extras were brought on: a proprietor, a waiter, and Rachel. The frames were designed to provide a context for the actual meal. Here the rich customers were invited by a fawning proprietor to enter his humble establishment. Here they were examining the food and drink on display. Here the waiter was removing Mendel's coat. And here the proprietor lit Sir's expensive cigar. Finally there was a cameo in which Rachel had to bend down, lick the toes of Alicia's high heels, then polish them with a rag. Alicia was told to give the servant a good kick for her pains.

Before she had finished polishing Rachel fainted. The smell of the food had been bad enough for Alicia and Mendel but for the emaciated ailing girl it had represented a stomach-griping torment. The arc-lights too made the already muggy atmosphere hotter. Alicia could feel the runnels of sweat pouring down her back. Rachel lay at her feet, ashen faced.

The riding crop was wiping his shiny forehead. He stepped over Rachel and went to the table. He took a quick swig of champagne.

—Damn Jew bitches stink worse than the men.

Then all at once as in some grotesque reversal of a dream-spool, the entire demonic artifice melted away. The rich banquet disappeared back into the crates, the clothing and the jewellery were torn unceremoniously from the major participants and packed away into suitcases. The equipment was dismantled and hurried out to the limousine. The cafe was bare again, a squalid vault stricken with the memory of a transient earthly paradise. The riding crop and acne were content.

—Wait till this is released back home.

—High life in the ghetto. How they treat their own. That girl fainting like that was a nice touch.

Then they were gone, demons such as the Kabbalists talk of, not made of all four elements. Mendel, who could have supplied more information on the habitat and rites of such beings, leant dumbly in his long johns against the table. His whole body shook. Rachel lay with her head in Alicia's lap. The real proprietor had miraculously returned. He wanted these fake customers out. The whole incident was bad for business. He threw down their clothes in a heap. Then Alicia noticed a gleaming fragment on the floor under her chair. For a moment she thought one of the seed pearls might have fallen off her borrowed necklace. She grabbed at it. A crumb of icing. Rachel was stirring now. Gently she popped the crumbling sugar pellet into the young girl's mouth.

It took him weeks to locate Bernard again. Every lunch break he would search in another part of the ghetto, picking up false leads, avoiding the eyes of the police, suffering rebuffs and threats. After the spring resettlements and her decision to live with the Rosenfelds, Rachel had lost contact with the underground. She was abstracted, especially after the barely alluded-to incident in the cafe, a sneezing shadow glued to his mother. She no longer even had a clear memory of where Bernard had been hiding in the spring. He would have moved on by then, perhaps several times. Yet Chaim persisted, fortified by the thought of Rachel's brief encouragement one evening beside Henryk's allotment; and by the chill weight of the cigarette case in his inside breast pocket.

It had been a thundery, overcast day although some said the rolling echoes in the east had more to do with the Russian advance than any innocent late summer storm. The air was dry and stagnant in the stairwell. How many such places had he visited over the weeks, all similar, all wrong? Yet he climbed to the third floor, as the little girl in the print frock on the corner selling ersatz chocolate had suggested. There was a low whistling. Once inside he realised with a disabling shock that this was the room where his family had lived when they first came to the ghetto.

Behind a table made from an upended tea-chest Bernard sat on Alicia's old three-legged stool. Chaim remembered her telling Josef to leave it behind. *It reminds me of those early days*. All the other furniture had long since gone. In the shadows where Grandma had died, a figure stood. Another squatted on the spot where they had rigged up the partition for the pot. Suddenly they were all around him, Henryk and his mother and Grandma. It was here he would make his decision, in this room of ghosts and mirrors.

—I saw you the first day of the resettlement. In the stable window.

Chaim broke off, choked with an emotion he could not express. His long rehearsed speech had already collapsed. Where he stood now he had lain once in bed, masturbating about the girl in the window. Yesterday. A century ago. Bernard was rolling a small metal cylinder up and down the table. A cartridge case. This was a room to him. Chaim's emotions were a world away.

—Do you have access to the Census Department?

The question was so unexpected, so lacking in formalities that Chaim, half sunk in the past, found himself taken unawares. He nodded furiously as if to shake off the swarm of memories.

—My father, I mean my stepfather, is Josef Rosenfeld.

There was another roll of thunder. It was still distant. The walls vibrated slightly. In this room Mendel and his mother had tried to change Grandma's name to Rachel. Strange presentiment. It would be better now if he changed his. Or lost it. A bluebottle droned round the single naked lightbulb hanging from its cord of frayed flex. They had laughed when Henryk came back one day with a lampshade. How he found it they never discovered. But it fitted. He could see him still, tottering and grunting on the three-legged stool, his brawny arms upraised, as if they had just caught the diaphanous shade with its rippling pattern of butterflies. It had been a cold day with driving sleet. This evening the room was hot yet clammy. Bernard's voice came low.

—We know there's to be another resettlement. No,— here he shook his head impatiently—those bastard words, official words. It'll be worse. A total clearance. The ghetto will be demolished.

The figure whose trunk stood rooted in the wraith of Grandma's bed stirred uneasily. Chaim half expected Henryk to blunder forward. He knew about the resettlement. But not the clearance.

—My father (he didn't bother to correct himself this time) says different. Not a total clear-out.

Bernard was rolling and rolling the cartridge case. Chaim felt a spasm of anger. Then helplessness. If he withdrew this time they would shoot him in the back. The choice had already been made.

—There will be plans. Which sector goes first. Who goes where. You can help us, a little.

Suddenly there was a louder explosion. The light flickered, dulled.

—They'll be cutting that off soon. A total clearance.

Bernard stopped rolling the cartridge.

—And Rachel. We heard she was ill.

Chaim froze slightly. He guessed Bernard's interest in her wasn't purely objective.

—Too ill to be involved, yes.

—Tell her—here Bernard coughed and dropped the cartridge on the floor—tell her I, we, think of her. When she should feel better . . .—For a moment their eyes met, in boyish rivalry. Then the old shields came down.

A few minutes later Chaim walked out to a stairwell where, in another life, he had come upon Josef proposing to his mother. Tonight that old misery rose up like an uncapturable joy.

'Weep O Daughters of Jerusalem. Weep my People. Weep

192

O Children of Zion. There is no end to the suffering of our people. Read and grieve.'

Josef looked up at Solomon.

—When did this arrive?—He touched the torn sheet of paper.

—Yesterday. Moses escaped on Tuesday. He only came back because of this. He knows the rabbi.

—The author.

—Yes. I know him too. We're from the same neck of the woods.—He dabbed his bald head. He was too old for all this.—Well I thought you should see it.

Where was Alicia? His stomach cramped. And Mendel? It was dangerous to be late for work. He turned back to the creased and grubby sheet of paper:

'All that follows is true. It was related by a plumber, a very reliable man, the son of (here followed a long and complex genealogy set out to prove the plumber's trustworthiness) who was summoned to mend a cistern. There by chance he met this Henryk. It is fatal to talk to prisoners. But this Henryk is evidently cunning in a simple sort of way. He knows of hiding places even in the depths of the fiery furnace. He told this plumber how the people are brought in railway wagons, every day, from different countries. At the siding they are unloaded and sorted. A few such as this Henryk are selected to work in the camp. The rest they drive to a sort of complex of changing rooms. At least that is what our people believe. But once they have stripped all are led into darkness. Rooms where something is thrown in and something else released. Some poison. No one is sure what. None last more than twenty minutes. This

Henryk is one of the poor masked unfortunates who goes in afterwards . . . the ovens . . . weep . . .'

Josef rubbed his eyes and looked up. Black mosaics. White.

—Has the Chairman seen this?

—We wouldn't dare. But we thought you . . .

—My wife had a relative . . . he was here that day . . .

Solomon touched the paper then swiftly withdrew his hand.

—We thought you could include it in the archive. Surely it must be included.

Josef nodded.

—And not allowed to get abroad.

—There are so many rumours now it would make little difference. And Moses is back in the ghetto.

Where were Alicia and Mendel?

—Do you think it's true?

Josef touched the creased paper.

—This? I don't know. Yes and no. Does it matter?

—You mentioned some good hideouts in the west sector.

Solomon's eyes were milky, old. He wanted to die an old man's death. Josef nodded. If his clerk should vanish he would not raise the alarm.

He lay on the stained straw mattress under the cracked ceiling. Beside him on the floor lay the ripped but neatly folded tallit that had been knitted over a hundred years previously by a cantor whose grandfather had been a pupil of Baal Shem. Above his head on a hook hung the tefillin which Alicia had rescued from the police station waste basket. They had been made by a leather worker whose great grandfather had witnessed the dispute between Iron Head and the Rabbi of Lublin. A Talmudic commentary on Exodus lay on the windowsill. It had been printed some fifty years ago in Vilna by the Jacob who now ran the ghetto printshop. Otherwise the room was empty, as if already unoccupied, stripped.

He could not uproot from his mind that morning's events in the cafe. The food and drink had not concerned him, inhabiting as he did a frame innured to privation. The clothes were an irrelevance. Even the heat had barely made him sweat. But Alicia. She had looked younger in that borrowed finery. Less innocent in the glare of artificial light, under the lecherous eyes of cameras.

When Josef came in without knocking (Mendel never bothered to lock his damaged door nowadays) he expected a dressing down. Why hadn't he reported for work this morning? Why this constant irresponsibility? Today he had an explanation he knew his protector would find satisfactory. Yet he felt disinclined to give it. Josef seemed preoccupied, wrapped in a mist of inwardness. He sat down on the mattress and drew something from his pocket.

Josef wondered whether prolonged isolation and hunger hadn't finally turned Mendel's wits. But he knew now what he must and mustn't do. His friend had revealed that to him, almost inadvertently. To show the paper to Alicia would be pointless. He must continue to work as he had before. The very hopelessness of his task, the hollow pragmatism of it all, was the only possible response. What had the underground claimed? Resettlement is death. Ah, but they did not say that resistance also means death. And passive acquiescence too. Only his way held out any hope of survival. The sheet of prophecy and lamentation and horror would be filed away for future generations. It was somehow irrelevant to them, who had lived knowingly or not beneath its shadow.

Josef had come like a messenger. Thunder announced his arrival. His words were of last things, a day of Wrath. Yet wasn't it written that behind the black fire of the Torah lay the white fire, unrevealed and waiting for the messiah? He saw Alicia again and wept. So much gross luxury and sin. So much that would have to be stripped away before the white fire could burn through the black. So much lost and given up and shed. And he who had meditated so often on that coming conflagration found himself filled with a tender love of ordinary things. He even loved this piece of paper and what was written on it in black fire.

They were on an island in the middle of the lagoon. The water was full of bodies. His father said: *these are the fossilised remains of creatures caught up in the last cataclysm. They are packed together in that way because of shifts in the earth's surface over countless millennia.* When he looked again the bodies had turned to a bed of oysters. Henryk came crackling across it. He was dressed in the robes of a Venetian doge and carried a small parchment scroll. He stopped and let the scroll drop open:

We are treated well here. Work is hard but we are allowed a nap in the afternoon. Please do not send food parcels. Looking forward to our imminent reunion.

Then the scroll caught fire, the robes turned to leaves and Henryk plunged naked through a hole in the oyster bed. It smoked a dull violet.

A sewage outfall pipe ran down the beach of the island. He limped towards it. Soft footsteps pursued him. *Give me back my cigarette case* his giant father boomed.

They took her away my little sharpeyed chick. When she fell on the ramp I picked her up and dried her cheeks. But they took her away. And what is this? It isn't a trowel. It's a sort of pick.

13

The thunder was almost overhead by the time he reached the Census Department. He had known where to find Josef's skeleton keys, tucked behind the skirting board in the closet bedroom they both shared. It was growing dark. He slipped the key into the door and turned. A jagged shaft of lightning severed the sky above the street, illuminating his solitude. At least there were few people about these days, a consequence of the resettlement. And now, because of that same thinning, the Census Department shut down completely after six. He turned the key again. The door was stiff. But gave. They would all be back at the apartment now. Waiting for him. Wait then. I shan't be long. A clap of thunder rattled the building like an empty desiccated pod. Not so empty. He climbed the stairs.

Another key let him through Solomon's office and a third into his stepfather's inner sanctum. He moved noiselessly with a stopped heart. There was something sacrilegious about touching all these complex, heavy, self-mirroring documents. As if he had found his way to the ghetto's dark shrine.

Anything about clearances, movement of people, anything like that.

There was another flash of lightning, a blue and white incandescence.

If you can't manage it we'll just have to break in.

But he could manage it. And Bernard would be proud of him. And less likely to ignore him where Rachel was concerned. He sat down at Josef's desk.

He climbed the stairs with weary deliberation. Mendel as usual had exhausted him. The folded sheet was in his pocket. He would paste it into the week's Report of Events. Another witness.

Chaim had found what he needed. An estimate of the numbers of people in each sector and a chart of how best to ease the flow from collection points to the Spur. This was followed by an estimate of the number of workers who should stay behind to form the nucleus of a fully efficient unit. It included several pencilled-in names. The family was all there. And Mendel. Was this one of his stepfather's desperate gambles? Or did the words 'efficient unit' originate with the authorities? And if so, why should they be trusted? Poor Josef. Always trying. Always gambling. What had Bernard said? *A total clearance.* Perhaps. Perhaps not. But it was the numbers that mattered and the order of sectors to be cleared. He closed his eyes trying to memorise it all. There was the thunder again. And another sound, softer, drier. A creaking. Shoes.

Mendel had burst in, excitedly confused. He said someone had come back. He said they would join him soon. Who? she had asked. Messiah son of Joseph of course. That is, Henryk. Rachel was resting in the bedroom. Alicia did not want her disturbed. She pulled the door to. Henryk? Where? But Mendel seemed not to be listening. Josef had the words. And the black fire that hid the white. He was going to put the words and the fire together somewhere. Alicia ran across the room and pulled on the coat without the lining.

Josef went across to the office window and lifted it slightly. Thrips shoaled there, black against a green pulse of sheet lightning. Still no rain. He decided not to switch on any lights. His hand felt sticky and slipped all over the place when he slid the filing cabinet aside.

She was running up the stairs despite her fatigue. The stormlight swayed her shadow across cracked plaster.

Chaim crouched and waited. After Josef had opened the window there had been a grating noise and then he seemed not to be there. He peered round the edge of the desk. Should he go the way he had come? He decided to wait.

Pasting the paper into the file he heard the footsteps on the other side of the cabinet and froze. Had he forgotten to lock up behind him? Then her voice floated through, muffled. She had the spare set of keys. He went over to the cabinet.

—I thought I told you always to give the signal.

—Henryk. Mendel said Henryk had come back.

Josef sighed.

—So he told you. I wasn't going to. But no, not come back. Here, you'd better read for yourself.

He pushed the file toward her in the stormlight.
Black fire. White.

Someone else had come into the office. There had been the same grating noises and then this person too was not there. He stood up, stretching to ease the cramp in his calves. Should he leave by the window? But now there was another noise, from behind the wall, a sobbing. Was someone hiding there? Someone who hadn't realised the last resettlement ended months ago? Or had decided to prepare for the next? He crept closer. It was coming from behind the filing cabinet. He peered over, round. There was a chink running down the left side. Through its white rift he saw into an unknown room. His mother and stepfather were clinging together in the secret archive.

Thunder again. It was as if they dwelt there apart from him in another world. Worrying still about Henryk and the coming deportations, lost in their tent of words, their temple of figures. He had all the figures and words he needed. How remote they were. And sad. Locked and swaying together in hopeless hope. The one trusting to fate, yet raging against it; the other half obeying and half subverting the authority that would eventually destroy them all. If only he could lead them from that dusty shrine into the new life beyond the wire. He could not. Sadness overwhelmed him. He would have stood rooted to the spot, his face to the white rift in the cabinet like a priest consulting an oracle, if another stab of lightning hadn't revivified the two statues locked beyond his reach. They were coming out. He would leave by the open window.

—That's odd. I hadn't realised I'd opened the window as much as that.

Josef was still holding Alicia's hand. They had found each other again.

So Chaim jumped as Mendel had jumped. Down onto the urinal's corrugated roof. Into another world.

The fast of Elul was halfway through. Once again he had been able to subsist on nothing but bread and water. It was not as spiritually perfect as total abstention but, coupled with the slow erosions of ghetto life, it tended to make all meditation and prayer overwhelmingly intense. Now after one such gruelling session he sank back exhausted but content on the straw mattress. Empty space opened all around him inside and out. He was like a mirror without edges waiting for the candle. The old tender love of created things returned but washed clean and simplified. He no longer raged or enthused. He did not want to dance. He did not want to denounce. All his surfaces were filmed with water of light. He was a child who, having lain down to read the old inscriptions in the village graveyard, rolled over and lost himself in the slow white wheel of the sky. The black fire had dissolved to reveal the white.

The bedding had gone but the church was not empty. Now the nave played warehouse to a cairn of thousands of pairs of shoes. Abraded and scratched by unknown currents, these leather and wood concretions had been washed up here, to lie as still as shells on a foreshore, beyond change. People moved among them, beachcombers of the wrack of shoes, sifting them for size, colour, quality. They were silently reverential in the presence of the mound. This was the church's new altar. What the shoes might announce nobody knew. Or wanted to know.

He found her sitting in a hollow of shoes, eating rye bread. He wanted to tell her about the information he had gleaned last night. He wanted perhaps to boast a little of his exploits.

—They don't do any walking then, further East.

It was meant as a provocation, a charm even, to raise the old Rachel from this pale, listless double. She munched slowly, deliberately, as Alicia had taught her.

—They all get regular issue.

This could have been his mother talking, through the wads of damp bread. But there was a gleam in her eye. He picked up the right shoe of a pair of child's sandals. The buckle was broken. There was a dark stain on the leather upper.

—Even the little ones?

She did not reply but motioned him to sit down. She tore off a greasy lump from the half chewed stump.

—No. You eat it.

He looked at her more closely. Her eyes were clear, even sparkling.

—But your allergy's better now. No more bedding.

She nodded and smiled.

—I feel better.

He couldn't restrain himself.

—You know I've made contact again. As you said I should.—Here he touched the hidden cigarette case.—You know about the uprising.

Again she looked at him with that slightly mocking gleam. This too had something to do with her new found health.

—My place is with your mother. And Josef. There was a rumour about Henryk. Moses had something to do with it. Even Alicia cannot doubt what resettlement means. In the old days—here she stroked the stump of bread as she had once stroked his cheek—the wilful ignorance of the ghetto dwellers appalled me. I wanted everybody to know. Now everybody does know. So it makes little difference.

This was Alicia talking again. Chaim tried shock tactics.

—Then why don't you come with me? If it makes little difference.

—You're strong. I fainted when they made me act in the cafe.

—But you're getting stronger. You said so yourself.

Silence. Beneath which he sensed the faintest of waverings. He would have to be patient. The ruined church reverberated muffled echoes. The air reeked fustily of shoes. Behind them, sticking up like a fossilised tree-bole out of stagnant marshes, a marble column rose from a mound of clogs only to end in cracked and jagged nothingness. Again she spoke.

—My place is with your mother and Josef.

And again he sensed the slightest ripple of hesitation. Now too she was offering him bread again, only this time in the form of a moist pellet on the tip of her tongue. He took it and felt a brief spurt of desire. Then fatigue returned. Once she had nourished him with more than bread. But those times were gone.

As he slipped through the scorched hole that had been a side chapel Chaim looked back and saw her bent over a mound of galoshes. Then he lurched against a piscina and vomited. Slopping there in the stone trough the thin greenish fluid contained no sign of the wafer she had so gently offered him. That at least would seem to have been miraculously absorbed.

Tenderly he stroked the horse's whiskery muzzle. He had glimpsed Ezekiel's chariot in ghostly silhouette against this rickety old cart. A charred stench filled the air. Black fire would reveal white. The time was close.

—Mr Chairman I beseech you. Remember the story of the desert islands as it is written in the Talmud. Once there was a master who freed his slave and the slave set off on a voyage. But the ship was wrecked and he floated to a strange country. There the inhabitants welcomed him as king and he lived in great splendour and authority. But a voice – even as this voice speaks to you now – warned him in a dream that when a year was over, he would be cast out by the inhabitants and sent to a desert where he would live in great misery.

The horse snorted. He stroked its muzzle. There were powers present. The angels of the sefirot.

Crown. Wisdom. Intellect. Love. Power. Beauty. Endurance. Majesty. Righteous One. Kingdom.

Harnessed to the cart. Pulling it.

Josef was running down the stairs. It was the last time he would do this. Up above in the Chairman's office the Amtsleiter and the council were waiting to decide the fate of another twenty thousand and here was Mendel telling the Chairman fairy stories. It was the last time.

—But the slave who was king did not ignore this voice as so many of his predecessors had. He made shift to cultivate the desert where he was to be sent and to establish a community there so that when the year was up and he was cast out, his new abode proved as congenial as the old and he lived on there in great splendour and authority.

He could see the chariot plainly now. And its fiery wheels. Like spirals. Shells. Black on white.

The Chairman was eyeing him.

—May I go now? Have you finished?

Josef plunged out of the Judenrat and dragged Mendel from the horse. The chariot began to fade. And the angels.

—Don't trouble yourself Mr Rosenfeld. It's been most instructive.

The Chairman was climbing down from his cart, helped by Schmoyl.

—On this important day I've been reminded yet again as to who is and who isn't indispensable. I'm surprised your friend Mendel is still there. He *is* your friend I understand.

Josef could not answer. The chariot had gone back to heaven. Schaefer stood in the doorway, listening.

As he came to the old Park allotments he heard shouts and curses. Beyond the protective wire mesh, among the bean poles and the green regiments, two or three elderly figures were stooping. Every so often they would jerk a left or right fist behind them in a gesture of disgust or surrender. From out of these fists, describing a high slow trajectory, tiny meteoric showers arced and fell. When he was almost level with the fence one of the showers hit him full in the chest. Black and yellow writhings spasmed and fell in every direction.

—There's even more than yesterday.

—Thousands of the bastards.

—It's the weather. Thunder. No rain.

—There's been a plague of butterflies.

—We need chemicals.

—Chemicals. In the ghetto.

—Nicotine would do. Boiled butts.

—Too late. Too late.

The figures continued in their doubled-up ritual. Josef saw where the cabbages had squirmed with caterpillars, their hearts holed and shredded, daubed with green excrement. What had Henryk said? *Be vigilant. That's my motto. If you examine the undersides of the leaves for eggs and crush any you find, caterpillars won't be a problem.* But Henryk was gone. Over the old gardeners' heads white butterflies danced, mockingly eager to lay yet more rafts of helmeted yellow eggs. Josef turned away. He saw Mendel's hand on the horse's muzzle. He saw the smoky council meeting. Schaefer's cobalt eyes. The ghetto was to be cut by two thirds. The war would be over soon. No need for excessive production. Unsafe buildings demolished. Less overcrowding. A sanitary measure.

The soft tireless munching jaws of caterpillars. Cater-pillars with human faces.

All essential administrative personnel will be exempt. There will be no yellow permits. Only thus can the Aktion be made to run smoothly.

The butterflies fluttered. Another cluster of caterpillars flew up helplessly into the air. Aktion. A new and darker word. A military word.

All administrative personnel.

Too late. It's too late.

They all knew. Their eyes said so before Schaefer had gone. He knew they knew. The ghetto could not last much longer. Even if they survived this resettlement. Yet all continued to indulge in the ritual of sums and allocations. The four sectors were mentioned. The methods of clearance. As if anybody or anything would remain behind for long. Yet none of them could face this fact. They continued to pretend, padlocked as they were to the skeleton of administration. Even Josef could not shake free. The water was rising.

—Herr Schaefer mentioned that there would be no yellow permits. How then are we to decide on the makeup of the new pared-down ghetto?

The Chairman had his arm on the mantelpiece. The Amtsleiter had gone. The other council members watched him. They had grown to trust Josef as a spokesman. The Chairman looked up. His old truculence had vanished. His eyes were dark.

—The authorities have already decided. This is not a matter of self-determination. The times are too critical. I would have given you the lists at the end of the meeting but since Mr Rosenfeld has pre-empted me . . .—Here he snapped his fingers and Schmoyl came into the room bearing a pile of documents. They were distributed in silence. The Chairman went on.—People on the lists will gather at dawn on the first day of Tishri at the Judenrat.

The papers rustled. Leaves munched by caterpillars.

—But where is my family?

—My mother.

—There are hardly any workers.

—Is this a resettlement or a pogrom?

The Chairman lifted his hand from the mantelpiece. The sleeve dropped away revealing a watch that splintered the sunlight.

—You will notice that all administrators are included.

—Do you believe in this charade?

The papers ceased to rustle. Josef flinched slightly at his own forthrightness. The Chairman moved closer and leant down. His breath smelt faintly of garlic. Where on earth did he obtain garlic?

—Belief doesn't come into it. You are on the lists Mr Rosenfeld. You are one of my top administrators.

At that moment Josef knew his family would not be spared.

The munching jaws, the faces. He walked away from the ruinous, dying allotments. Yes, Henryk would have had an answer. A remedy too, no doubt.

When Chaim arrived back at the apartment they were sitting round the table. The candle was unlit. Josef motioned him to sit.

—The council has met.

Chaim grew attentive. He might glean a little more information to take to Bernard this evening. His mother stared at Josef as though he were about to perform a miracle. Rachel was upright but pale. Her chest still sounded bad, despite the remission in her allergies. Mendel rocked slightly, to and fro.

—There is to be—here he coughed as if forced to blurt out an obscene word—an Aktion.

Alicia put her hand in his.

—You have done your best. Not everyone can be spared.

Josef looked up. He was laughing. Alicia drew away, frightened.

—Not everyone. No—Josef was almost shouting—no. The chosen have been listed. I am on the list.—His words dropped into the room and lay there, smouldering.

—I have failed you all this time.

Alicia put her hand out and touched his arm, tentatively, a girl.

—No you haven't Josef. No. There has been a mistake surely. Let me go to the Chairman.

—Josef shook his head. The first of Tishri. An Aktion.

—Lord how much longer will this separation make me a homeless fugitive. The fires of wandering are ablaze and I am ready for the stake.

Mendel was standing at the window, a black, brooding bird. No one had the strength to hush him.

Unseen, Chaim slipped away.

Bernard was staring out of the window where Chaim

himself had often stared in the early days. A warm slightly damp evening breeze blew through the broken panes. It would rain soon. He had come back to this room of ghosts to plead for their living doubles.

—Can't be done. Family means burden. Our cells are all complete. No elders.

Chaim stared up at the black swinging socket where the lightbulb had been. He had hoped this at least might work. His family's safety for the census information.

—But if they lie low in the dugouts?

—You could. And Rachel. With my cell. We lost a member yesterday. But not the others.

—They'd prevent you from fighting,—Chaim said dully.

—We don't even fight until after the Aktion. Any involvement with non-participants (here he meant the deportees) would be disastrous. I couldn't trust some of us not to try and save relations. Our task is to kill the enemy and fight our way out of the ghetto. Until the Aktion's over we all lie low.

Chaim knew he was getting nowhere. He tried another tack.

—I have the information.

—We don't need it. We had a contact at the meeting today. It's total liquidation. Those who stay on will be made to clear up. Then they'll be disposed of. Which leaves us.

Bernard came away from the window. He touched the socket.

—Power's off. They'll sweep this sector first. The day after tomorrow. But we'll be in the sewers. Waiting.

So even this attempt at bargaining had failed. Chaim felt close to tears.

—What shall I do?

Bernard's face softened a little.

—Decide between your family and us. You and Rachel know where to go. But no one else.

With a little pang of the old jealousy Chaim suspected that Bernard longed to cut him out of the equation too. There was a distant muttering to the east.

—Still no rain.

—That's not thunder. It's the Front. They have to close this place down as soon as possible.

When she heard the door click she instinctively thanked God. She had thought Chaim gone for good. They had failed him, the adults. There was nothing Josef or she or Mendel had to offer. She wouldn't have blamed him for going. But now he was back she determined to go to the Judenrat in the morning. She would plead as Josef hadn't. Surely they could be granted some sort of immunity. She held Rachel closer to her. The girl's head felt hot.

Josef was dreaming of a giant caterpillar when Chaim crept in beside him. The caterpillar was lying along the length of the nave in St Mark's. Its jaws oozed a black milk.

Mendel lay in his garret. He was no longer a mirror. He would be again. He would enter the mirror with Alicia.

Why didn't they let me go with her? What do they want me to do with this pick? What are those buildings, those chimneys? A giant chicken factory. All we need now is wings.

14

The gunfire was intense and close at hand. There had been a breakout down at the main gate. Instinctively her gloved hand sought his. He was staring at the Chairman.

—But you said yourself I am one of your most important administrators. I have a family Mr Chairman, a family.

The man whose word had decided so many people's life or death seemed paralysed by thought or its absence. All that had accrued to him since the foundation of the ghetto was shredding away. He had long since lost sight of any moral goal. Now the very illusion of authority was gone. The arctic breath of the Amtsleiter's commands had reduced him to nakedness. Yet he was not ashamed.

—Then you too want to go, is that it Josef? I could easily arrange for one more.

The ghost of a joke hovered in the air between them.

—If you can increase the number of deportees you can reduce them. Let my family too find sanctuary in the Judenrat.

The Chairman sighed as if their senses of humour were at variance.

—Your family Josef? Mendel a zaddik. The boy a ZOB spy . . .

It was time for her to intrude.

—Mr Chairman. Do you remember when I first arrived here as one of the Western deportees?

The Chairman brushed an imaginary veil from the air before his face. It was not his business to remember.

—You told Josef to employ me, guessing I had secretarial skills. If it hadn't been for that we might not have married. You married us Mr Chairman. We are your responsibility too.

More gunfire. The breakout was turning into a massacre. The Chairman walked across to the window.

—Nothing can be changed. Josef must stay. But if—and here he almost winked at his Census Officer—if you can find a way of protecting your family, who is to say? The war might end soon or the ghetto might receive new settlers.

—You mean you want us to hide. Like rats.

Alicia looked from the Chairman to Josef. Already on his face she saw the signs of a new immersion in the ghetto's muddy pool. He was an official still, addicted to compromise. She stood up.

—We have our dignity. Do you expect us to cower in darkness? Emerge into the light, blinking?

She had hoped this would rouse Josef but he seemed lost in abstraction. The door opened and a sweating Schmoyl burst in.

—We've got them all. And sealed the gate. No need for the SS.

He looked hopefully at the Chairman. Next day at least one ghetto policeman's family would be given sanctuary at the Judenrat.

He listened as the footsteps of his mother and stepfather faded down the staircase. Rachel was outlined against the milky light of the window. She seemed almost transparent these days. And hot. He thought with a moment's longing of how, in peaceful times, this morning alone together in the apartment would have led inevitably to bed, then a bath, then bed again. But today was the eve of the Aktion. The two adults who had attempted to be their guardians for so many months of hardship had ventured out on one last mission. No factory would be open today. Those who had been given sanctuary in the Judenrat were already packing up belongings and preparing to move later that afternoon. For the others, the majority who would be deported, there was little choice. Most sat together or alone, in their rooms or in passageways and yards, blankeyed and listless, gripped by physical and emotional paralysis. Some, no less despairing but with a certain hopeless practicality, had begun searching for suitable hiding places. Cellars were a favourite, as were lofts. But failing these, even the dusty space under a bed would do. Finally there were a few who had decided to act then and there. Without family ties and too old ever to have been attracted to the underground movement, they gathered dementedly at the main gate. In the confusion of their weaponless onslaught some broke through only to be gunned down by the German Criminal police in the wasteground between the fence and the city. The rest who had retreated at the sight of blood were left to the tender mercies of Schmoyl and his men. The cries could be heard in the Rosenfeld apartment. Rachel shivered, hotly.

—They may persuade the Chairman.

Chaim's moment of boyish desire had long since passed. Yet he could not accept Rachel as she was. Through her transparent form he saw again the figure of a fiery and uncompromising girl framed by a glassless window at dusk. It was to her he spoke now, humbly.

—I saw Bernard again. After what Josef said. Last night.

Did she quiver slightly? Or was it the light, cut by a pigeon's wing?

—We can go tonight Rachel, you and I.

She looked at him, her eyes hooded in shadow.

—I cannot abandon them. Not yet.

Then it was as if the pale shadow and the flaming girl were one, sitting on his lap, clasping him tightly round the waist, pressing a dry mouth to his. What knowlege, soft as a masticated lump of bread, hard as a cartridge case, passed between them as they swayed there in the dim rain-heavy light? Chaim never knew, but when at last he drew back and looked at those cracked lips and the long thin nose and the black coiled hair held up by his mother's green dolphin comb, he understood that he too must stay.

—Ow that's hard.

—I don't think so.—He was embarrassed. Erections were few and far between when you were as hungry and tired as he was.

—I didn't mean down there. Silly.

She could have been a real girl again and not this fiery amalgamated phantasm.

—This.

And with her slender hot yellow fingers she drew out his father's cigarette case.

At first, stumbling blindly out of the Judenrat into the eerily silent streets, worrying about Alicia (had she gone straight back to the apartment? Would she do something ill-advised?), he was possessed by the secret archive idea. They could all hide in there: his wife, Chaim, Rachel, Mendel even. But then doubts had crept in. Solomon had not taken his chance with the bunkers in the western sector. He was still around and knew all about the archive. As did one other surviving secretary. Although they were all exempt from deportation they might talk. And then, if his family were discovered, the documents would be too. He had a duty to those words and figures, so laboriously amassed. Perhaps when his plan for their final resting place had been put into action he could think about the room again. But for the moment it was out of bounds.

Then almost immediately, as though he were in high fever, one thought gliding out of another with inexorable clarity, he remembered the wall in the apartment. Where the wardrobe was. One end seemed deeper than the other. He had noticed it when he first arrived in the ghetto. A partition of some sort. It had been obscured recently by the Kurdestan rug he had bought from Abram's fence in the market. As a wedding gift for Alicia. If he could get his hands on a hammer and some other bits and pieces. Half running back to the Census Department he became absorbed in memories of the woodwork classes he had attended as a boy. *Josef you will never make a practical man. You are an intellectual. A bookworm.* Well, he would show his father now. He would create the most important thing of all: a place to hide.

The hammer was Solomon's. Why he kept it in his bottom drawer was a mystery. It was lucky he had found the bunch of skeleton keys that had gone missing the other day. Solomon was already at the Judenrat, squabbling with the other clerks about sleeping places. The nails and the saw posed more of a problem, until he remembered Jacob. It hadn't been easy getting there. The little printing shop lay on the edge of the almost deserted south sector. Tomorrow it would be demolished. Today, trucks were being driven in to be stacked with anything of use or value. There were police about and a scatter of kapos. But Josef's well-known status gave him a certain authority. He had been right to expect to find Jacob in his work place. The two pre-war Heidelbergs were his family. On this last day of days what else could he do but polish and oil them, tending these dark uncomprehending structures as if they were beasts, needing food and nurture. In earlier times he had been a master printer, creating elaborate editions of Talmudic texts, the Zohar, rabbinic commentaries. But for the last two years he had been obliged to turn his hand to darker mysteries: ghetto money, Judenrat proclamations, copies of the Chairman's speeches, leaflets, ration cards. It was Jacob who had overseen the printing of what would turn out to be the ghetto's last major announcement, a timetable of the great October resettlement which already flapped on every available wall and pillar. For this job he had shown the same attention to detail as when dealing with the most complex biblical annotations. Only the slight flick of his tongue, the glitter of his eyes behind their thick rimless spectacles, suggested he had an opinion on the matter. Now he sat, his workers having gone into hiding or simply fled to their apartments, fingering the metal type in a tray on his knee. Gothic not Hebrew. He had what Josef needed. Later that day when the special detail came to take the Heidelbergs away, they found the body of an old man swinging from a rope that hung exactly equidistant between the platens of the two machines.

Hearing the clatter on the stairs they pulled apart like any young couple surprised in an illicit embrace. But their guilt was aged and listless and complex.

Dropping everything like that only increased his sense of angry purpose. He would show Alicia that he could be a man as well as an administrative cog. He would show the Chairman that he had hidden resources. They would survive this resettlement too. All of them. He groped on the stairs for the tools he had so carefully secreted in a leather pouch strapped to his waist. It was fortunate that the belt hadn't broken sooner, outside Jacob's for instance, when the special detail appeared. That too he decided was a sign.

She had meant to go straight back to the apartment. It wasn't Josef she had married but the whole crumbling ghetto edifice. Now she saw herself and her family beneath that tottering wall, cowering, naked. What protection was her marriage now? Where had her love led them all? To think that once or twice in the early days, when it was still possible to believe in strength and well-being, they had actually made love in the secret archive. To have been locked together in that room full of dust and memories when they might have been planning escape, freedom. But Josef would never escape the ghetto. It was a part of his flesh and blood. He was melting day by day into the words he stored and collated and hid away. The archive had become the dark double of the thesis he had never completed. But, unlike the thesis, the archive would not be abandoned. Josef would make sure he placated his father's ghost. So she reasoned, walking along the deserted street, the sound of gunfire becoming more and more sporadic, helpless in her love and pain, unable to reason.

The shadow with upraised arms might have been angelic if it weren't so thin. Sickly, helplessly, she realised how far out of her way she had come. Or intended to come. This was the man who could say what Josef never said. Yet she loved Josef.

—It is the promised land. They banquet there. As in the old pictures. Men and women with the heads of chickens. He has told me.

She had begun to mouth her usual doubts, already drawn into his stripped flaming world, when there was a scream overhead. It came from an open window.

—No. I won't go in there. It's too small. I won't.

Mendel was unseeing, deaf.

—He has lost his trowel. But he has something else. I can't quite see what. We are to go to him. You and I. Tomorrow.

—I won't. I get claustrophobia. You go in. I'd rather they came for me. I can't breathe. Oh.

Silence. Mendel's coat flapping. A few drops of rain pricking her cheeks.

—Who Mendel?

'Him. Henryk, the Messiah son of Joseph. He who is to announce the revelation; white fire behind the black.

The shouting in the upstairs room had ceased. Were they all to end up like this, squashed into dark spaces, listening for voices, boots, gunfire? Mendel was demented. She knew now. Yet he would not be walled up. He would stand out in the light he so longed for. And she shared that longing. She too wanted the broken vessels to be restored. Not in a dusty archive. Not behind a wall or under a bed. But outside for all to see. She had met Josef without flinching. She had married him. Now it was her duty to walk alone out into the hard final fire of light. Behind her own thoughts and Mendel's muttered repetition of the Passover song he had sung the night before she glimpsed, faintly, the chance to save her children.

Once he was through the jagged hole Josef had sawn in the hollow partition wall, Chaim wanted to laugh. It was such a childlike thing to do. Like the time he had hidden from his father in the cupboard along the hall. Somehow the little door had bolted itself on the outside and his secret pleasure had turned to panic. But it was not Oskar who pushed his head into the darkness. The time for games was long past. Josef peered:

—Is there room enough for three?

—I don't know. Rachel, you come in too.

And again he was smiling. That time down at the lake in the ruined lock-keeper's house. They had surprised a couple in the cellar, he and his friends. He still remembered the pale flash of a thigh, the man's stifled imprecations. The same smell of damp and plaster. The same constriction and excitement. And now Rachel was beside him, trembling, hot.

—There's room. If we stand side by side.

Rachel gave a little scream.

—There's something in here. I can't see. Oh horrible.

She had staggered out. Josef's head returned, haloed by a match-flame. The clotted swag of a cobweb floated towards him. Rachel, the underground activist, afraid of the dark. Yet suddenly he felt miserable. Why hide when you could fight? Why not go alone to Bernard in the sewers? Then Rachel's head replaced Josef's.

—Don't stay in there too long, Chaim. Come out into the light.

He needed her still. As he stepped from the hole in the partition he heard Josef half talking to himself about batons and nails. He was like any father on a holiday, doing jobs around the house.

—I'll have to make it look as if the wardrobe's fitted.

Rachel's hand sought his, trustingly.

He had decided about Mendel, he realised, long before. On the day he had found him addressing the Chairman in his cart. Now, when he saw Chaim and Rachel in the hole together, he was certain. Mendel could not hide there. He was too volatile. He would shout. Or pray. Or simply

223

laugh. And yet, he told himself with a new rush of guilt, he couldn't just abandon his old friend. He had worked on the wardrobe for an hour now. He felt sweaty and dizzy. It was fixed into place, completely obscuring the jagged hole. He had sawn the back out and fitted it in again with removable screws. This would be their entrance and exit. The whole of the back would be hung with the Kurdestan rug. To hide the screws. Shaped lathes ran round the wardrobe like beading. He was almost proud of his handiwork. *Call this carpentry, Rosenfeld? The dovetailing's all askew. Make it again.* Rachel was sweeping up the sawdust and the discarded nails and the white splinters of wood. Evidence. She would pour it all into the stove in the front room. He looked up. Alicia was still not back. It had begun to spot with rain. Should he go out looking for her? Then he heard her familiar footstep on the landing. He gathered up his tools in the leather pouch. Explanations would have to come later. Now he had one more task. He met his wife on the stairs and told her to wait for his return. She was not angry now. She kissed him and told him to be careful.

The saw and the hammer, the screws and other tools lay on the straw mattress. Mendel and Josef pored over them like archaeologists over a newly discovered hoard.

—It's all I can do Mendel.

—They catch the light. Those blades. Like fire.

Josef suppressed a gesture of impatience.

—The floorboards will be easy to take up now. And you should be able to slip them back from a lying position. It's lucky you're so thin.

Mendel was running his fingers along the toothed edge of the saw.

—Last night I heard the ineffable name. It was a vibration in the air. And then I saw the garment of the universe, decorated with stars. Each star was a part of the name. Each point of fire a letter. This is not a time for hiding.

Josef felt a great sadness descend. The rain-drops pattered on the roof of the tiny attic. Black stars. This was almost their last meeting. They had always spoken different languages, lived in different times. Yet Mendel's knowledge was no less rooted than his own. Who was to say which man would be the stronger, in the end?

—It's all I can do.

With sudden feeling he put his arms round the tall thin kabbalist. How bird-like he had grown, a feather to be wafted away. Yet sinewy and taut. Josef even felt a little afraid, standing there in the half light, his hand patting Mendel's sharp protruding shoulderblades. On his way home through the ghetto he came across several families making for the Judenrat. Earlier that day he would have wondered bitterly why them and not us. But now he felt different. It was the hiding place partly. And partly Mendel. Already many strands that tied him to the administration had begun to fray and run loose. Soon he might be as free as Mendel. And as strong.

Alicia peered into the open wardrobe. On one side stood Chaim clutching the Kurdestan rug in a scroll to his chest. On the other side Josef knelt, Jacob's screwdriver in one hand, a pile of screws in the other. The back of the wardrobe had been removed and leant against the wall. The trick had been performed. Something or somebody had become invisible. As a sceptical member of the audience, Alicia must be allowed to examine the machinery that had facilitated this legerdemain. Gingerly she touched the wardrobe, tapped the wall, stroked the beading. She could not help but admire Josef's handiwork. Yet even this seemed a part of the great lie of the ghetto. What were they hoping to hide for? What would they emerge into, a week or two weeks hence? Josef seemed unconcerned with such trivia. His mind was on important matters.

—So each evening I come and let you out. There's enough food in the apartment. You can even have some of it in there with you. It'll be damned uncomfortable but you'll be safe.

—And calls of nature?—She was smiling but pale.

—You must take the bucket. But perhaps you'll only be in there a day or two. This is the most populous sector, that's why they're starting here tomorrow. After they've cleared it I might be able to persuade the Chairman.

—After what he said this morning?

Her tone was sharp but confiding.

—Why not hide us all in the archive?

Josef dropped a screw. He wanted to hush her. Chaim looked over his scroll but said nothing. Josef whispered.

—No. Others know of it. I can't risk . . .

—And you say it's only big enough for three. That Mendel . . .

—Can I come out now?

The voice was thin and muffled. The person who had

226

been made invisible was about to be magicked back into the world.

—Do you like it mother?

Rachel was brushing a cobweb out of her hair. She seemed stronger this evening. But flushed.

—Like? It's not a word I'd choose. It's certainly ingenious. But why all of us? Tell me that.

Her tone had changed. She seemed suddenly exalted. And pressed on:

—If I stayed outside they'd be less likely to search. I'd be a decoy. The children . . .

Chaim felt the rug grow heavy in his hands. If his mother was going to let herself be taken then he might as well go to the underground tonight. And Rachel. But Rachel had stopped shaking out her hair.

—If you stay out so must I.

There was a knock on the door in the other room. They all stiffened. There had been a change of plan. The Aktion was beginning. No. But it would be advisable to conceal the hiding place before anybody was allowed in. Unfortunately Mendel pushed past Rachel before she could stop him. He caught a glimpse of the hollow space in the wall. And knew.

The fire came from there. From the dark hole. It braided out and wrapped the three adults in its long molten ropes. They were becoming mirrors now, Alicia and Josef and himself. He saw how it must be: himself and the Princess of the dusk together out in the street; Josef the Prince of the ghetto burying a white star in the earth. But the children, they were not mirrors yet. Their candles had not guttered. So he danced now before this Ark of a wardrobe knowing who would be saved and who must wait. Even as Josef told him to get out he danced. Only the children would live. For him and Alicia and Josef the light was elsewhere. He kissed Rachel goodbye and he kissed Chaim goodbye. How hot their heads felt. They were not ready yet for the cold light of being saved. Nor the white fire behind the black. He had no need to kiss Alicia because he would see her again.

Chaim's father has come back. He is wearing Schaefer's suit. He strides through the streets of the ghetto which have turned to canals. He is walking on the water, carrying a shofar and a photograph of his son as a baby. The one where he lies on a rug naked, clutching a string of costume pearls. The pearls have turned to collar studs and now his father is blowing the shofar. Here come Alicia and Josef and Mendel, following him, dancing, out through the un-guarded ghetto gateway which is also a Romanesque arch in a wardrobe.

Josef is a child again, hiding in the shed at the bottom of the garden. Father is angry because he stole and drank the milk. He will never come out again. What are those voices, far off down the lane? They are not searching any more. They have gone to live in another house, without him.

Alicia must row her entire family across the lagoon to an island. There is a cathedral on the island. They will seek sanctuary there and confess to the blood of the firstborn.

Chaim is a baby. Josef is her lover. Rachel is as old as Grandma. Mendel is a statue carved from jet. The water thickens, swirls. She loses an oar. The lagoon is a boating lake. The Chairman walks across the water, rattling a leather pouch full of coins and shouting *Your time is up*.

Rachel crosses but does not cross the bridge of sighs of shoes.

The name you seek is not in chapters. Nor in verses, nor in words, nor letters. The name you seek is between. Says the angel in the purple-black bottle, buried under the floor.

The last night of Elul; Tishri's first dawn. It is the New Year again. A wheel revolved, the ghetto lies under slant shrouds of rain. In Henryk's plot the runner beans hang, brown dripping thongs. Inside, their seeds are marbled mauve and scarlet. Although the caterpillars have long died or stiffened into chrysalises their frass still badges the riddled hearts of cabbages. Its soft jade is dissolving with the rain. In the yard where Mendel danced long ago the dry well echoes as the hard bright pellets of rain plunge to the shaft's bottom. Rainwater runnels down the steps of the church of St Mary and All Saints where a sodden bootsole lies, a onefooted ghost's footprint, running nowhere. The window of the Census Department streams rain. Rain is everywhere. The ghetto lies still under its relentless unquenching barrage.

He had not gone to the underground. For better or worse he

had thrown in his lot with his family. After Mendel's unexpected appearance Alicia had become adamant. She would not hide behind the wardrobe. It was another official ruse. The Chairman probably knew of the entire pathetic plan. Better to sit quietly and wait. So the argument had raged until Rachel had broken down, insisting Alicia hide with them. Even then, Chaim thought, his mother seemed peculiarly abstracted, as if she already knew exactly what she was going to do. How he pitied and loved her at that moment. Yet felt apart. As though their lives were diverging in spite of themselves. So she had gone to bed, suddenly old, in Rachel's arms. Now it was the dark before dawn. Josef would have to get to the Judenrat before the Aktion began. He had the back off the wardrobe again. Alicia and Rachel, barely awake, stood shivering in their night-gowns, watching.

—We'll put this bread inside. And this jug of water. Oh, and the bucket.

Chaim glanced at his stepfather's pale face and red eyes. What would it be like for this man to wall his family up and walk away?

—Who's first?

It might have been a fairground amusement, a ride on the ghost train. But the real ghosts were outside, approaching. There was no time for more than a brief embrace. All avoided each other's eyes. Then suddenly his mother was struggling. And slowly, dreamlike, in the waxing light, the three of them began to wrestle the frail greyhaired woman into darkness. All were weakened by hunger and apprehension. All were determined. The moment lasted hours. A rewind of a scene occurring all over the ghetto, with innocents becoming tyrants, forcing other innocents into places where they did not want to go. Then all at once Alicia relented. She stepped in, followed by Rachel. Chaim went last. *I'm counting on you* he heard his stepfather say and felt his hand on his back. *You're the man in the family now.* Josef's would-be jauntiness reverberated hollowly in the boy's mind.

Muffled by the hardboard and the rug Josef had heard her voice as he swivelled the screwdriver in the last screw.

—Remember Josef. Remember. For the children.

Remember. Josef could hardly drag himself away. Yet had to. If he didn't survive today who would find them? Horror stories from his youth of virgins walled up alive rose to haunt him. He felt like a cross between a gaoler and an executioner, he who had never been either. He was on the stairs now, having hidden the tools in a stove already crammed with sawdust and slivers of wood. And what if the whole plan failed? The squads would be here soon, moving from block to block, kicking in doors, reining in their dobermanns. He had left the door ajar. To suggest abandonment. Would they keep quiet? Would the cobwebs bring on Rachel's allergy again? She might sneeze. And Alicia, his angel from the West. What would she do? Last night Mendel had offered to accompany her to the Spur. He seemed to have some confused idea about saving the children too. Mendel. For all his otherworldliness he had a preternatural grasp of cause and effect. Suddenly an inexplicable anxiety assailed him. What if . . . ? Perhaps he should check his friend too. Would he use the hideout under the floor? He doubted it. Yes, he must check. But at the first corner he came face to face with the Chairman's dog-cart. As it was raining so heavily he was invited to accompany his superior to the Judenrat. The ghetto administration swallowed him once again.

He had seen the chariot a second time. Josef and the Chairman were riding in it, hunched against the rain. The dark chariot that presaged the end of days. Dark flakes of fire in the wheels, turning, swishing. And the demons of air and fire, they were everywhere this wet morning. Some had reached the landing of Josef's apartment. They had already counted to a hundred. Now they shouted: *We're coming ready or not*. An answering shout from inside the apartment. Her voice. That wasn't in the game. The cheat. He quickened his pace, jumping three steps at a time, avoiding the wet dark footsteps of the demons.

Chaim was holding his mother's arm. His other hand was on Rachel's head. They had all stood up in the darkness. He whispered.—They're in the block.—Rachel snuffled back another sneeze. This was bad. But much worse was his mother's repetitive low chant of Mendel's Passover song.

It had been hell so far and it was only eight o'clock. The last lot had been dead when they broke down the door. The smell. Suicide. Days old. They wouldn't make up the numbers at this rate. And the SS were everywhere. You felt like a deportee yourself, not a policeman at all. And the rain.

With water still dripping from his cap into his scarf, Schmoyl launched a kick of rage at the next door. It was unbarred and he almost fell through. His rage increased. Another empty apartment. They'd see about that.

His mother had stopped chanting. She turned in the darkness.—Go further along the cavity. If they come near the wardrobe I'll shout.—No mother.—Yes. But only if they start breaking it down. I might save you that way. They may not look.—Rachel sneezed in her throat again.

They were shouting incoherently and smashing things. The sound of a shattering plate. He felt his mother flinch.— Don't shout mother. They're drunk. They may not . . .

The cries of the demons playing hide and seek drew him onwards.

—What's this, a wardrobe? What's behind it? Open it up. That's right. Get rid of those clothes. What's this, a rug? What's behind it? The back of the wardrobe what do you think? Stop. Listen.

Silence. Rachel pinching her nose between thumb and forefinger. A muffled thumping.

—It's hollow. Kick that bloody wood in. Hell I'm soaked.

—Here I am.

—No mother you.

—Yes here. Here I am.

A little girl afraid of the dark. Longing oh so longing to be found.

But as the wood splintered, blurting a light that sucked his mother through, Chaim felt strong hands drawing him deeper into the darkness. Now Rachel had her palm cupped to his mouth. It smelt of lavender.

—Others in there with you are there? That kid of yours?
—He's with the underground. He's got your name on a bullet.
A slap. A cry. Silence.

Still breathing in the darkness. What?

That huddle of demons. Air and black fire. But the time of the angels was at hand. The time of white fire. And the demons were already wet. Especially the one wearing dark glasses.

—When Nebuchadnezzar held our people in slavery Jeremiah said 'Think not that of your own strength you were able to overcome the people of the Lord. 'Tis their iniquities which have condemned them to this sorrow.'

—Another one.

234

—With a prayer shawl.

—At last we meet again. Remember me. Remember Schmoyl. Remember this.

For a second and last time his glasses flew off his face and shattered into many glittering fragments.

—Is this the man who shook the earth and made kingdoms tremble?

There were more blows, more imprecations. But somehow Mendel's presence dissipated the searchers' momentum. Schmoyl could think of nothing but what he'd do to him between here and the Spur. Now he dragged him downstairs personally, leaving Alicia to be pulled along half unconscious by his second-in-command. The kapo detailed to examine the hole in the wall was left alone. He had no dog. He made only a cursory examination of the hiding place, seeming almost abashed by so much ingenuity and ruin. His truncheon brushed Chaim's leg but did not register the fact. Then the kapo was himself distracted by a shout from Schmoyl to get down to the floor below and stop those two escaping through the window. The apartment door swung shut. For a moment or a millennium Rachel and Chaim had worn the cloak of invisibility which Mendel had fashioned out of faith, delirium and love.

She clung to Mendel all the way to the Spur in the rain. Or he clung to her. His face was badly bruised from the beating. He could not see clearly without his glasses. If there had been time it might have been even worse. But today time was harrying Schmoyl more venomously than the ghetto policeman had ever harried his victims.

Chaim and Rachel clung together, upright. They merged in the half light. As the afternoon wore on and the cries and shots and barking faded, they climbed out of the wall and lay together on the bed under the rug from Kurdestan. They were too exhausted and overwhelmed now to care who found them. The patter of the rain on the window soothed their fever.

Josef found them. He thought they were dead. He touched their heads sorrowfully. They stirred. The wardrobe still stood against the wall but its door had been ripped off, its back smashed. The floor was covered with tangled clothes and coathangers. Then he knew. She was not there. He clung to the two children in wordless misery. Chaim was the first to speak.

—She gave herself up you know. For our sakes.

—And Mendel did too.—Rachel's voice sounded stronger than Chaim had heard it for months. It was as if without Alicia she had been thrown back on herself. And him.—They did it together. We should honour them.

But Josef was still caught between rage at his wife's obstinacy and guilt at having sacrificed his friend. He wept.

—You should have all hidden in the archive.—He had forgotten they were not supposed to know.

—No father.—Chaim had never used this title to Josef's face.—No father. Mendel I think wanted to go and mother . . . she knew what we had to do. You and the archive.

236

Rachel and I, elsewhere.

—She said remember. And for the children. It was her message to me.—Josef's voice was old.—Look they broke our best plate. The one your mother brought all the way from Venice.

It was the plate with dolphins round the edge. The shards caught the dying light. They were mixed with slivers of broken lenses.

So Alicia and Mendel were taken. So Chaim and Rachel broke their ties with their protector and friend. Nothing was said. But as they sat in the apartment in the gathering dusk they knew their life together was at an end.

They don't eat meat here they eat fire and ash. When will Alicia come? And Mendel? Must I be the only one to see them eat?

15

Josef leaned against the filing cabinet and pushed. As always it moved grudgingly. Beyond, in the secret room, light was beginning to curdle and dim. He stepped in and slid the cabinet back. Behind him the two desks waited, the archive in the cupboard, the typewriters. Everything was the same, the shape of things, the smell of paper and dust, the taste of the chill damp air on his tongue. Only he had changed. He squatted numbly by the cupboard and leant his head against its scratched walnut veneer. Here they had celebrated their profane Sukkah, argued about Henryk, been reconciled. Here they had brought the miseries of the day and shed them off. She moved here still, gliding between the desk and the cupboard, helping him to collate, to write up the weekly report, to copy and record. But she was gone. Not until this moment, confronted by all the uncountable silent cries and complaints of the ghetto, had he realised how truly she was gone. What had Mendel said? My Princess of the dusk. Gone. The dusk was for him alone. And the words he had stood guard over for so long. Mendel's kabbalah would live on without its disciple, a version of the universal reality. It could not be expunged by any human act. But this archive was wholly dependent on its creator. What Josef did now and in the next couple of

238

days would decide its fate. Now that he had no family these millions of words were his dependants and his descendants. Slowly, wearily, he stood up and opened the cupboard. The September entries were lying loose in a box file. They had not been typed up or sewn into a separate volume. He carried the file over to the nearest desk, sat down and took out the last sheets. Some were in his handwriting, some in hers. He did not look at hers. But reached for a pen and began:

'The first of Tishri. New Year. Heavy rain. The Great Clearance has begun. Today the east and southern sectors. Tomorrow the north and the west. On the third a fullscale demolition will begin, removing a substantial number of derelict and unsafe buildings. A skeleton staff (he grimaced at his choice of adjective) remains in the Judenrat to oversee operations and prepare for the new small streamlined ghetto that will (we are told) be set up by the authorities in lieu of the old.'

He paused and read over what he had written. Here as usual there was no cry from the heart, no anguished lament. All must be kept objective and cool however hotly his face burned. He continued:

'People are saying –

That this is the end of the ghetto.

That the ghetto has become such a decayed and dangerous place it will be better to go East.

That the war is over (but this is patently untrue).'

He paused. Outside all was silent. Where were Chaim and Rachel? Had he abandoned or freed them? He saw again the single red high-heeled shoe lying in the gutter outside the Department. Though scuffed and scratched and with a fake gold buckle that had tarnished badly in the rain, this shoe would never have been allowed to lie there a week ago. It would have disappeared to be used in some pathetic bartering transaction for bread or sugar. Now there was no one to pick it up. No one to barter with. What had she looked like, the woman whose shoe this had been? She had dropped it perhaps from a bundle that, having been humped laboriously all the way down to the Spur, would be unceremoniously snatched from her in any case. And why did people, even in times like these, insist on packing a pair of red fashion shoes? Alicia had gone. And Mendel. Soon he would be gone too. To describe that shoe now, in the archive entry, would be to make all that had passed before redundant. Perhaps all the future needed was a description of a court shoe in the gutter, smeared with mud. He could not do it. The pen his father had given him shook in his hand. In larger scratchier letters he wrote 'She is gone. The entire archive will be buried in her memory. No more. Josef Rosenfeld. Ghetto Registration and Census officer, Solicitor and sometime Scholar of Ashkenazi messianism.' At that moment journal and archive flowed together. He carried the file back to the cupboard, locked the door and lay down on the floor to sleep under his coat, dreamlessly.

Halfway into the night they began to argue. The sewer entrance Chaim had been told about was blocked by a pile of fallen masonry. Rachel led the way to a second smaller tunnel but this petered out in an empty maze of gullies and pipes. They had managed to find two boxes of matches in the apartment but their supply was beginning to run low. As they came up out of the second entrance, Rachel tripped over something soft and swollen. A dead man's head lolled sideways against a kerb. She gave a little cry and squatted down shivering. The rain was still heavy, draping silvery folds on the cool black air. They were alone.

—We should go back.

She was hot still. He felt hair plastered to her temple under the scarf.

—To be found today instead of tomorrow? We couldn't repair the wardrobe anyway.

—You're shivering. We'll never find it.

—Why do you give up so easily?

—I don't but I keep thinking of her. And you're not well.

—I'm a burden is that it? If you'd gone to Bernard when I said we should . . .

—When *you* said? If you'd had your way we'd have all been on the transport by now.

There was a cough in the darkness. A policeman walked past the entrance to the alleyway where they were sheltering. The memory of a similar encounter in the spring caused them to clutch at one another. They realised they needed rest.

After a dreamless interlude curled in each others arms like wet fox cubs they woke to the first glimmer of dawn and began searching again. There was nobody on the streets. In the distance rose a faint rumble of goods wagons being shunted. They moved in short spurts between one shadow and another. After what seemed like hours but was only in fact ten minutes they reached the yard of Isaac's clothing factory. In the middle lay the plinth of the unknown warrior. It was as Chaim had expected or hoped. The plinth had been moved slightly. A sodden pile of torn blankets lay heaped against one side. Beneath them was an inspection pit. A shaft led down, serviced by a metal ladder.

For an agonised ten minutes Josef fully believed that he was going to suffer the same fate as Alicia. He could hear police bumping about in Solomon's office. He had the cyanide capsule ready. They were in the room. Then he heard Schmoyl say *He isn't here. We'll fetch the Chairman.* Evidently they had missed him at the Judenrat.

A hundred yards along the tunnel that ran away from the bottom of the shaft they were caught and held. Chaim's match fizzed in the slime at his feet. There was a click and his eyes dazzled.
 —Like two flowers in the wasteland. Like two who are lost, . . .
 —Who's that?
 —Bialik. My favourite.
It was Moses. They had been found.

The gunfire suggested that the selections were beginning in the northern sector. No one had returned since Schmoyl had kicked down all the doors. They must have assumed at the Judenrat that he was dead or missing. Which, in a sense he was, puffing slowly upstairs with the milkchurn from the cellar. This was the fourth and last. Somehow he would have to take them all down again, crammed with papers.

Henryk's old barrow stood in the hallway. Why had Schmoyl said We'll fetch the Chairman? On the last landing the milkchurn slipped and hit his toes. Pain diverted him from all further speculation.

Bernard sat on the floor of what had once been a chamber where the sewage maintenance teams stored their tools and materials. The tunnel which connected it to the main pipe had been blocked with wooden spars. Moses stood guard there. Behind Chaim sat six other youths, – five boys and one girl – all dirty, all armed. Together they made up the first of four underground cells affiliated to Hehalutz. In front of them sat Chaim and Rachel, half prisoners, half guests. The roof dripped continually onto their heads and shoulders, as though the earth was drizzling. Rachel shivered.

—And so your stepfather couldn't save you and now you're back.

Bernard was talking to Chaim but looking at Rachel. Grief for his mother was ousted by jealousy and resentment. He was being made to look a fool. Unwisely he launched into a minute description of their attempt to hide. As if the ingenuity of the hole in the wall might cancel out Bernard's thinly veiled imputation of childish helplessness. But Bernard just laughed.

—And so you did what they all do. It was a wonder you weren't dragged out too. I heard they took the hasid.

Chaim nodded, burning with shame despite the cold and the dankness. He could still see the broken lenses on the floor. But it was Rachel who spoke next.

—Chaim wouldn't have hidden in the apartment if it

hadn't been for me. He wanted to come down here. He put me and the family first.

Which was half true perhaps. But Chaim was grateful for this support. Bernard was not laughing now.

—We put no one first down here. Tomorrow they will begin to demolish the entire ghetto. There are bulldozers on the perimeter already. They've already dug a pit for the last fifty police. Or rather the police have dug it. They've been told it's for a party of gypsies. The rest of the administration, that includes your father, sorry stepfather, will be going out at dawn on a special Judenrat transport.

Chaim bridled again at Bernard's attempt to link him with corrupt authority.

—My father won't be on it. He also has work to do.

Bernard was looking at Rachel again.

—I've heard about that archive. It'll disappear with everything else. We have one treasure left, the daring after despair. Yitzhak Lamdan said that. And these are our treasure.—Here he tapped his semi-automatic.—I want you to go to the Census Department, Chaim.

This was unexpected and suspicious. The drips from the roof grew louder, more metallic. The six fighters behind Bernard sat like idols. Moses shifted in the blocked tunnel.

—Methinks our knight will not abandon his princess.

Bernard did not turn.

—You on lookout keep your mouth shut.—Then, turning to Chaim—What we want to know is: can you snipe at the Judenrat from that office? When the Chairman comes out tomorrow we want him dead. And any other functionary who happens to be with him.

Chaim stiffened.

—My father too I suppose.

—You say he isn't there. And if he is we might make an exception.

—You want me to go alone?

Bernard smiled at Rachel.

—Of course. We work in ones until tomorrow.

Chaim was trapped. To go would be to leave Rachel behind. Yet he wanted Rachel to see he was capable of action, after all this time. Bernard too. As he was stooping along the low passage to the main tunnel he had a premonition of absence. The cell would be elsewhere when he got back. Rachel would have vanished. He felt a pat on his back.

—Go in safety. I shall be lookout.

Moses tossed his head back in the direction of Bernard. Chaim knew that at last he had found an ally.

He had got as far as the filing cabinet when the commotion began downstairs. There was no time to hide the milk-churn. They were already in Solomon's office. It was a larger group than last time. Among many others he recognised the voices of Schmoyl and Solomon, contradictory, intermixed. They were evidently appealing to someone. And threatening him. Suddenly there was a loud silence. The Chairman had heard enough.

—Schmoyl says the place is empty. Josef Rosenfeld must be dead. Herr Schaefer assures me the list was here. We – I – must search for it. Schmoyl you stay here and see no one touches anything. Solomon come with me.

So began the last interview between the Ruler of the ghetto and his Census Officer. Thinking to find the upstairs office empty, Solomon did not bother to knock. At the sight of Josef he started back. He was guilty about having done nothing to save the archive. Soon, under cover of darkness, he would make a break for that bunker in the western sector. The Chairman too looked pale.

—We were told, that is, Schmoyl . . .—Slowly he drew himself up to his full height.—Why did you not return to the Judenrat? I needed you there. The special transport, the one that leaves tomorrow. They want to know who's on it. I can't tell them.—Here he began to shrink a little.— They're murderous Josef. Solomon here had the idea of giving them the list you drew up last week. That includes everybody. It may pacify them.

For the first time in two years Josef felt contempt for the old man who shook opposite him. Yet the contempt could not be prevented from rebounding on himself.

—They took my family.

The Chairman looked blank.

—You refused to save them and now they've gone.— Josef omitted to mention the whereabouts of the two youngest members.—And now you want me to help you.

Again the Chairman was drawing himself up. There were faces at the door now. Pale and threatening. Josef saw Schmoyl among them. He laughed.

—Very well, here is the list.

The box file on the table contained blank foolscap. It had been intended for the rest of October. Now time itself had been erased. He handed it to Solomon. Solomon knew.

—Here is the list.

The clerk had turned to the crowd at the door. They clamoured.

—Not here. Back at the Judenrat.

Solomon too hated the Chairman. He whispered to Josef.

—I see you're getting the milk ready. Can you do it alone?

Josef nodded.

—You'll be coming back with us I take it.

The Chairman was entering his final nightmare. He shook his fist at the faces in the doorway.

—No.

It was Josef's first act of disobedience. The Chairman was too distracted to notice. In any case one less at the Judenrat meant one extra seat on the special transport. Herr Schaefer had told him it was a luxury train. All mod cons. He looked forward to the dawn. He'd had enough of ghettos. He took one last look round the room.

—What *do* you need those milkchurns for?

Josef no longer felt obliged to answer.

He loved the rain. Made him feel so clean. Soon this place would be clean, Judenfrei. He began to whistle the Woodbird's song. A job well done. Promotion. Perhaps to Berlin. Though the bombings were bad there now he'd heard. Still mother would be proud of him. And Lotte. Dear Lotte who had at last accepted his proposal of marriage. The last few stragglers were being driven to the Spur. Judenfrei. Now they had only the Judenrat to deal with. How he had enjoyed telling that old fool about the luxury train. But Josef hadn't been there. Had vanished, they said. Nevertheless, he must see the Census Officer again, must revel in his utter humiliation. A shoe lay in the gutter. Red. A woman's. He picked it up and ran a trembling finger down the damp heel. If . . . But no.

The childman who came plunging out of the alley was both younger and older than he looked. He caught only a glimpse of blue stained overalls and a whiff of sewage before the blade flew up flashing. Then what happened? He had expected at that very moment to feel a dull pain but instead nothing. And the childman was fleeing. Herr Schaefer was too stunned even to draw his luger fully out of its holster. Then trembling, laughing, swearing, he understood. He was Siegfried. He could not be touched by a mere Jew. Slowly, contemplatively, he dropped the shoe back into the gutter. He would make a diversion to that office after all.

When Chaim half ran half fell into the room Josef was sitting at his desk panting. He had only just managed to push the milkchurn through the gap and reposition the filing cabinet. Seeing it was only his stepson he could not disguise the irritation in his voice.

—Oh it's you. Isn't the underground worth it?

Chaim, also panting, stood irresolutely just inside the door. First the worry over Rachel, then the botched and childish attack on Schaefer and now his stepfather's anger. As if this were a normal encounter in a normal pocket of time. Outside, the last deportees were trudging to the Spur. It was the end of things. Mendel had been right. Yet here

Josef behaved like a man beyond history. A flake of dried excrement fell from his trousers to the floor. This was his existence now. Yet he had to warn Josef.

—It was the underground that sent me. They'll be here tomorrow, if the angle's right.

Ignoring Josef's bewilderment he went over to the window. No. The Judenrat porch was obscured by several buildings, including, he now realised, the tenement where they had all lived. He would tell Bernard that. He turned back to his stepfather.

—I shouldn't be telling you all this but I must. You'll be in grave danger if you leave the ghetto from the door of the Judenrat tomorrow.

Chaim couldn't prevent a certain pride creeping into his voice. Now he was privy to secrets Josef would never share. Yet he had not expected laughter.

—Tomorrow. What is tomorrow. She is gone. And in there . . .

But suddenly he stopped. For the fourth time that day the office was receiving a guest. Before Chaim could argue he had been whisked into the room behind the filing cabinet. He stood there clutching his knife, just in case.

Splashing now through the thick slime of a side tunnel she ran on. They had given up running after her now. At least their whispered *stops* and *comebacks* (even this deep the tyrant might be alerted) had faded. There was no light except from the match she would occasionally strike and hold up. Once in the darkness she fell, her hands plunged to the wrists in cold ooze. She saw him then, the underground leader who was in league with the Chairman. She must tell Chaim. Samael was down here. The dark angel. And she had no intention of becoming Lilith. How hot it was. Yet freezing too. She knew the way. Like Ariadne. Yes. Like in the story she had read as a girl. The Minotaur was behind her. Its breathings had died out. How far to Theseus? She had the thread, the thread of her mind that had rolled up into a ball the day Alicia was taken. Now all she had to do was unravel it. Then it would run ahead of her, a hot shining thread in the darkness. Up and out. So she continued splashing and singing that song Alicia had taught her: 'La ci darem la mano'. She did not notice a shadow always behind her.

The voices were remote yet close, as if all the words that lay in the room around him wadded the air and filtered it. He pressed his ear harder to the back of the filing cabinet, avoiding the rusty milkchurn that lay on its side near the entrance. Schaefer was asking Josef why he wasn't at the Judenrat. Then something about the wheelbarrow. The one old Henryk had used. It certainly was strange to have moved it up from the cellar to the hall. Schaefer's voice was soft and smooth. He betrayed no sign of his recent encounter with the mad knife boy. Yet there was an edge to his voice, a nervousness. What was he saying now? Something about a shoe, a red shoe. *If only you would.* Would what? What did he want Josef to do? Silence now. The rustle of blood in his ear. Should he rush out now? And finish what he had started in the street. Impossible. And in any case the knife was shaking in his hand. He did not have

Bernard's coolness. The silence continued, buoyed up on the undercurrent of trudging feet. Then the voices began again, if they were voices and not echoes in a cave. *You know I can't. But she has gone hasn't she? You won't be reunited for a while. Why not? You know you want to.* Here in the cave's inner sanctum, the ark of the wardrobe at his back, Chaim listened as in a nightmare to the bargaining of two tormented souls. Another silence in which he distinctly heard the sound of sobbing. Then Schaefer again, nearer, clipped, deflated. *There have been rumours of a secret archive.* Now the click and glide of a drawer in the filing cabinet being slid out. Again Chaim tensed. *No matter. I personally will be supervising the demolition of this sector. After I have seen you off on the special transport of course. So we shall see what we shall see. Until tomorrow.*

Josef had been weeping. Now he was quiet. He rolled up another sheaf of papers, tied them with twine then inserted the roll carefully into the milkchurn by the entrance.

—You'll help me then. It's not a command. But he'll be back. I must do it this evening.

Chaim went over to the other milkchurns. He must get back to Rachel. But his stepfather needed him. Josef was no longer an official. He had shed his ghetto garments. Furiously, with all the rage of lost innocence, he began to wad one of the milkchurns with paper from the archive cupboard.

She followed the thread from room to staircase to room. No one. This was part of the maze. It led nowhere.

Offices. A sort of closet piled with empty box files. A typewriter on its side, a stranded crustacean. Then the voices down below, climbing. Angry men. Servants of darkness. *Where are you Census Officer? Blank paper that's all you gave us. And you know it. The Chairman's paid and so will you. Crawl out of your hole or we'll drag you out.* The air in the open window was cold then hot. Rain bounced hotly from the urinal's corrugated roof. *Elsewhere* it rattled, *elsewhere*.

In the deserted Park allotments two figures gardened through the rainy dusk. Henryk's patch had not looked so fresh and clean for months. Gone were the weeds, the fragments of bean pole, the upturned wheel-less pram. But this was no ordinary turning over of clods in preparation for the cleaving frosts of winter. Already both men had vanished halfway beneath the earth. A wet loose mound lay to one side, constantly growing. Soon the trench was so deep only heads arms and spades were visible. They worked in silence, pausing once to glance at some sodden earth-smeared pages Henryk had buried here. Illustrations from what had once been a valuable manuscript. The Coming Age. Feasting in the earthly paradise. Revellers with animal heads. In earlier times Josef might have been excited by such a find. Who could have smuggled it into the ghetto, from what long razed genizah? Then how had it been lost again, lost for Henryk to find? But now his mind was set on another kind of manuscript. He threw the pages on the mound and continued digging. A little later he stopped again to wipe rain and sweat from his forehead. *This must be deep enough. Come on we haven't got much time.*

Then both men were climbing out of the trench and running to where a wheelbarrow stood bearing four rusty milkchurns, their necks wadded and tied with sacking like vast pickle jars. These they carried back one at a time with much grunting and straining to the side of the trench. Then slowly they lowered them in, the heavy tubers of churns, until, too deep to be held any longer, they slithered out of wet numb fingers to drop on the tamped earth with a soft thud. Then the men were shovelling again, burying what they had planted or laid to rest. The earth that would not go back into the still unsettled trench they spread all over the allotment, fetching weeds afterwards to heel in where they had worked. The broken batons were replaced too, along with the pram. Then without looking back, they pushed the wheelbarrow to Mendel's yard, hoisted it up on to the well rim and pushed it in. This was followed by the spades which they had wrapped round with sacking to minimise the noise. The task was finished. And so too, it seemed, whatever had existed between these two men. After a brief hug they parted ways, Josef to go back to his office and Chaim to return to the sewers and Rachel. Behind them they left a million words germinating or rotting in the earth.

There was one witness to this Egyptian scene of toil amidst rainy darkness. In the half ruined chancel of St Mary and All Saints, Rachel perched on the altar peering out through the socket of the smashed Rose window. Demons were out there, burying treasure. Behind her on the chancel steps old Isaac lay dying, swaddled in blankets from his own defunct clothing factory. He groaned. She was afraid the demons might hear. And she had lost her thread.

The shadow was in the vestry, watching.

Why does Josef want those old pictures out of the earth? I buried them for compost. Chicken-headed people. Are they going to bring them here? What for? Mendel can't look at them now. Nor Alicia. I had to pull them apart. With the pick they've given me instead of a trowel. Their faces were blue. Perhaps he wants me to see the pictures. But I have a chicken-head already. I wear it when I go in after they've all stopped writhing. It helps me breathe.

16

Josef stands looking out of the window. It is open for some reason. The rain has drifted into the office and soaked the floor. He too is soaked and muddy from the digging. Had they buried the archive deep enough? How heavy the churns felt, yet frail somehow. He had handled each one as if it were alive. Alicia. They had met in the ghetto and touched. Briefly. Gone now. The trampled earth puddled with rain. A red shoe in a gutter.

Josef stands inside the secret archive, in a drift of box files. She glimmers before him. He lies down. She is astride his hips, naked. The cries when they come are hers then his. He clutches the warm cyanide phial.

It is summer in the submarine city. They are swimming together along pillared arcades. They are about to get married again. Suddenly the water turns purple. The white palaces and the towers, the trumpets of chimney pots and the bridges are all leaves, afloat on a muddy pond. Summer is old in the city of the drowned.

First you close your eyes then you bite. Like this.

leaves teeth milk black

bitter almonds

black

Moses had gone as well as Rachel. He would have to find her. Bernard was evasive, then dismissive. But thankful for the information. When they trudged off through the tunnel Chaim hung back then took a deliberate wrong turn. His membership of the cell was over. But he had a mauser.

Isaac is an angel and I am his servant. These white things are clouds. It is heaven. Listen to the thunder of praise. Listen.

Bulldozers and tanks and flamethrowers. The sectors are being razed. Smoke of dust. Fires. Melting tar. A red high-heeled shoe.

Schaefer has the shoe in his jacket pocket. He is standing outside the Judenrat talking to the Chairman. Where is our elusive Census Officer. The Chairman does not know. His face is swollen from the beating Schmoyl and the other policemen gave him when they realised there was no list. The Amtsleiter leaves his second-in-command in charge and runs off down the street. The Chairman climbs into his dog-cart. The ghetto police hound the last officials out of the Judenrat with kicks and curses. They know they will have to stay behind. They guess and don't want to guess who the pit is for. Suddenly a shot rings out. It comes from the direction of the old Rosenfeld apartment. In the act of beating Solomon with his truncheon, Schmoyl crumples to the ground. A detachment of SS return the fire. Unseen, Solomon slips back into the deserted building. The Chairman's horse rears and the last deportees leave for the Spur.

The drowned city steams in the sun. Bonewhite. The roofs are caked with seaweed.

Thunder of destruction. They have moved on to the north sector. The Chairman and the other officials are walking up the ramp into their luxury coach. The ghetto police have been relieved of their truncheons and are themselves being assembled in the goods yard to march to the cemetery. Smoke and heat ripple the grey October sky.

Everywhere the rich smell of burning tarmac. Bernard and the others are still sniping from the old Rosenfeld apartment. They have hit several demolition workers and a couple of soldiers. But their fire has been pinpointed. And they are desperately low on ammunition.

Chaim has left warm tar on the stairs. He might have just come back from the beach. Josef is already rigid. He closes the eyes and leaves by the window Rachel used. He must find her. There is a building on fire nearby.

Too late for the dugouts. In the cemetery maybe. Among the headstones. This is Solomon's wisdom.

The Amtsleiter sees and does not see the tar on the stairs. He is shaking. Damn Lotte. Damn mother. He stops at the door, calling *Josef are you there?* Silence. And, when he enters, something different. As though the room had expanded. It has. He stands shaking at the door. The secret archive. Gone. And Josef too.

Bastard. Before I came. Killed himself. He kicks Josef's ribcage. All around the empty box files lie. Bastard. He holds the red shoe. I would have saved you if you'd . . . He strokes the red shoe. Very well, Mr Rosenfeld. He undoes his fly and takes out a rapidly stiffening member. He strokes it with the shoe. Faster. Semen spurts over Josef's face. There is an explosion and then the sound of falling masonry.

If Isaac has ascended to heaven why is she still in hell? Chaim has gone underground with the other demons. She must look for Alicia and Mendel. They are somewhere in this inferno.

Moses, her shadow, runs out of the vestry and follows.

A tank has taken up position outside the Judenrat. It is firing at the tenement where the Rosenfelds used to live. Suddenly the side of the building collapses in a slew of rubble. The roof is on fire. Someone can be seen briefly in an upper storey window. He has draped something round his head and shoulders. Like a giant prayer shawl. A Kurdestan rug. He falls. Bernard.

She is standing about a hundred yards from where the police are lined up next to the long hole. The soldiers have not noticed. She weeps into the rain. Where is Alicia? Where is Mendel? Perhaps they will rise up out of the hole and fly away with her. Then the noises start. Hard and sharp and loud. The noises make the policemen disappear backwards into the hole. She must tell them to get out. Alicia and Mendel are coming. They must get out.

The black basalt headstone commemorates a follower of the Baal Shem Tov. The basalt is rifted and chipped. Time. He has no time. He cannot save her. She is shouting again. They hear her now. They turn from their shovelling.

Josef's stepdaughter. Why is she shouting? Solomon stands up. He shouts too.

Shouts. Shots. Chaim closes his eyes.

Moses drags Rachel behind the wall. The clerk has drawn their fire.

When Chaim opens his eyes she has gone.

The city is drowning for the last time. Some can no longer live beneath the water. They flounder on the surface or float while the buildings disappear beneath red and black bubbles.

Siegfried Schaefer has personally overseen the transportation of the Registration and Census Officer's body to the cemetery. He has wiped the white liquid from the face. A separate grave is being dug by two kapos. He weeps. When the body is thrown in he tosses something after it. A red shoe.

Warte nur, balde
Ruhest du auch.
He mutters.

The dusk sky is lit with the ghetto's fires. Soon no building will be left standing. Ash covers Henryk's vegetable plot with its hidden clamp of words. Chaim peers round the headstone. The Amtsleiter is alone.

A shot. The solitary mourner falls with a grunt. His solitary executioner threads his way among headstones crying *Rachel*. Soon he turns reluctantly away and makes for Isaac's factory yard. Splashing through darkness he surfaces on the outskirts of the city. Two others meet him there in the grey dawn light.

First it is light then it is dark. I saw them in the dark burying black milk. What will grow there now? Black fire Mendel said. White fire.

Three hands touch the cigarette case. It is cold then warm.

Afterword

The Nazis established many Jewish ghettoes as they tightened their grip on Eastern Europe during the early years of the Second World War. These sealed cities within cities, products both of casual bureaucratic improvisation and ancient racial enmity, loom up in the twilit zone between exile and extermination, crystallising and 'fixing' many elements of the historical nightmare which elsewhere can seem blurred, confused or simply ungraspable. Fearful overcrowded places where disease, starvation and murder were the norm, these communities nevertheless played host to extraordinary human endeavour and achievement: the Warsaw ghetto nourished several string quartets; Vilna was the scene of intense literary activity; in Lodz a great archive was established. Some ghettoes, such as Lodz, developed into large closed industrial complexes; others, like Radom, were smaller and more open to the outside world. There were ghettoes that survived almost to the end of the war, while others disappeared more quickly. Attempting the impossible task of mediating between the inhabitants and the German administration, the Judenrats or Jewish councils were themselves paradoxes in microcosm. Occasionally (for example in Vilna), a Judenrat could throw up a leader so domineering as to seem himself a sort of tyrant. Deportations out of the ghetto could be sudden and overwhelming. The infamous 'kesl' Aktion in Warsaw between late July and early August 1942 is now estimated to have sent some seventy six thousand people to Treblinka. In Lodz on the other hand, 'resettlements' occurred over a greater timespan and seem less of a haemorrhage, more a slow bleed. And the end, when it came, could be equally various. Kovno was set alight, Lodz simply emptied of its inhabitants; while the heroically suicidal underground uprising in Warsaw was followed by a destruction more thorough than anything dreamed of by Scipio Africanus outside the gates of Carthage.

There was never any Jewish ghetto exactly like the one evoked in this story; the people who inhabit it too are all imaginary. But I have tried to suggest how it – and they – might have lived and died, fifty years ago, in Europe.

My title derives from Paul Celan's poem 'Todesfuge'.

The epigraph is taken from 'Ovid in the Third Reich', Geoffrey Hill, *King Log* (London: 1968).

The quotations on pp. 67, 132, 133, 142, 145, 149 and 242 are from T. Carmi ed. and trans., *The Penguin Book of Hebrew Verse* (London: 1981).

The quotation on p. 89 is from Martin Buber, *Tales of the Hasidim: The Early Masters*, trans. Olga Marx (New York: 1975).

David Hartnett